The Author is Dead

Ches Smith

Literary Wanderlust, LLC | Denver, Colorado

Published in the United States by Literary Wanderlust LLC, Denver, Colorado. www.LiteraryWanderlust.com

ISBN print: 978-1-942856-30-6
ISBN digital: 978-1-942856-31-3

Cover design: Ruth M'Gonigle

Printed in the United States of America

Acknowledgments

I would like to begin by thanking the faculty and staff at Meyerland Performing and Visual Arts Middle School. It's important to me that you know no one in this book was inspired by any of you. I promise. Unless, of course, it's a character you're particularly fond of. You know that despite my school-wide emails that border on verbal abuse, I have an unyielding respect for what you all do. One teacher (and fellow author), in particular, was instrumental in the development of this book and that's Mark Dostert. Thank you for your wisdom and encouragement in all things literary, Mark. To Dr. Stephanie Sim, you saved me from myself. To my online rogue's gallery of INTPs (you know who you are), thanks for encouraging me, precisely the kind of person your mother told you not to. To my parents, Roger and Susan

Vernon, sorry for all the bad language in the pages to come. If you start to wonder if you raised a degenerate, be comforted by the fact that I didn't write it in prison. I love you both. To my dad, Gary Smith. Thanks for all the great lunches and great conversation. I can't even imagine the horrors of Vietnam and the demons that returned with you. I suspect that damn war is never really over, but the tremendous gains you've made these last few years have been inspiring. And to Carolyn Smith, thanks for being right there with him. To Susan Brooks at Literary Wanderlust, thank you for your kindness, patience, and most of all, for giving me a chance (this sentence should conclude with an exclamation point, but I know you're not fond of them). To Julie Paris, my rock star of an editor, your dedication to this novel has meant the world to me. And finally, to my wife, Silvia, and our wonderful kids, Sarah, Cristian, and Max. Sometimes, it must feel like you live in the eye of Hurricane Ches, but you manage to keep me at a perfectly manageable category 1 by giving me an inexhaustible supply of laughter, love, joy, and most importantly, cheese enchiladas. I don't deserve any of you.

CHAPTER 1

Near the doors that led in from the parking lot at the edge of Macy's casual-wear section, a mannequin was dressed like a bum. Ratty fake beard, frayed trench coat, greasy red ball cap, and the coup de grâce, a T-shirt advertising a local band called the Zombie Cowgirls. A fetid stench emanated from the display such that store employees held hankies over their noses at a distance, no doubt wondering how it was set up unnoticed and, more importantly, how they were going to take it down without gagging. At the mannequin's feet, a homemade sign suggested customers check out Macy's new iBum line out back by the dumpsters.

I slipped by holding my breath as long as consciousness would allow. Whatever anti-social miscreant had done it had my respect. Anarchy. Revolt. Insurgency. *Viva la revolución.* All that shit. Given came out, she'd changed her appearance, something more conspicuous. Gorgeous. But not like a swimsuit model. More like a swimsuit model's corpse after one hell of a Halloween party. Dark eyes ensconced in dark eye shadow, a nose ring, lips like the skin of a black moccasin, and blonde hair with crimson-tipped pigtails that brushed the shoulders of her puffy coat.

She bought a drink and wandered the crowded court looking for a free table. She caught me staring, noticed I was alone, and approached, acting all nonchalant and innocent, weaving between people carrying food trays with shopping bags hooked on their pinkies.

"Hey man, can I sit here?" she said.

She plunked her sweaty fountain drink on the table in front of me and sat down without waiting for an answer.

"Place is crowded," she said. "I found an empty spot by the yogurt stand, but the guy at the next table smelled like ass."

I hesitated to make eye contact, striving instead for an impression of her the way one might look at an eclipse. She leaned in and examined my face, the ghastly scar on my cheek in particular. "Holy shit, what happened?"

Deliciously straight to the point, social convention be damned.

"I...shot myself."

"Jesus. On purpose?"

I nodded—yes, yes, on purpose.

"Are you a masochist or were you trying to kill yourself?"

I shrugged as if to indicate the latter was the obvious and embarrassing answer.

"Well, either you didn't try very hard or you're a terrible shot, man. I mean 'Can't hit the broad side of a barn' bad. How hard is it to miss your own brain?"

I chortled. She was clearly no stranger to suicide and failed suicides have an unspoken bond. A mutual appreciation for the absurdity of life and death as a punchline to it.

I finally looked directly at her. Dimples and a small scar above her right eye. "The gun slipped. My fingers were greasy," I said.

"Was the gun *inside* your mouth?"

"Yeah."

She cringed and wrinkled her nose exposing her teeth, white and pink against midnight lips. "Why didn't you try again?"

"I was already shot. Blood was everywhere."

"Oh, please, you were shot through the cheek. That's like...like the paper cut of gun wounds. It's not even a real attempt, just a"—she made dorky air quotations—"cry for help." She said that last part in a mocking tone.

"I lost two teeth," I said as if that somehow legitimized the whole thing.

"Ouch. I had my wisdom teeth out under anesthetic and thought I was gonna die. That must've hurt like a *sonofabitch*. Tried pills myself. Never been so sick in my life. You on meds?"

"Not currently. Used to take fluoxetine."

She rifled through her shoulder bag, pulled out an unopened bottle of fluoxetine, and rattled it. As she put the vial back in her bag, she pulled out her phone. She'd received a text. She read it and glanced over her right shoulder at the glass doors that led to the parking lot.

Whatever she *didn't* see seemed to provide some small measure of relief. Over her left shoulder, however, I noticed a man in black leather pants, tattered military jacket, and combat boots outside the floor to ceiling windows peering inside, looking in our direction. He was nowhere near the doors and she didn't see him. It was cold outside, and he paced back and forth holding a phone in his left hand while using his breath to warm up his right fist.

"I saw you watching me," she said.

"Sorry. It's a thing I do. Watch people."

"Am I interesting?"

"You stand out. Especially for the kind of shenanigans you're getting into around here." I waved a loose finger back and forth to indicate the mall at large.

"Shenanigans? Is that a word people still use?"

"It's a good word. I like to keep it alive." Mall security walked by, eyeing her. She reached out and took my hand, kissing it intimately as if we were lovers. Her touch ignited my heartbeat. Security saw this and decided she wasn't their girl. Perhaps they assumed the perp wasn't the PDA type. She watched them as they walked away and then gave me a lit-eyed, manic smile. "Guerilla marketing," she whispered.

"How'd you pull off the bum mannequin?"

She laughed and leaned forward. "The clothes were cut open along the back with Velcro sewn in for a quick dress. Then I spritzed it with deer piss."

"Deer piss?"

"My dad uses it for hunting."

I nodded, impressed by her ingenuity. I moved my attention to the binder open on the table before me and seesawed a pen between my fingers. I'd definitely transcribe this little episode later. In fact, this woman had all the makings of a great character.

"Why do you watch people?"

"They're interesting."

She looked over my shoulder at the Burger King counter, at teenagers on break from their jobs at the lowest levels of middle fashion, at a security guard who looked as if he wanted to go home, get drunk, and rethink his life. "They're horrible."

"Horrible's interesting."

She rolled her eyes. "I guess." She patted my binder. "What's this?"

"My loose-leaf chronicles."

"Ah. And what do you do that it must be chronicled?"

"I'm a writer. I have a day job, but I'm a writer mostly."

"Lemme guess—you write about the malaise of being a white, middle-class man in America."

"No. Well ...shit."

"Anything I might've read?"

"Never published."

"Ah."

"I also write sci-fi," I added in a lame attempt to seem less predictable.

She sipped her drink and left a splotch of black lipstick on the straw. God, what I wouldn't have done to be that straw.

The man outside had his hands pressed against the window now, looking through them as if through a porthole.

"How many books have you written?"

great civilization. You know them by their art. In two thousand years, what will they know of—"

"Wait. There's a difference between someone who's *creative* and someone who's truly an artist. Just because someone can design a soda cup doesn't mean they have anything meaningful to say about the world."

She looked to her right and tilted her head. Facing me again, "I disagree. Even the most mundane designs reveal a core understanding of color, balance, and shape—all observations related to the real world. It's *all* meaningful."

"I don't know. That seems like a rabbit hole that goes straight through to China. At what point do you dilute the word 'artist' into nothing?"

She furrowed her brow and slunk back in her chair. "That's true ...I think you just fucked up my argument."

"Sorry."

"Don't apologize. I need people to call me out on my bullshit."

"We all do." I thought about what she said for a moment and then shook my head. "Aren't creatives greedy in their own way? They can't always be bought with money, but they *can* be bought. With adulation. It's not as immediately powerful, but greater down the stretch."

"Is that why you shot yourself? For the dream of posthumous headlines that might showcase your talent? Did you think you were the next John Kennedy Toole? The next David Foster Wallace?"

A hint of cruelty accompanied her words. I wondered if my tainting of her pure artist archetype bothered her. She relented and asked me my age.

"Thirty-four. You?"

"Twenty-six."

The man I'd seen outside came in and stood just inside the door with his hands in his pockets. He was definitely staring at her now, watching her the way a wild dog considers meat it's not allowed to have.

"Someone's interested in you, I think."

She looked over her shoulder, sighed, and turned back. Picking at the deep purple nail polish on her pinky, she said, "Ever feel like every day is the end of something?"

"Sometimes, when I drive, I listen to music and imagine the end credits rolling over the final frame."

"I do that too. What would your story be like up 'til now?"

I didn't even have to think about it. "A tale of mundanity and madness."

"I like that." She smiled. "Mundanity and madness. You on Facebook?"

"Social networking isn't my thing. Not big on technology, in general. It's making the world too small. Too familiar."

"I don't disagree, but when in Rome. Do you at least have a phone?"

"A work phone. Purely out of necessity."

"Give it to me. Let's get you on Facebook. I'll be your first friend." She held her hand out as if declining wasn't an option. I pulled the phone out of my pocket and handed it to her. She expertly tapped a few things with her thumbs and waited. She held it out to me. "Password." I took it, entered the password, and gave it back.

"What's your name?"

"Ches. Smith. Spelled C-h-e-s."

"Short for Chester?"

"Nope."

"That's what it says on your birth certificate?"

"Yep."

"Job?"

"I'm a computer tech."

She laughed. "A neo-Luddite computer tech. That's awesome. Education?"

"Some college."

"Birthday?"

"Four eleven seventy-nine."

"Mine's in April too. Relationship?"

"No."

She raised her eyebrows and smiled with restrained jubilation. Sneaky little minx. Was she just trying to tease that out of me? No. Probably not. I thought it best not to mention the divorce.

She held up the phone. "Smile."

The flash blinded me. She looked at the photo, zoomed in, and then deleted it. "Let's try again. Turn your head to the left so your scar's harder to see. Right there. Now, look into the camera like you've got a *delicious* secret."

I tried. Another flash. Blinded.

She examined it. "Well ...your secret's less about sexual prowess and more about the woman trapped in your basement, but it'll have to do."

She set it on the table in front of me and then tapped some things into her own phone. Mine dinged with a friend request.

She leaned in. "Well?"

"Seems like I shouldn't accept friend requests until after twenty-four hours or so. Don't want to seem desperate."

"Oh my God, I'm sitting right here. Just accept it already."

I accepted and noticed her name. "Thalia Tanner. My great-grandmother on my dad's side was a Tanner. And did you know Thalia was the Greek Muse of comedy?"

"You know your Muses. Well, Ches, I'd better go." She pushed her seat back and stood up.

"Yeah, me too. Places to be," I lied.

She inspected me as I stood up, seemingly top to bottom. "You're in shorts. It's too cold for shorts."

I looked down at them. "It's Texas. There's no right way to dress for the occasion."

She looked at the man by the doors. I was glad he didn't come over. He looked like he had the will and the means to kick my ass. I was going to do my best not to give him the occasion.

She turned back. "Did you know John Lennon wrote the song 'I am the Walrus' to fuck with people?"

"Really? I just thought he was on LSD."

"He was, but that's beside the point. He heard about a professor who was assigning Beatles songs for student analysis so Lennon thought it'd be funny to write something completely beyond analysis."

"But it wasn't."

"No. That's what's so damn crazy about it. The greater point is that this creative genius meant so much to people, he actually started writing songs to mean *less*. That's a creative supernova, there's just no other way to describe it. Inspiration will strike. You'll see."

It already had.

I watched her saunter the sixty-foot distance between the table and the door, past the bank of trash receptacles and the counter service Taco Bell. Like meerkats, men turned their heads and looked her up and down until sensing their girlfriends' stern stares. Thalia paused at the Dippin' Dots kiosk, examined the flavors, and continued to the door. She had this swagger, a devil-may-care way of moving her hips while maintaining an air of confidence and dignity. She walked out of the mall doing her best to ignore her stalker who now followed close behind, barking something at her. She slapped one last sticker on the glass door as she left and held out both middle fingers. The man slapped one of her hands down—I heard the smack—but she put an even more rigid birdie back up in pure fuckoffishness. I watched her walk away down the sidewalk and into the parking lot, still being followed until she disappeared behind a passing SUV.

On my way home, I passed police cars with sirens on, going the other direction.

CHAPTER 2

At home I was restless. I walked to Full o' Beans, a coffee shop on the corner, and sat at one of their tall, brushed nickel tables by the window. The place smelled like cappuccino and chocolate and a hint of the disinfectant wipes used to clean the counters. The bulletin board by the door had local concert info and advertised guitar lessons with little tear-off phone number strips. They rustled in the breeze every time someone opened the door.

People came in and went out and passed by the windows outside. I had contempt for their hurried lives, their abruptness, their failure to stop and appreciate what they had, but I also longed to be one of them, to move in their circles, to think less and do more.

I believed Thalia was a kindred spirit and I obsessed over her from the moment she walked away. She was true religion. I stared at each photo on her Facebook page hoping those fractured moments could reveal something meaningful about her. She liked to dye her hair weird colors. She had a cat. She could fit at least three ping-pong balls in her mouth at a time. Judging by the ping-pong picture, she might have had a drinking problem. Her relationship status was complicated and my dream was to be the source of that complication.

Just after six o'clock, ominous messages flashed on her feed in internetese, a butchered and abbreviated form of digital English.

"Pray 4 Thal."

"OMG, wat hppnd?"

"John shot her."

I thought it was a sick joke. Who the fuck is John?

"WTF!?!?!?!"

"WTH!?!?!?!!?!?!?!?"

"WTF & WTH!?!?!?!?!?!?!"

It continued like that, post after post, cheap and superficial signs our species is de-evolving into jungle whoops and hollers. Had they no decency? Shouldn't it be social convention to convey such news with reverently proper spelling and punctuation?

Then, like a "FUCK JESUS!" belted out at a Pentecostal tent revival, one phrase stood alone:

She didn't make it.

She didn't make it?

A television mounted on the back wall of the shop usually displaying pictures of coffee beans and sunsets was tuned to *Portlandia* reruns at the request of a few of the more hipsterish patrons. The words "Breaking News" flashed across the screen accompanied by a shock and awe music cue that got everyone's attention. Under images of police officers doing police officer things it said, "Shooting at Sugarville Mall." A search was underway.

The news didn't provide Thalia's name or show a picture of her. Too soon. They were probably still notifying her family.

The man I'd seen was her ex, John de la Muerte. Apparently, his birth name was Leslie Olenbacher III, but he changed it when he became the front man for a death metal band called Anal Tear. You can't do death metal with a name like Leslie.

"Too close to home," the barista said, looking over at the TV. She was a tattooed beatnik with matted hair and Wayfarers.

I felt raw. My world was turned up in some ways, turned down in others. In my mind, the shooting wasn't something that had happened to Thalia, it was something that had happened to *me*. I'd been wronged, the punchline in some cosmic joke.

Stunned, I sat in a downward spiraling psychological mutation, staring out of the coffee shop window until the barista asked me to leave. I hadn't noticed my chair was the only one not upside down on its table. It was dark out. How long had I been there?

"Sorry," I said as I left.

"Careful out there," the barista said. "That maniac is still on the loose."

Indeed.

❖

Most people would get shit-faced after news like that, anything to forget for a while, but I didn't drink. At my eleventh birthday party, my grandfather on my dad's side had undiagnosed cirrhosis of the liver and heaved blood on my Batman birthday cake before collapsing onto the gift table. That ruined drinking for me. And birthday cake. He died three days later. He was a bastard anyway. Back in '72, he turned a sixteen-year-old into a paraplegic when he crashed into her Volkswagen on his way home from the pub. He put my father in the hospital twice. My grandmother, his wife, disappeared in '54 under "mysterious circumstances." My only lingering impressions of him were that whiskey made him a dick and then whiskey made him a dead dick.

No. Alcohol was never an option.

I sped down to the coast blaring angry music— Nine Inch Nails, Metallica, Public Enemy—parked on a secluded beach, and sat on my hood looking out at the water. The Texas side of the Gulf of Mexico was always brownish-green and too opaque to see your feet if you stood in it. Some people think it's because of oil drilling, but it's actually because Louisiana and Texas are on the business end of the Mississippi River's diarrhetic ass. Under a low-hung, nickel-sized moon, however, the gulf might as well have been home to a path of sparkling diamonds that cut through a black void and led beyond the horizon.

Something about the beach at night drew me to it. It felt like the end of the world, a frothy line between the living and the dead, a place where one's lot in life came into focus with nihilistic lucidity. Nothing on the horizon. No promise of safe passage. Nothing permanent. Small waves crawled up the beach to impotently slide back out with an untidy rhythm that only nature can produce. The air was salty and pungent with the smell of seaweed and dead fish, the wind aggressive. Some unseen suicide siren tempted me to walk out into the surf until that

Mighty Miss filth swallowed me whole.

I didn't know how I felt about Thalia's murder. I was drowning in what seemed to be an inappropriate amount of grief over a stranger.

Another car pulled up about forty feet away. The headlights cut off and the driver, a middle-aged white man, stepped out and sat on his hood.

Shit. Was I a cliché?

He nodded and held up his beer to acknowledge our mutual presence. I gave him an uncertain wave and then slunk back into my car and called my psychiatrist.

After four rings, he answered. "Hello?"

"Dr. Norman? This is Ches. Smith." Speaking to him made me nervous. All true intellectuals made me nervous. I guess I worried they'd expose me as the pseudo-intellectual I hoped I wasn't.

"Oh yeah, Ches." He sounded mildly annoyed, probably because of the time. "Haven't heard from you in a while. How are you?"

"Not too well."

"Oh?"

I felt stupid calling him. "Umm," I said. "Did you hear about that woman who was shot at Sugarville Mall today?"

"Mmm-hmm. Saw it on the news. Why? You didn't shoot that poor girl, did you?"

"No. No, of course not, but ...well ...I knew her. I mean ...I met her. Today. Right before."

"Oh?"

"Yeah and ...I don't know."

"You're having a tough time processing it. You don't sound well. Are you at home?"

"No. I'm at the beach. Alone."

He didn't respond.

"Hello?"

"Do you have a firearm with you?"

I didn't respond.

"*Ches?*"

"Not at the moment. No."

"Pills?"

"No."

"An uncontrollable urge to drown yourself?"

"I wouldn't call it *uncontrollable.*"

"Do you need immediate attention? Someone I can call?"

"No. Can we meet tomorrow? I'll be okay until then."

The line was silent for a long moment. "You sure?"

"Yeah."

"9:00 a.m. I can squeeze you in."

"Okay. I can take half a day. Thanks."

"Take care, Ches."

I hung up and tossed the phone on the passenger's seat.

If Dr. Norman were cereal, he'd be the three-pound bag of Froot Rings on the bottom shelf of the breakfast aisle. He cohabitated office space with a psychic and a personal injury lawyer, for Christ's sake. He was cheap, though, and that's what was important.

I stared at the surf. "Fuck it."

I waded out into the surf, shoes and all.

CHAPTER 3

"It's been a while," Dr. Norman said. He sat forward in his chair like a pudgy owl, sunglasses entrenched in a tuft of gray hair on top of his head. A sympathetic face marred only by a glass eye that made me nervous to look at. It took at least four sessions before I felt reasonably certain it wasn't going to plunk out of his face and stare up at me from the floor. I had to remind myself to make eye contact with the live eye, not the dead one.

Live eye. Live eye. "Money's been tight."

He held up his hand like Jesus in one of those old Catholic paintings. "I've told you, don't ever let money be the reason you don't come to see me. You know I'll work with you."

I shrugged. I still smelled like seawater. I'd changed, but not bathed.

"You feel it's charity?"

I nodded a little.

"You don't like that."

"The only people who like charity are the charitable."

"How's Libby?"

"Next question." I wasn't in the mood to discuss my ex-wife.

"She still keeps her bi-monthly appointments. We talk over the phone, except when she's in town and can come in. Which is rare."

"Then why are you asking *me* how she is?"

I leaned back on his golden ochre couch, a relic from the seventies. The curtains were open a crack, the trees outside still. African masks gazed at me from the narrow bits of wall between his fully populated bookshelves. On his desk sat a Jesus-fish paperweight and an open Bible with a highlighter resting in the middle. He used to recommend church but must have concluded that I was a lost cause.

"Still off the meds?" he said.

"Yeah. I don't like the way they make me feel. I lose the lows, but I lose the highs too. I like the highs. I need the highs. They're all I've got."

"What good are the highs if the lows kill you?" His dead eye was piercing, unrelenting, like a soul x-ray. "When we spoke on the phone you told me about having met this young woman from the papers."

"Yeah."

"How are you doing with that?"

"Thalia. Her name was Thalia." It seemed important that he know that. "I feel numb. Like something's been taken from me. Like ...like I'm a mouse caught in a trap, still alive, but unable to get free. And the cheese is right there within reach, only it's being eaten by ants."

He raised his eyebrows. "That's weird." This from a

man who makes a living listening to weird people say weird shit. "You felt something for this girl. You felt something for her and thought maybe there might be something between you if given time. You were robbed of that."

"Story of my life."

"Do you really think there could have been something between you? After so brief an encounter?"

"I don't know. We clicked, I think. She wasn't like anyone I've ever met. Not like Libby at all. I felt like a different person with her."

"That's infatuation. Given time, you would have felt like yourself again and she would have become clearer to you. Warts and all."

"Is that a bad thing?"

"Often it is, yes. These kinds of lightning-strike relationships are fraught with dreamy-eyed delusions. This brand of ...love, for lack of a better word, happens fast and ends faster."

"It sure ended fast for me."

He stared at me as if reading the truth in the lines of my face. "Over the last few years, we've talked at length about your tendency to obsess. Your obsessions hurt everyone around you. Yourself, most of all. It's often how your melancholia presents itself. You'll focus on anything to keep your mind off your own self-hatred."

He went on psychoanalyzing me awhile and making me feel decent about myself until I became consumed with the irrational idea that I was his least favorite client. Not necessarily the craziest, but definitely the whiniest.

"How's the writing?" he asked. "Is it still good medicine for you?"

Good medicine? It's my actual obsession. Well, that and now Thalia, of course. I thought obsessions were bad. Maybe I can merge the two. One obsession must be healthier than two. "I've been stalled," I said. "Something new might be cooking, though. I don't know."

"Perhaps this girl, this Thalia, could still serve you as a muse. That's no small thing."

"Yeah, maybe," I said.

Yes.

Most definitely.

His good eye grew wide as if he'd had a revelation. "I want to give you an assignment. I want you to write about her. Get to know her posthumously. It will allow you to see what might have been and what probably wasn't. Might give you closure."

"Closure? I'm not really looking for closure." I lowered my chin and bit my lip searching for the source of turmoil in my present situation. "This isn't just about Thalia, I don't think ...It's about needing a change."

"A change from what?"

"From life. From nine-to-five living and Facebook and smartphones. Talking about the weather or *sports*— fuck all, I *hate* sports. Politics is just a shell game. Moving money around to screw over the people least capable of doing anything about it. Religion is worse. It's all meaningless. I'm tired of living my life under the expectation that my single greatest hope lies in what I'm going to do next weekend."

"And you think Thalia could have changed these things?"

"I don't know."

"Your problem—well, one of them—is you want the

world to adjust to you. You try to use your creativity to incite changes in others that you yourself aren't willing to make."

Huh?

"You should start by going to the funeral," he said. "You need to ground yourself in reality. Flights of fancy are okay on the page, on the canvas, but it's no way to live."

He went on and on. I had little else to say. I wondered if he saw nothing but a cliché when he looked at me. A dreamy-eyed and depressed thirty-something barreling toward a mid-life crisis.

I feared he was right.

❖

Thalia's obituary made the paper. Her picture was there, one of the ones from her Facebook page. Not the ping-pong ball one. Seeing news of her death in print transformed the dreamlike quality of her demise into something tangible. She was in fact, dead. She'd been snuffed out, terminated, liquidated. She'd laid down her burden, joined the majority, gone to Davy Jones's locker, kicked the bucket. I didn't cry—hell, I hardly knew her. I'd have had to spend a few more hours with her just to call her an acquaintance, but things between us seemed so unfinished. Eternally so.

Maybe the shrink was right. Maybe I needed to commit this whole thing to paper. Get some closure. Suck the venom out, so to speak.

I went to the funeral. The old Baptist church was packed. I stood at the back as an outsider wearing the same black suit I'd worn at my father's funeral—tight in the crotch, sleeves a little too short. Others stood back there too. No pews available. It smelled like musty books and old people. Maroon carpet. Walls covered in cheap wood paneling. The sun shone through narrow, blue and green stained-glass windows on the right. Thalia's casket sat closed before a fan of yellow and white flowers and a 16x20 photo of her, also not the ping-pong ball picture.

The preacher tried to make sense of what happened by searching for answers in his holy book. He spoke of Job and of Jairus's daughter and of Jesus on the cross. He spoke of a time to come when tragedies like this would be made right. I couldn't escape the feeling he was trying to convince himself this was God's plan. The truth, as I saw it, was worse. Emptier. Truth often is. That's why lies are so popular.

Regardless of whether I thought the preacher's stories were true, they were applicable and spoke to the longings of the heart. The holy writers understood the dread of death, but they provided no answers, only murky loopholes. Answers are illusory, but still we grasp at them through campfire stories and on cave walls and in books and on movie screens. We keep telling them because the conditions never change. We tell them to make some sense out of it, to document our complaints as if the very act of expressing it can register our voices out there in the dark.

"Amen," some of the people said as the preacher spoke. Lots of sniffling. One woman excused herself, crying uncontrollably on the way out, the drama queen.

Thalia ran in unorthodox circles. Many of her friends donned black lipstick, crazy hair, and deep blue eyeshadow. Mascara ran down their porcelain cheeks like streaks of sludge. A disturbing number of them were missing eyebrows. They were dressed to look like death at a funeral, yet seemed out of place. Nonconformity as a style is just another kind of conformity. Show me the guy who shows up to a funeral in a pink bunny suit and I'll show you a *real* non-conformist.

The other half of the crowd were small-town folk. They looked across the aisle at their co-mourners as if witnessing the crimson tide of the apocalypse. A turkey-necked lady in horn-rimmed glasses rose and moved when a skinny, leather-clad kid with two different colored eyes tried to sit next to her. A cowboy, maybe fifty-five, sixty, watched the freak show with contempt on his face. A spiky-haired fat guy in a Sex Pistols shirt whispered mocking country-isms to the pink haired girl next to him. She let him know he was being rude with an elbow to his ribs.

The congregation sang "Amazing Grace," and the freaks and geeks capped it off with an impromptu rendition of The Ramone's "My Brain is Hanging Upside Down." The country folk walked out in droves during the latter, but I overheard someone say it was Thalia's favorite song.

What exotic stew birthed and nurtured Thalia that this motley mixture of people might turn out for her funeral? The tragedy of her death had given way to the intriguing paradox of her life.

My abbreviated loose-leaf chronicles were in my pocket, hungry for words.

❖

After the memorial, I stood in the dimly lit foyer trying to decide if I should follow the procession to the graveside when a young woman in a black dress came over. She had hair the color of grease, self-cut from the look of it, and a gaunt face. Her eyes were like Thalia's, but uglier. She'd been sitting in the front row and was almost certainly Thalia's sister. She held out a hand to introduce herself.

"I don't think I've met you," she said. "I'm Calliope."

We shook. "Your parents had a thing for Greek Muses, huh?" I said.

"What do you mean?"

Thalia must have been the smart one.

"I didn't know her very well," I said. "We met right before ...ya know." It seemed inappropriate to specify.

A look of recognition crossed her face. "Did she friend you on Facebook right before?"

"Yeah."

"Some of us were wondering who you were. Other than that asshole, you're one of the last people to see to her alive. It's easy to get hung up on her last moments. Why'd you come?"

"I don't know," I said. "Trying to understand."

"There isn't much to understand," she said. "Just one of those things. Johnny was obsessed with her. It didn't help that she toyed with him endlessly."

I didn't like the idea that Thalia was one to toy with people. Had she toyed with me? If given enough time, would *I* have shot her?

The foyer was clearing out as everyone migrated to the parking lot. An old woman in a wide-brimmed hat followed the others, pushing a walker in front of her. Tennis balls on the feet of the walker helped it slide across the floor. A skinny old fellow, more bone than man, held the door open for her.

"See you in a bit, Granny," Calliope said.

Granny grunted.

We walked outside. A long procession of cars was forming. The afternoon sun watched from above—no clouds, warm even though it was November. Texas has at least three hundred and sixty-five seasons a year. We stopped under the awning a few feet from the hearse.

With one eye squinting in the sunlight, Calliope took her first good look at me. "Oh, shit, what happened to your face?"

"Fishing accident."

"Jesus," she said, and cringed. She looked back. The pallbearers were loading the coffin into the hearse. "It's almost time to go. You going to the graveside?"

"Haven't decided."

She tilted her head. "Can we meet up sometime? I'd like to hear about those last moments."

"Yeah, sure," I said, though I didn't really want to.

We exchanged numbers.

She began to walk away but stopped and turned back. "Ya know, she probably would have slept with you." She said this as if stating a plain fact, as in "I'm going to have steak for dinner" or "The weatherman says it's going to rain tomorrow." She looked down at the phone number on the bulletin and then went to the second-hand limousine parked in front of the hearse.

I decided to follow the procession.

❖

At the graveside service, I kept my distance, standing under a sprawling live oak on a hill carpeted with bright green Bermuda grass. Cemeteries are never boring. It's fun to give stories to the names on the grizzled tombstones. Sally Quintanilla, 1954–2002, was beaten to death when a group of children mistook her for a piñata. Jack Fillmore, 1908–1967, swallowed his tongue trying to chase a renegade grape down his own gullet. Ernest P. Johnson, 1892–1995, died of autoerotic asphyxiation. He was one hundred and three at the time.

I swore I saw Thalia's killer, John de la Muerte, in the distance, watching, but realized it was just a tall, skinny bush swaying in the sporadic breeze. Maybe he was behind it, I don't know. I was always paranoid.

"Did you know Thal or are you rubbernecking?" someone asked from behind me. Startled, I turned, half-expecting de la Muerte to knife me in the gut, but it was only Thalia's father. I knew who he was because he'd given the opening prayer during the service. I was still worried that I might have a knifing coming to me, judging by his tone. Thalia's mother hadn't been at the funeral, maybe she was dead too. Those in attendance at the graveside service were dispersing. Thalia's dad sheltered a cigarette in the palm of his hand and his moss green eyes locked onto me like Death Star tractor beams.

"I was at the mall that day. She sat with me and we talked awhile. She was a good person, Mister Tanner."

He spurted out a stream of smoke and considered me. He was a real Texan—mustache, slicked-back hair, button-down shirt, jeans. I thought I smelled the faint bouquet of a late-night bender. His eyes were bloodshot. He'd thrown on a greasy Budweiser cap.

I knew a guy in college who was from a small Texas

town. Everyone called him Chicken Bone for reasons I never understood. Chicken Bone told me that country boys signify their mood by the way they position their cap on their head. "If the bill's off-center one way or the other, they're in a playful mood," he told me, "If it's backward, they're ready for something, work or sports or some damn thing. If it's centered in the middle of their forehead, everything's cool. But if it's down low over their brow, well sir, that means you're about to get your ass kicked."

"What if it's sideways?" I asked.

"Then they're from the city and have a well-placed knock to the jaw comin' to 'em."

Presently, the bill of Mr. Tanner's hat sat well above his hairline, bill tilted up as if he couldn't be bothered to pull it down. That, according to Chicken Bone, meant he was resigned to a bad hand.

Mr. Tanner gave me one of those *What's up?* nods. "What happened to your face?"

"Tried shaving with a straight razor on a train." I loved making up weird explanations for the scar. Failed suicide was nothing to be proud of, either because I'd attempted it to begin with or because I'd failed, depending on which day you ask me.

"Jesus." He looked down at the ground awhile. "Did you see *him* there? Johnny?"

I nodded.

"What'd she talk to you about?"

"Writing, mostly. I'm a writer." I should have stopped right there but I continued, "I'm thinking of writing about her. About her life."

He held up his hand to stop me. "This isn't your

fuckin' business." He flicked his cigarette at me and walked away. The ashes burned my forearm and I batted them away like I was fighting off angry bees.

Dead daughter or not, what an asshole. At least I now have the satisfaction of knowing that some months later, he'd die on my living room floor.

CHAPTER 4

Thanksgiving.

Empty house.

One place setting at the table.

Ravioli spinning on the microwave carousel at five minutes, half power.

No better way to spend a Thanksgiving. The traditional dinner sucks—turkey is chicken's fat, dehydrated cousin, cranberry sauce looks like pureed viscera, pumpkin pie is just a really shitty shade of orange. The annual seven hours of football is a neutered echo of the ancient coliseums. The Macy's parade is pop-culture ejaculate. And as for entertaining a house full of extended family, I'd rather get scrotal piercings, one for every day of the year.

The microwave dinged and I pulled the little plastic bowl out, peeled back the film, stirred, and put it back in for another minute at full power.

The second to last time I attended a traditional

Thanksgiving was just after Dad died and my aunt and uncle on my mom's side flew me to Ohio to spend it with them. Two days later, I was on a plane back to Texas because I told their grandchildren that Disney is run by a cabal of wealthy pedophiles and cited the company's long and checkered history of hiring gorgeous, hyper-sexualized teens who grow up to become gorgeous, hyper-sexualized adults with psychological issues commonly associated with childhood abuse. I assured the kids that *all* their favorite shows began with a felonious blowjob. They were watching *The Little Mermaid* at the time.

The last time I attended a traditional Thanksgiving was when I went with my ex-wife, Libby, to Fort Worth and told her über-devout Catholic grandparents that Mother Teresa was a masochistic cunt.

But in my defense, if *I* didn't tell them, who would?

I pulled the tray out of the microwave. A burned gasket of marinara sauce stuck to the top perimeter of the bowl and the middle was still cold. Another quick stir and the temperature would even out to something tepid but tolerable.

How had Thalia spent her Thanksgivings? How was her family spending *this* Thanksgiving? Were they sullen, sitting around a table with turkey and all the trimmings, eyes downcast, appetites slight to nonexistent? Did they call it off? What could they possibly be thankful for?

After I finished the ravioli, I called my grandparents to get my annual check-in over with. They didn't know I'd divorced. I had deliberately neglected to tell them because marital obligations made fantastic excuses not to visit them in Ohio. My mother, their daughter, died of cancer and they never quite recovered from it. They'd become mopey and prone to random bouts of quiet whimpering. I did depressed just fine by myself without being in the company of two old prunes miserably waiting to die on their plastic-covered, flower-patterned furniture.

As we muddled through the obligatory small talk, I phased out of the conversation and sketched a picture of Thalia. Soon, I snapped back to reality and realized I was listening to a dial tone. Had I said goodbye? Did my grandparents think they'd lost the connection and simply hung up? Had I even made the call to begin with?

It didn't matter.

We'd have next year to talk about the weather.

Maybe.

Thalia's Facebook page became a kind of cyber-memorial where a Black Friday benefit concert starring the Zombie Cowgirls was announced. Calliope, Thalia's sister, was going to stand in as lead singer. I needed to go. Needed to feel close to Thalia.

The concert was at Crazy One-Eyed Bill's, an underground punk rock venue near downtown. I went after work, carrying my loose-leaf chronicles, still wearing my nice jeans and a pale-yellow golf shirt. The doorman looked at me as if to say, "You're in the wrong fucking place, money," but when he saw my scar, he nodded me in. Ghastly scars and disfigurements, wild tattoos, and prolific piercings hold sway with freak show folk. It's perhaps the only advantage the mark ever afforded me.

Except for glowing neon posters that hung beneath ultraviolet lights in the entry tunnel, everything inside

Bill's was black. The floor was black. The ceiling was black. The tables. Bar. Stage. Instruments *on* the stage. One of the only things that *wasn't* black was a Warholesque painting of Thalia that hung on the wall behind the drums. Perfect likeness. Like maybe it was screen printed. The place smelled. Though the city had an ordinance against smoking in such establishments, Crazy One-Eyed Bill's patrons reeked of smoke and escorted that stale aroma in with them to add to the already aromatic medley of beer and rubber.

I sat at a table in the darkest corner, willing myself to be invisible. I'd never been to a club before. Or a bar. Or a concert, for that matter. Crowds dizzied me, drunken crowds more so, a boiling anxiety that peaked in the prehistoric impulse of fight or flight. The crowd kept growing, obstructing the free flow of air in the room, a suffocating precursor to a full-blown panic attack.

A mousy little man in black leather pants and jacket and glasses with Coke-bottle lenses sat at the table across from me. He smiled and nodded. "Sup?"

"Hey," I said. He was what I needed to calm down a bit. Provided something to focus on. Someone small, unimposing, and friendly, like an antelope with a broken leg should the lions come our way. "Been here before?"

"All the time," he said. "Practically live here. First name basis with the owner."

Shit. He wasn't an antelope with a broken leg. He was a stringy, unappetizing antelope that tells the lions where the other, juicier antelope are. Antelope like me. I looked around at the crowd forming on the mosh pit/ring/killing floor, whatever it's called, and became lightheaded. Back to the little guy. "Did you know

Thalia?"

"Who?"

"Thalia."

"Who's that?"

"This concert is a benefit for her family. She was murdered."

"Oh, shit. Nope. Didn't know her."

The crowd was getting loud. I had to raise my voice so he could hear me. "Ever heard the Zombie Cowgirls play?"

"Yeah."

"She was their lead singer."

"Oh, okay. No big loss. They suck."

Asshole.

"Why'd you come then?"

"Wait, what day is it?"

"Friday."

"Damn. I thought it was Saturday. Saturday is karaoke." He stood up. "I'm out. See ya."

Alone again. The band, all women, was taking the stage, Calliope out front behind the mic. They had the requisite drummer, guitarist, and bass player, but they also had someone with a banjo, someone with a harmonica, and someone with one of those blow jugs that made me think of *Deliverance* and squealing pigs and the phrase, "You got a purty mouth."

They played and were awful. Really, really bad. The auditory equivalent of a hammer on bare teeth. The instruments didn't go together at all, like a shake made of any damn thing—ice cream, tomatoes, unpeeled lemons, dog shit. But if I squinted and the light was just right, Calliope looked a bit like Thalia which made the music endurable. It was like seeing an old friend again.

I wrote down ideas and notes in my loose-leaf chronicles binder and drew sketches of Thalia in the margins. After about forty-five minutes, I'd had enough. I pushed my way to a table with the Zombie Cowgirls shirts, CDs, and hats. I bought one of each to support the cause. A girl with gauged earlobes bagged my merchandise and as she handed the bag over, someone bumped into me from behind. Beer spilled on my back. I turned to look and there I was, face to face with Thalia's dad. He was drunk.

He didn't recognize me at first. "Sorry about that, man—"

There it was. A look of dismay gave way to a look of annoyance and then one of disgust. He put a finger in my face. "You're that fucker from the funeral."

I turned away to leave, but he grabbed my loose-leaf chronicles out from under my arm and opened it. It might as well have been called *The Big Book of Thalia.* I had the distinct impression that this man hadn't thought about me since the graveyard, but he wanted to brawl and I was an easy target. If he looked at the situation just right, he could make a case against me, punishable by a severe beating or at least a nasty talking to.

"Creepy ass son of a bitch," he said. "Are you *stalking* my dead daughter?"

I held my hands out. "Come on, man. I'm not stalking her. Just here to show my support, no need to get all worked up." I hadn't been in a fight since grade school.

The music kept playing. Only those within earshot noticed us.

He had the lumbering right hook of a lush and while

his knuckles grazed my nose, I managed to lean back enough to prevent a square hit on the jaw. Maybe it was a flashbang of rage or sheer desperation, but I punched him the way you might punch a feral dog if it attacked you. He fell back like a plank of wood, feet hinged to the floor.

An alpha male would have been empowered by a one-punch KO, would've used his fallen prey as a step stool, pose like a hunter after bagging a lion, but as a life-long omega male, I was terrified. Terrified I'd hurt him. Terrified of the repercussions. The words "single-punch homicide" came to mind. And what if he popped up and snapped my neck with a two-handed twist the way they do in the movies? I'd crumple down, head on backward, die kissing my own ass.

As he started to wake up, I grabbed the chronicles and the bag of merchandise and dashed out of the club, smacked my shoulder on the doorframe, and almost tripped in the gravel parking lot.

I just hoped he was too drunk, disoriented, or both to chase me down.

CHAPTER 5

The next afternoon, I woke up, went outside, jumped my back fence, and climbed into the tree house next door with my loose-leaf chronicles and a pen. The neighbor was out of town. I enjoyed the childish, rustic environment—three shabby windows, a crooked door, gaps between the wall slats, a No Gurls Alowd sign on the door. The ceiling was too low to stand up straight. The wind shook the leaves and the gentle swaying always set my heart at ease. I took a deep breath and tried to think of something other than Thalia's dad.

Thalia had said, "These days, you have to do something sensational to *make* them listen."

I guessed that was what was behind her guerilla activity at the mall that day.

That played over and over in my mind.

The obituary had said she was born in California but moved to Texas when she was two. She always made honor roll, was captain of the debate team and graduated with honors. She was enigmatic, charismatic, and sarcastic, and her poetry made the school newspaper an unprecedented *three* times. The obit didn't mention the fact that she was the lead singer of the Zombie Cowgirls. Though I didn't care for their music, her lyrics were beautifully transcendent. She was a writer, a rebel, a beautiful, unbound soul. Given time, she would have made us all listen.

The wind picked up. Branches scratched the roof. Camo patterns of diffused sunlight swayed on the plywood floor.

I longed to see her again and wished the casket at the funeral had been open so I could have savored one last glimpse.

The casket was closed. *My God. Did he shoot her in the face?* A horrible thought. A likely possibility. Nothing ruins a face like a well-placed bullet; that much I knew for sure. Ever since it happened, I had been plagued with uncontrollable visions of how it must have gone down. I could see the gun, hear the shots, experience the burn of the bullets. I saw her lying there bleeding, heard the sirens, saw the crowds looking on in disbelief. My mind's eye was pried open, *A Clockwork Orange* style, forcing me to watch a raw, unfiltered event I never actually saw.

I was trying to shake off these grotesque images when Thalia, that beautiful savage, my muse, appeared to me sitting on a blue milk crate by a rack of wooden guns. She wore a white dress shirt, sleeves rolled up, which made her lipstick and eyeshadow appear even darker against her china-doll skin.

"Jesus Christ." I jumped up and hit my head on the ceiling. Doubled over, I rubbed the quickly forming bump. Was she a ghost? A delusion? The byproduct of meds I used to take? A symptom of my condition itself?

"I bet you're glad you didn't walk me to my car," she said.

I looked up at her. Still there. I let out a gasping, nervous laugh, but said nothing.

She looked around. "Do the neighbors know you squat in their kid's tree house?"

Shock gave way to some semblance of familiarity. "No. It's not like I live here, I just enjoy the ambiance. My neighbor is out of town for Thanksgiving. He doesn't have a family. The tree house came with the property. I think he might be a serial killer."

She looked out the window and down at my place. "Ever mow your lawn?"

"I'm morally opposed to mowing. It's an affront to the natural world."

"Just say you don't have a lawnmower and you're too cheap to pay someone to do it."

"I'm not cheap."

Soft light washed the right side of her face into luminescence.

"Met your family," I said. "Delightful."

She nodded. "Dad's an asshole, Calliope's an idiot. Almost everyone I know is one kind of bat-shit crazy or another. *Especially* my ex." She swiped her hand over her forehead. A bullet hole appeared, bloody and throbbing. I looked away until she moved her hand back over it and made it disappear.

"I can't believe he shot you. *Why*?"

"You don't know, so how should I know? Maybe you should try and find out."

"Maybe I will." I hesitated. "Calliope said something odd to me."

"What? That I'd sleep with you?" She gave me a look filled with defiant attitude but then softened. She tilted her head and spread her legs over the edge of the milk crate with her hands between them. She arched her back and started unbuttoning her shirt, bottom to top. The inside edges of her breasts were just visible—

I squeezed my eyes shut and turned away. She wasn't that kind of muse. I respected her too much to dishonor her memory with cheap, self-indulgent fantasies. I needed her to be more to me than mental fodder for masturbation.

"What's wrong?" she said. When I looked back, it was as if it had never happened.

"Nothing."

She looked down at my loose-leaf chronicles. "Been writing about me?"

"Just notes. Random thoughts."

"Still searching for inspiration?"

I nodded.

"Still looking to change the world? To write the next great American novel?"

"At this point, I'd settle for an op-ed piece in the *Sugarville Examiner*."

"You're riddled with self-doubt. That's a start."

"A start?"

"The masses see the world as a single, unbroken plane. Everything is black and white. Their perspective unbending. Others, much fewer in number, brilliant minds, see things from many perspectives. View the world in ways unimaginable to others. It's that tenuous grasp on reality that makes them brittle. They walk the fine line of madness, always seeking to understand and be understood, yet the one perspective they lack is the very one they attempt to connect with: that of the masses."

"Are you saying I'm brillia—"

"Don't say it. To declare yourself in one camp is to demonstrate that you belong to the other."

I rested my head on the wood planks behind me. "Madness."

"Your intellectual prowess is at the mercy of the world and it's the world that will declare which one you are."

"This is madness."

She crossed her legs, put one hand on her hip. "Listen. We've got a story to tell."

"Your biography?"

"Humph. How boring can you get?" She held her hand out and panned left to right. "I think we're living it. Right here. Right now." She pointed at me. "Make it interesting."

"Where would I begin?"

"At the mall, dumbass."

"Oh, yeah. Okay."

"Don't worry, it'll be good, you'll see. With my help, of course."

She presented me with a knowing and mischievous smile, and I was sure she was real.

❖

I went for a morning walk because walks are dreadfully boring and force me to think about the next writing hurdle to pass the time. The hurdle was the first sentence. Every author's dream is to write the perfect first sentence. One like Bradbury's "It was a pleasure to burn" or King's "The man in black fled across the desert, and the gunslinger followed" or Vonnegut's "All this happened, more or less."

Brief. Perfect. Inviting.

Thalia followed a step behind, speaking to me over my right shoulder. "It's one sentence. What's the big deal?"

"That one sentence can win or lose a reader. When they're standing in the bookstore, it's probably the one sentence that can make them want to buy it. It's arguably the most important sentence of the book. At least where the business end of writing is concerned."

The sidewalks in my neighborhood were old and uneven, reclaimed by nature in sporadic patches. Low hanging branches and unkempt bushes caused me to occasionally duck or take a detour off the curb and into the street.

"How did your last book start?"

"Uh, let's see if I can remember. 'Nodi—' "

"Who's Nodi?"

"The protagonist. 'Nodi wasn't sure what he expected of the temple scriptorium, but whatever it was, this wasn't it.' "

Thalia sang, "Boooriiing."

"I guess. Maybe that's why I couldn't get it published. I could base the first sentence on my first and only encounter with you. How about 'It was a cold November day—' "

"I'd be amazed if anyone was still reading after that."

"Okay. 'I met Thalia Tanner thirty minutes before she died.' "

"Not bad, but shouldn't the reader be just as shocked by my death as you were?"

"Yeah, I guess. I know,"—I held out my hands as if reading it off a marquee—" 'Near the doors that led in from the parking lot at the edge of Macy's casual wear section, a mannequin was dressed like a bum.' "

"Meh. You'll think of something."

"I think I'll go with that one for now. Just to get started."

" 'kay."

I stopped to jot it down in my pocket-sized notebook, but two squirrels were humping in the grass to my left. I moved down to give them privacy. After committing the sentence to paper, I put the notebook back in my pocket, and we walked ahead to a time-worn concrete bridge over a bayou. I looked down over the edge and counted three turtles' heads poking out of the water. A few baby turtles were on a branch near the east bank. Dragonflies hovered around them.

Thalia leaned against the bridge railing, her back to the bayou, wind pushing her hair into her eyes. "When did you first know you wanted to be a writer?"

My mind went back to high school. "I was fourteen and wrote a short story about a kid who could close one eye, lift his right hand, make a backward *C* with his thumb and pointer, and pop his classmate's heads like pimples from his desk at the back of the classroom. I read it in front of my English class and they all just stared at me, wide-eyed and gape-mouthed. The teacher wrote me a pass to see the counselor. Held it out to me as if to say, 'You know the drill.' "

"Nice."

"That was when I realized words have power. Whoever said, 'Sticks and stones may break my bones, but words will never hurt me,' was an idiot."

She nodded.

"Writing keeps me—I don't know if *sane* is the word—but I guess ...I guess if my mind had poles, the South Pole would be despair and the North Pole would be contentment. The intensity of my creative impulse—to write, draw, paint—determines how far above or below the equator I am. Despair has its own gravitational pull, you know. Writing keeps me above the equator—the next word, the next sentence, the next paragraph."

A snake weaved through the water. I watched it while trying to get back on topic, but snakes terrified me and I lost my train of thought to a series of involuntary visions of all the worst ways to encounter them—snake drops on my head out of an opening umbrella, snake slithers up the toilet and pokes its head up between my legs while I shit, snake writhing out of a chicken pot pie as if from a placenta.

Thalia was gone.

"Near the doors that led in from the parking lot at the edge of Macy's casual wear section, a mannequin was dressed like a bum," I muttered, happy to have started. From then on, I tried to make decisions—not on what made sense or was in my own best interest—but on what I thought a potential reader might find interesting. *Alice in Wonderland* could keep her six impossible things each day. I was going to do six impossibly stupid things each day. Just getting up in the morning counted as the first. Five more to go.

CHAPTER 6

Showing up at work was impossibly stupid thing number two and staying there was number three. Most writers have day jobs, even moderately successful ones. I was the computer tech at a public middle school. I hated technology, but I was good at it. Unlike people, it made sense. Through a series of vaguely personal connections to my father, who ran his own fix-it shop, I just sort of bounced into the job like one of those Plinko discs on *The Price is Right*.

For a computer tech, the simple act of walking down the hall can play out like one of those zombie movies where the protagonist is cornered by one zombie, then two, then a hundred.

"I can't get on the internet."

"My computer won't start."

"My laptop is slow."

"Do you have one of those thing-a-ma-doos that plug into the ...ya know?"

"Can you watch my class while I run to the bathroom?"

They might as well be saying, "Brainnnnnssss."

Can't shoot them in the head, either. Can't even *joke* about shooting them in the head.

The monotony was exhausting. Same questions, same people, over and over. Every day was my own personal *Groundhog Day.* You'd think educators, who give instructions for a living, could follow instructions themselves, but they can't. Nor do they understand that video and sound can't float through space and magically appear on whatever device they will it to. And many of them certainly don't know that computers have to be plugged in to work, or that, as a rule, they aren't liquid submersible and that plugging one in *while* submersing it in liquid could be fatal. Monitors aren't made of Teflon. Laptops don't grow on trees. Oh sure, they *pretended* to pay attention and learn, to eagerly look over my shoulder with an eye towards self-sufficiency but dismissed all thought of it only to call me in for the same thing a week later. Many of them perpetually played the damsel in distress—even the men—and I can tell you this, had I been Rapunzel's fair-haired prince, I'd have left the bitch up there. If she couldn't get down on her own, fuck her.

The nice thing though about being a tech at a public school is that it almost requires being several years behind the technological times, which I was. Due to budgetary constraints and bureaucratic red tape, techs on the cutting edge couldn't handle the job, like a Formula 1 driver forced to race in an RV.

The bell rang.

If there were a hell, it would consist of wandering a

crowded middle-school hallway for all eternity. Middle-school children are brain damaged—incapable of walking in straight lines, speaking at normal volumes, or keeping their hands to themselves. And the smells, my God, the smells. Cologne worn so thick it stings the eyes, dirty gym clothes, pee, vomit, low-cal soy meat in the cafeteria. If I were to design a school, I'd lay it out like a rat's maze—one entrance, one exit—and the corridors between classrooms would be soundproof and only a foot wide. They'd eat Ritalin for breakfast.

I ducked into Mr. Hemingway's room to wait out the five-minute class change. That was impossibly stupid thing number four. John Hemingway—absolutely no connection to Ernest—was a friend, I guess. A friend of a non-close and personal nature. We got along, had mutual interests, but didn't go for beers after work or anything like that. I always thought his head looked like the moon would if you sprayed it along the equator with brown silly string. Round melon, bald on top with long hair on the sides and back and acne craters he tried to cover with a beard. He always wore a short-sleeve button-down, slacks, and a tie worn loose. It looked as if he'd dragged himself into work after an all-nighter with Japanese businessmen. He smelled like coffee would, if coffee could sweat.

"Go on to class," he said to a child who popped his head in. The kid popped back out like a frightened cat. "Little turd, that kid. He's in my second period. Every five minutes he wants to go to the bathroom or get a drink of water or he has a headache and wants to go to the nurse. Even when he's in here, he doesn't do anything but stare straight ahead and I swear to God, sometimes he touches himself. And then his orc of a mother wants to know why he's failing. Like it's *my* fault."

I sat snugly down in one of the little student desks that were scarcely big enough to contain me. Posters of book covers, parts of speech, and famous literary quotes were on the walls. The whiteboard had homework assignments written on it. A code of conduct was on the door. His desk was unnervingly messy with a newspaper laying on top with a headline about Syrian refugees.

"How was your Thanksgiving break?" he asked.

"Productive."

"Go out of town? Visit any family?"

"No. You?"

"Went and saw my mom up in Dallas. She's in a home. Place smells like piss and a nurse stole her billfold. Jesus Christ, I must've heard about that billfold a hundred times. I was glad to leave. I'm not going up there for Christmas, it's too much trouble. I went to a wedding when I got back into town. This chick I used to bang in high school got married. I'd say she graduated *at* the top of our class, but it's more like *on* top of our class. Half of it anyway. She wore white and everything. Jesus, she got around back in the day. Anyway, they did this weird thirteen coins thing during the ceremony. Ever heard of that?"

"No."

"Each coin represents something, I don't remember what—one of them was love I think and, maybe good hygiene. The groom handed her those coins and I thought, oh look, she's finally getting paid for what she's been giving away for free." He started laughing and it took a moment to regain his composure before he continued. "I got to chuckling and had to go to the bathroom 'til it passed."

I mustered a polite smile. "I finally started writing that book I've been talking about." Saying that to Hemi was impossibly stupid thing number five and it wasn't even two o'clock yet.

"Hey. Good for you."

A girl popped in, fourteen, maybe fifteen, who should have already been in high school but couldn't get past the eighth grade. Hemi looked at her, looked at me, and then back at her. She ducked out sheepishly.

"Rosalita Montez," he said. "She's in my fourth period. Don't get me started on that one."

"Wrote the first chapter. I feel good about it. I thought it would be fiction, but it's turning out to be more of a memoir."

He turned and looked out the window. "Never did finish my novel."

"Why not?"

He rolled his eyes. "Everyone's writing a novel these days. Everyone has a computer. The internet is full of free advice for writers, good and bad. There's self-publishing. It's too easy and done to death. And people don't even read like they used to. People love to write, but no one's reading. It's the same with conversation. Everyone wants to hear themselves talk, but no one wants to listen. Nah. You know as well as I do that the age of transcendent writers is over. Like God, the author is dead. We've had the misfortune of being born as the party's winding down."

"That's defeatist."

"It's not defeatist. It's realistic. I think it's nice you're writing, but don't hang all your hopes on it, ya know. You've got a decent job here. A paycheck, anyway. Learn to be content with that. You'll be happier in the end."

I hated hearing him say that and imagined Thalia standing behind him with a straight razor. She held it up with her right hand, pulled his head back with her left, and slit his throat. Blood spilled out across his desk, over his keyboard, around his mouse, and soaked into stacks of ungraded papers as if they were sponges.

"It's just hard to accept this might be all my life amounts to," I said, dismissing the image.

"We're Americans. We're supposed to die disillusioned and wondering what happened to our childhood dreams. Unless we get Alzheimer's first." He put his arms behind his head and leaned back in his chair. It had duct tape on the armrests and made fart sounds when he moved. "Nah. No one cares about literature anymore. It's all about reality TV and blockbusters and video games."

Impossibly stupid thing number six in three...two... one.

"Would you be willing to look over it?" I said. "My book?"

He pooched out his bottom lip, nodded. "Love to."

Had he known then what I know now, he would have uttered an entirely different two-word answer: "Fuck" and "no."

CHAPTER 7

After three weeks and one-hundred twenty-six additional impossibly stupid things—petty theft, vandalism, casual arson—fire without the commitment, like casual sex—nothing interesting enough to recount, John de la Muerte still hadn't been caught. Or if he had, the paper had zilch in the way of information about it. I didn't want to go anywhere near Thalia's dad again, so I went to the local police precinct to see if I could get an update.

I expected the lobby to be filthy and unkempt in the manner of any space populated by too many blue-collar men—stale coffee and doughnuts, floor scuffed beyond all reason, things duct taped to other things—but it was actually quite clean and modern. The floor was shiny, the plants alive, and it was well lit and pleasant smelling. I approached the gruff and grossly overweight desk sergeant who sat on the other side of a bullet-proof window and asked about Thalia's case.

"Who the fuck are you?" he asked.

I'm the guy whose taxes help pay your fucking salary fifty-two paychecks a year, you ungrateful prick. "Just a concerned citizen."

"Got some ID, looky-loo?"

"I'm not a—forget it."

I handed him my driver's license through the little half-circle hole at the bottom of the window. He inspected it, looked something up on his computer, and then loosely handed it back sandwiched between two fingers. "Well, Mister Smith, as much as we appreciate your concern, if you don't have information about the suspect and you're not immediate family of the deceased, go take a long walk off a short fucking pier. A murder investigation is *not* a spectator sport."

"But if I had information, it would be valuable to you?"

"*Do* you have any?"

"No. Well, don't know. Maybe."

He grumbled something under his breath and told me to hold on. He picked up the phone and dialed an extension. "Kuklinski? Some guy here, name's Smith. Chaz Smith—"

"It's Ches," I said. His look said it didn't matter.

"Says he might have information on the Tanner case." He hung up. "Third floor, hang a left, and wait on the bench. Detective Kuklinski will meet you there. Don't waste his time."

"Yes, sir," I said and rolled my eyes as I turned away. I always had a problem with authority. Every time I saw cops, I instinctively worked up a plan to wrestle their gun off them in case the shit went down and we had to see what's what.

I'd only had two substantial interactions with the police in my lifetime. The first was when I was twenty and they came to the house to investigate my father's suicide. They had all the sensitivity of a cheese grater. The second was when I was in the hospital getting the hole in my face stitched up and some fresh-faced lady cop wanted to know where I'd gotten the gun and what I'd done with it. Didn't tell her a damn thing.

Detective Kuklinski was about what I expected. A hard-on in business casual dress with a gun and a badge hooked to his belt. He walked me back to a plain-gray cubicle in a large room full of plain-gray cubicles. I didn't see anyone in handcuffs, no grisly crime scene photos, no urgent briefings about an imminent and potentially violent takedown. No one put a gun to anyone's head and demanded to speak to the mayor.

He sat me down, took my name and number, and listened to my account of that day at the mall. When I finished, he asked if I'd like to be arrested for obstruction of justice.

"Obstruction, sir?"

"Every minute I sit here with you is a minute I'm not doing my fuckin' job."

I figured we were about done at that point. Someone pulled the detective aside and he told me to show myself out. I noticed a picture of John de la Muerte and paperwork that pertained to Thalia's case pinned to the far side of the cubicle. Strolling out, I snuck my phone out of my pocket and snapped photos of them. Screw him and his fuckin' job. If he wasn't going to find de la Muerte, then I sure as hell would.

CHAPTER 8

It was the first week of December and I stayed home as much as I could. Ah, the time of year when the masses invade the commercial sector like cockroaches under cover of dark. Someone out there was being trampled over a doll. Someone was getting her ass kicked over a hundred-dollar TV. Someone was being shot over a parking space. All for the celebration of the birth of a man who said maybe we should stop being dicks to each other.

My home was classic hovelesque architecture—one bedroom, one bath, one half-bath off the living room— built in the mid- to late fifties. All exterior paint was original, as were the floors, walls, and countertops. According to the previous owner, portions of the roof had been replaced in '61, '83, '01, and '08, all due to inclement weather. The landscaping was naturally robust with a wide variety of regional weeds scattered about the yard. A few pieces of vintage machinery sat abandoned for ambiance. The driveway was perhaps its most endearing feature, reminiscent of the cracked and broken highways in film classics like *Mad Max*, *The Omega Man*, and *Planet of the Apes*.

Other than the roof, the only significant renovations were in the form of murals I'd painted in the time I'd lived there. Depending on the wall, there were futuristic cityscapes, fields of moon-bathed lavender, and superheroes—V, The Crow, Kabuki, Rorschach, Aquaman—arranged in mundane poses. Aquaman, for instance, sat at a bus stop reading a *National Geographic* special on sea turtles. The Crow was clipping his toenails. Native American tribal designs were in the hall, stars and swirling vortexes were on one ceiling, a sunny sky on another. The kitchen was painted like an Italian café after an alien invasion.

The north wall in the bedroom had my version of that famous photo of the Buddhist monk burning to death after he set himself on fire in a busy intersection in Saigon. The only person other than myself who'd ever seen the mural was an exterminator. He asked me why I'd painted it. The truth of it was I didn't know, but what I said was, "Such a principled person is a rarity these days. If only we could all believe something so strongly."

"Sounds like a bunch of hooey to me," the exterminator said. "The guy needed Jesus. If he'd had Jesus, he wouldn't a set hisself on fire. He's in the fire fer good now, though." Before he left, he told me if I'd cut the lawn every now and then, I wouldn't have so many pest problems. This, too, had something to do with Jesus.

I was proud of the paintings when I painted them,

would stand back and admire them, but as time went on, all I could see were the flaws—poorly rendered proportions, mismatched colors, bad design elements.

Writing was like that too, I'd discovered. I could wake up in the dead of night with the greatest sentence ever crafted in the English language running through my mind. It was like finding Bigfoot or spotting a UFO. I could hear Mozart playing, it was that good. I'd write it down in my loose-leaf chronicles, go back to sleep, and find it incomprehensible the next morning.

My old tan rotary phone was ringing on the end table, just beneath a photo of John de la Muerte. I'd printed pictures of him and hung them around the house. I'd never forget his face. No idea what I'd do if I ran into him, but it made me feel proactive.

Ring...ring.

I sat in a lawn chair between stacks of unshelved books, staring at the flaming monk. Light poured in through the filthy glass patio door on my left, dust mites chased each other around in it. My analog TV was on behind me for noise, news reporting something about a bombing in Iraq. Mosque. Many dead.

My loose-leaf chronicles were in my lap. What might the painting look like if I added people standing around him roasting marshmallows?

"It's beautiful," Thalia said. She appeared at the door.

"It's horrific." I reached down to the floor and grabbed a shoe box full of paintbrushes.

Ring...ring.

"You going to answer that?" She pointed at the phone.

"No. I only answer the mobile. Anyone I'm willing to speak to has the number."

She stepped closer to admire the painting, inspecting the brush strokes, rubbing her fingers on the monk's burning head.

"Terrorists have it wrong," she said. "Righteous indignation is the bane of human civilization. It's just a retaliatory swing that leads to even more righteous indignation. Nothing is ever solved. This monk had it right. Righteous indignation turned inward leaves nothing for the indicted to strike back at. They're just left with themselves, they're own reflections, and the horror of their own actions. Imagine what it would be like if terrorists would take this monk's example and only kill themselves—in splendid public fashion, of course. As it is, their message is negated by a mountain of death and destruction. Without all that clutter, the message is all that's left."

"Are you some kind of terrorist sympathizer?"

"Are you?"

"I'm nothing, is what I am. A patient in a psych ward of my own making. A man with no voice."

"Oh, you have a voice, alright. It's an audience you lack."

She looked back at the burning monk and rubbed her fingers over his face again.

I went into the living room where I'd sketched a life-size image of her on the three-foot-wide slice of wall that stood between my front door and the window. I squirted some black acrylic into a paper cup, thinned it with water, and began to outline her face.

"Why bold black lines?" she said.

"Going for a comic book aesthetic."

"Does this mean I'm your hero?"

"I thought that was obvious."

"Kinda creepy, don't you think?"

I stepped back and analyzed it. "Creepy? Is it?"

"A little. I mean, what's next, candles at my feet? Little statues? Incense?"

"It's not an altar. Jesus."

"Not yet, it isn't. Next thing you know, you'll dig up my rotting carcass, dress it in kinky lingerie, and make it your lady."

I couldn't help but laugh. "I'm not a necrophiliac."

"Whatever you say, *Mister Bates*."

"This is my process, it's what I do. I paint a picture of my protagonist. It helps me stay focused. The main character of my first book is behind the bookcase over there."

"Why behind the bookcase?"

"Novel was an unpubbed failure. Don't need the reminder."

She watched as I traced the features of her face with the paintbrush—eyes, nose, mouth. I loved the feel of properly thinned paint slipping off the end of the brush and onto the wall. I moved down to her neck, then her shoulders, her breasts.

"Easy, tiger," she said, "Don't exaggerate them. I'm not some scantily-clad warrior woman straight out of a Frazetta painting. And for the love of God, don't paint hard little nipples poking out of the shirt. Nothing says *mommy issues* like a dude with a nipple fixation."

My mobile rang. Caller ID said it was Calliope. "What's she want?" I dropped the brush in a jar of water, wiped the paint off my hands with a paper towel, and answered.

"Ches?"

"Yeah. Calliope, right?"

"You remember. I want to meet up."

Oh, for fuck's sake. "That's ...probably not the best idea, all things considered."

"What? You talking about what happened at the concert? Don't worry about it. Dad was drunk off his ass. He gets like that. Nothing personal. Probably doesn't even remember what happened. *I'm* glad you came, if it's any consolation."

"Oh." I still wasn't sure. "You said you want to meet?"

"At the mall. Tomorrow, say five?"

"Like ...a date?"

"A date? *Really?*"

"Sorry, I misunderstood. If you were asking me on a date, I was going to refuse."

"Whatever. Look, I just want to know more about those last minutes of her life. I'm working on some things. It'd really help me out."

I really didn't want to go, but felt obligated somehow. You can't deny the wishes of a grieving family, can you? "Okay. I guess. Sure. Tomorrow at five."

❖

A makeshift memorial was still in the parking spot where Thalia was shot—pictures of her, well-wishing posters, dead flowers. The car in the next spot, one of those eco-friendly clown cars, was parked crooked, its front tire sitting on top of a stuffed unicorn.

Calliope was in the process of carving "Asshole" in

its front fender with a nail file. She'd already spelled it wrong, forgetting the H in the middle, scratched through it, and was almost done with her second try. Before we went inside, she tried to pierce the tire with the file, but it just bent in half.

"Thanks for meeting me. Call me Calli," she said as we walked toward the entrance. She wore a pink jumpsuit with white lines down the sides and she'd dyed her hair purple. Now I knew what purple grease looked like.

I could already smell the delightful amalgam of food wafting through the parking lot. A young Jimmy Olsen type followed us with a camera, snapping photos.

"Who's he?" I said.

"He works for the college newspaper. He's doing a feature on me." She told him to wait there and we went inside.

She ordered us vegetarian gyros and curly fries dusted with Cajun seasoning. I pointed out the table I'd sat at with Thalia, but three teenage girls were there, sharing a carrot and a diet soda. We sat at the next table over.

"What did she eat?" Calli said.

"She just had a drink."

"What was she wearing? Was it that puffy coat?"

I nodded.

"Of course, it was. We got it back from the coroner. It had holes in it."

I started to tell her everything I could remember about that day, but not far into the tale, she held up a finger and put one of those Bluetooth things in her ear. I hated those. They forever removed all possibility of differentiating nut jobs who talked to themselves from nut jobs who didn't.

"Hey, what's up?" she said and listened to whoever it was on the other end. She started laughing and looked at me as if I was hearing the joke and might be entertained too. I wasn't.

"Really?"

"Okay ...Yeah ...Okay ...Maybe ...No ...Really? ...Can I call you back?"

I thought she was finished. She was looking right at me. I resumed, but then she burst out laughing again. It took me a second to realize she was still on the call. I drummed my fingers and waited.

Finally, she disconnected with a "See ya," and allowed me to continue. The longer I spoke, the more bored she looked. She gave me the distinct impression she was humoring me. Humoring *me*. You asked *me* here, you bitch. I wanted to scream, but I tried to keep in mind that she was still grieving.

As I finished, she looked out the window at her reporter friend and sniggered about something. She saw me watching and straightened up.

"I guess maybe this isn't the kind of stuff you're looking for," I said.

"No. It's good. It's fine." She stuffed a curly fry into her mouth. "You mentioned you talked to her about writing."

"That's right."

"Dad said you mentioned writing about her."

"He didn't seem fond of the idea."

She gave me a wave of reassurance, swallowed the fry. "He's an asshole. Have you started writing it yet?"

"Um. Yeah."

"I wanna read it."

I leaned back and considered her. What was she up to? I could understand her interest and I was probably obligated to share it with her since it pertained to her sister, but I didn't want her looking over my shoulder the whole time.

"You know," I said, "what I'm writing really has very little to do with her. It doesn't even have to be related to her at all. Maybe it's better—"

"Nah-uh," she said, mouth working on a chunk of gyro. "I want you to ...what's it called? *Ghostwrite* her story for me. I'll make it worth your while."

What in holy hell was she talking about? "How?"

She sized up my disposition on the matter. "Those touched by profound tragedy can make millions off it." She actually held her hand over her heart when she said that. "I'm not missing this opportunity. Book deal first. Then TV deals, movie deals, self-help seminars down the road, maybe. I'll cut you in, of course."

I need a shower. I shook my head and stood up. *What a whack job.*

As I turned away, she said, "I'll tell Daddy."

I turned back. "What?"

"I'll. Tell. Daddy." She over-articulated each word.

"The asshole?"

"The asshole with a fully stocked gun cabinet and a drinking problem. I'll tell him you're writing it anyway. I'll tell him you're embellishing it too." She leaned forward and whispered "*Sexually.*"

I couldn't imagine Daddy being too enthused about that. "If I refuse to sell out and ghostwrite it your way, you'll tell your asshole dad that I'm turning his baby girl's life into some sort of sensationalistic porn escapade?"

"Yep." She popped the P for emphasis.

"And he's as dumb as you, so he'd find this reasonable?"

"Dumber."

I looked at the little condiment bar by the trash cans, the one with packets of ketchup and plasticware. How long it would take to hack through her jugular with a plastic knife? I sat back down. "Not interested. You're wasting your time. And mine. No one cares about anything I write, anyway."

"Why do you keep writing?"

"I just need something to keep my mind occupied, lest I shoot myself again."

"I thought you got that scar in a fishing accident."

I shook my head and drummed my fingers on the table in pure frustration. I gave her the stink eye, jumped up, and walked away, satisfied I'd agreed to nothing.

"I know where you live," she called after me. "Got your address off the internet. I've seen that little rat's nest you call a home, and I'll be in touch. I'd better see some pages."

On my way out, Jimmy Olsen took a casual picture of me with his digital camera. If tabloid TV had taught me anything, it was how to handle paparazzi. I shielded my face from further photographs, took his camera, and shoved him into a large, raised flowerpot near the door outside. I fumbled around with the camera, but couldn't figure out how to remove the memory card, so I dropped it in a garbage can on my way to the car.

The benefit of gun ownership comes sharply into

focus at moments like that. Where *was* my gun, anyway? I always swore that the next time I shot someone, it wouldn't be myself.

CHAPTER 9

The phone was ringing again. I ignored it.

Initially, I was proud of the way I'd handled Calli, but the more I dwelled on it, the more I was riddled with thoughts of all the ways it could go wrong for me.

"You're blowing things out of proportion," Thalia said, standing over me as I knelt and pulled a book off the bottom shelf of the bookcase in my living room. "Overreacting. Try to keep it in perspective."

My gun was stashed in a hardbound edition of *Infinite Jest*. I'd cut the shape of the gun out of the pages in the middle of the book deep enough to conceal it. I didn't know what kind of gun it was, all the pertinent information was filed off. All I knew is it looked like one of those guns gangbangers shoot sideways. The only bullets I still had for it were some of the ones I got when I bought it from a Vietnamese guy at the gas station down the street. He had a few weapons in the trunk of his car. Blind luck I ran into him, really. He didn't speak much

English but kept saying, "It never kill nobody." Said it at least fifteen times.

That was the night before I ate fried chicken and shot myself in the face.

The night I shot myself, I'd purchased the largest single bucket of chicken available, planning to eat only the skins and assorted crunchy bits. Fuck the diet. I also had an extra-large carton of crinkle fries and an extra-large sweet tea in one of those huge cups you can almost wear as a hat. A last meal before dying. I remember listening to a breaking news report on the car radio about a whack job shooting up a school and blowing his own brains out. I hated hearing news reports like that because of my own sickening, yet inevitable empathy for the shooters. The only other casualties that would be tied to *my* death would be of the chicken variety.

I took the gun and the chicken home and sat at the dining room table. The apartment Libby and I shared had been dreadfully quiet since she said she wanted a trial separation and packed up and moved in with her sister in Fort Worth. She left because I was depressed and depression is psychically contagious to all who live under the same roof. It was an act of self-preservation on her part, but to me, it felt like murder.

I sat at the table listening to "Hurt" by Nine Inch Nails and sucked down the rest of my tea and swabbed one last fry in ketchup, ate it. I grabbed the gun, put it in my mouth, and aimed for the sweet spot where the spine meets the base of the skull. I squeezed the trigger—it only takes about six pounds of pressure to fire—but the trigger didn't budge. Safety was on. An intelligent person would have pulled the gun out of his mouth, turned the safety off, and put it back in. Not me. I switched it off with my thumb, the barrel cool on my tongue, when my index finger, lubricated with chicken grease, slipped. The bullet shattered my first molar on the bottom left side, dislodged the molar next to it, pierced my cheek, and found a home in the bookshelf by the credenza. The muzzle flash left blisters on the roof of my mouth. I leaned over to let the blood gush onto the floor. I was surprised I'd had the guts to do it yet strangely relieved I'd fucked it up. I just sat there for a minute trying to work out my next step, weirdly worried about ruining the carpet. I'd dropped the gun and couldn't figure out where. I found it later on the floor in the pantry. It'd slid, or was perhaps inadvertently kicked, under the door.

My neighbor heard the shot, ran over, and saw me slumped and bleeding through the window. He kicked the door in, took off his shirt, and held it to my face as he made a one-handed call to 911. I remember thinking two odd things at the time: that his shirt smelled like onions and that the son of a bitch had better not try mouth-to-mouth.

The only emergency contact number they had for me was my home phone, so Libby had no idea what happened. While I was still in the hospital, she returned with an eye toward reconciliation, but when she saw the dried blood caked deep in the white Berber carpet, she left for good. A little quality down time for me at the nervous hospital after that.

Now Calli was bringing the worst out in me. I hadn't touched that damn gun again until *she* paraded into my life. I walked to the folding table in the dining area, laid the gun down next to my loose-leaf chronicles, and looked back and forth between the two.

Thalia covered the gun with her hand. "There'll be plenty of time for that later. You have a story to tell first."

"I'm just so tired," I said.

"You have to see it through."

"What about your sister? Your dad?"

"What can they do to you that you don't already want to do to yourself? Self-destruction is power."

I sighed and put the gun back in the book.

"And if they do it before I finish?"

When I sat back down, she kissed me on the cheek. I closed my eyes while her lips were still there. They felt like two moist fingers and I wish I could have recorded the little pecking noise they made when she pulled away so I could play it in a loop for all eternity. She ran her fingers across my shoulder as she faded.

"They're all talk," she said before she left. "You have no reason at all to think they're capable of the sorts of horrors your mind can conjure up."

Unfortunately, she was wrong.

CHAPTER 10

Mr. Ribbeshaw looked like you'd expect if a fairy formed a man out of a guinea hen—freckles, bird-beak nose, skinny legs propping up a beer belly. I didn't have a nickname for him because Ribbeshaw already had a farcical ring to it. Riiiiiiiiiiibbeshaw. Ribbeshaaaaawwww.

He was one of our science teachers and every time he saw me, he said, "Hey computer dude, how's it hanging?"

Every. Single. Time.

I've never understood what it means when one man says to another man, "How's it hanging?" but I can only assume it's an inquiry into the state of the penis. What confuses me is that the kinds of men who say this are precisely the kinds of men who act least concerned with other men's penises.

In the morning rush to wrangle his coffee, his duffle bag, and his keys into a manageable pile, Ribbeshaw left his school-issued laptop sitting on top of his mid-eighties

Corvette in the parking lot. The car was royal blue with racing tires and an aggressive scoop on the hood. No way could he afford that on a teacher's salary. Was he a dealer on the side? A pimp? I bet he was a pimp.

"Steal it," Thalia said. She was lying on the hood of the next car over as if sunbathing, fully clothed. I had just arrived at work myself.

"The car?"

"The computer, idiot."

"Human civilization survived millennia without them," I said.

"Can't fight progress."

"Who says this is progress? Show me a bit of technology that changes the human condition and I'll show you *real* progress. Everything else is just convenience."

She sat up and crossed her legs, facing me. "But you need the laptop. It'll make your job easier."

"Shakespeare didn't need a laptop. Plato, Aristotle, Chaucer, Dante, Mark Twain. Wait ...Mark Twain might've had a typewriter."

She shrugged, unconvinced.

"Damn it." I looked both ways, grabbed it, and stuffed it in my satchel. On my lunch break, I would go home and stash it under the couch.

#

Hemi sat back in his chair with his feet propped up on the desk during his planning period, reading what I had so far. Rosalita Montez sat in a cubicle at the back, making up homework. I was anxious to hear what Hemi thought and waited impatiently.

He mumbled the words on the page in the manner

of someone giving only the most cursory consideration to it. "...grabbed the gun, aimed for the sweet spot, squeezed. The bullet shattered first molar on bottom left side. Muzzle flash left blisters...leaned over to let blood gush onto the floor. Jesus, man."

He put it down and stared at the clock awhile then looked at me.

"You still seeing that therapist?"

"Yeah. Sometimes, but—"

He stopped me. "You're an incredibly smart guy. I think. Sometimes I can't tell."

"Do you like it?"

"It might have potential, but I'm looking at what you have so far, at these notes in the margins and here at the back, and it's really unfocused. It's kind of grim. To be honest, I'm not sure if this is even fiction? I mean, that scar on your face and this attempted suicide passage. What's that about?"

"I like to think of this book as embellished non-fiction. It's a new genre I'm coming up with."

"It's not a new genre, all non-fiction is embellished. The bottom line is that I'm not sure what the point of it is."

"It's hard to put into words," I said.

He lowered his chin and stared at me. "That's one of the dumbest things you've ever said. 'It's hard to put into words'? What the hell kind of writer says something like that?"

It *was* dumb.

I thought about it. "I guess it's about finding my voice in the midst of the incessant clamor of our times."

He put the palm of his hand to his mouth and made

a fart sound. "A writer writing about finding his voice? Done to death, man. While you're at it, why don't you write about a Prohibition-era PI, or a zombie holocaust, or horny vampires, or...or star-crossed lovers having a doomed affair set against the backdrop of war-torn ... wherever."

"All stories boil down to one of only a handful of underlying things. It's *how* the story is told that matters."

He rolled his eyes. "Why don't you paint anymore? You were good at that."

"I'm not passionate about painting."

"Sucks when passion and skill are misaligned."

I saw Thalia behind him, only this time she produced a long line of piano wire, wrapped it around her hands a few times, and sliced through the top of his head as if it were a cantaloupe. She pulled the top of his skull off by what little hair he had and scooped out a bloody IOU signed by God. She slapped the gory paper down on his desk and crammed my loose-leaf chronicles in the empty cavity. The binder didn't quite fit.

"Keep at it, if you want," Hemi said. "It takes time."

"I will. Nothing better to do, right?"

"Hey, that's the spirit," he said, with no enthusiasm at all. "One other thing. Type it up. What are you, in third grade? Writing a book on loose-leaf notebook paper is, ya know, really goofy in this day and age."

"I don't have a computer at home, but I'll see what I can do."

"A computer tech that doesn't own a—? Anyway, they say it takes like ten thousand hours to master something. Don't give up." He gave me one of those "I'm trying to tell you what you don't want to hear so you'll leave me alone" smiles.

I nodded. I didn't think I had ten thousand hours left.

When I left his room, I pulled out the paper with de la Muerte's address on it. I needed a distraction.

CHAPTER 11

John de la Muerte's home address was on the paperwork I photographed at the precinct. I drove to his house, parked across the street, and stared at it menacingly as if that alone could exact some kind of revenge. My car was a late model Japanese two-door— late '70s, that is—and if the sun hit the top of it just right, the dents looked like Jesus at the Last Supper. I showed it to a priest once. He was *not* impressed. The gun was in the glove compartment. Thalia in the passenger seat.

A woman in a light blue housedress sat on the front porch with her bare feet propped up on the half-rotten handrail. She kept a lit cigarette in her right hand, hovering about three inches from her lips. Her underwear was plainly visible but she seemed like the kind of woman that didn't care who saw what. Fuck 'em. Let 'em look.

"Is that his mom?" I said to Thalia.

"Don't know."

"The paperwork said he lives with his mom."

Thalia crossed her legs, tilted her head, and stared at the woman. "Probably is."

"Think she knows where he is?"

"Don't know."

"It's his mom. She must know."

She turned to me. "What are you going to do with him if you find him?"

I leaned forward in the seat and hugged the steering wheel. "I might be too chicken shit to confront him. Not chicken shit enough to merely turn him into the cops. I just want to find him. I'll deal with what's next later. Should I go talk to her?"

Thalia shrugged. "It's a start."

"I'm gonna go talk to her." I took several deep breaths, psyching myself out. "Should I take the gun?"

"Jesus, Ches," she held out her hand toward the woman. "She's a little bitty lady. What do you think is going to happen?"

"Right." I nodded and took one last deep breath before exiting the car.

I crossed the cracked, dirty street, approaching the cracked, dirty house. The sky was overcast with gray, low hanging clouds that would fail to bring rain. It was windy. The woman didn't look at me, just stared straight ahead and spurted a stream of smoke out of her mouth.

I hesitantly approached. "Um. Miss de la—"

"Don't you dare call me de la Muerte. It's Olenbacher." She kept staring straight ahead. Her voice oozed with the phlegmy charm of a lifetime of cigarettes.

"Right. Sorry. Just wondering if Joh …uh …Leslie is home."

She finally looked at me. "No," she said as if I was a complete moron. "You a cop?"

It was a strange question considering my attire. Did cops often show up at her house in Pink Floyd T-shirts and jeans with holes in them? "No. No, of course not. Just an old friend. Haven't seen him in a while."

"Can't be too old a friend if you're callin' him Johnny de la Muerte." She said the name with disdain. I didn't like it either. I decided to call him Leslie from then on because I assumed he wouldn't like that. "He only changed his name 'bout two years ago."

"Right. He, uh"—I had to think of something quick—"borrowed some CDs of mine and I was just hoping to get them back."

"Haven't heard from him in over five months. Don't expect to see him neither, now'd the cops are after him."

I tried to look surprised. "Oh? Why on earth are the cops after him?"

She looked dead in my eyes to see if I was serious, thought maybe I was, and laughed as if to say, "Boy, you don't know the half of it."

I knocked nervously on the column at the top of the steps. "Alright. Sorry to bother you."

As I started to walk back to the car, she called out to me.

"His room's upstairs. First door on the right. All his shit's up there if you wanna look for your CDs."

"Oh. Oh, okay." I wasn't sure I wanted to go in the house. What if Leslie was in there and this was just a ruse to get me to go inside so he could club me to death with a baseball bat? It'd look suspicious *not* to go in though. "Thanks."

I let myself in through the frazzled screen door, climbed the red-carpeted creaky stairs, and went into his room. I assumed the police searched it because it was in complete disarray. It smelled like weed and old pizza. His walls were covered with heavy metal posters, occult symbols, and anything else that might make one think he was the Antichrist. Three empty bongs sat on the bookshelf. Blacklight tube fixtures lined the top of the far wall. Blood-red curtains covered the window. The rug on the floor had a wolf on it and was crusted with something white and flaky that I feared was a fine veneer of dried semen.

A Post-it note on his desk said, "Band Practice @ Don's. 514 Rutherglen. Last Thursday of every month." I slipped the note into my pocket and noticed a picture frame lying flat on the dresser, picture-side down. I flipped it over. A photo of Leslie and Thalia together, his arm around her, both beaming. My eyes watered at the sight of it. It stung. I wanted to burn it.

Thalia appeared on his bed, lying on her side, head propped up on her right palm. "Don't be jealous."

"He shot you. Yet there was a time when you two were, I don't know, in love? How *should* I feel?" I went back downstairs.

"Find 'em?" Ms. Olenbacher asked.

"No, ma'am. Thanks, anyway."

When I got back to the car, I pulled my phone from my pocket and looked up the address from the Post-it note. I pulled the gun out of the glove compartment and released the clip. Still loaded. I popped the bullets out one by one into the ashtray, and reloaded it again.

CHAPTER 12

A book laid open in front of me on the kitchen table, a half-eaten hot dog in my left hand and a glass of iced tea in my right, resting on the table. The kitchen was cramped, dark and dirty, accentuating the alien invasion motif on the walls. The table was old, white laminate with a chrome ring around the edge.

"Whatcha readin'?" Thalia sat across from me.

"*A Confederacy of Dunces.*"

"Good?"

"Very. I've been wanting to read it since Day Zero."

"Day Zero?"

"The day you died. You mentioned John Kennedy Toole."

She nodded, then said, "Who are the dunces?"

I took another bite of the hot dog and washed it down with tea. "I think it's the people who stand in league against Ignatius, the protagonist. Society itself, maybe. I guess we're all dunces in our own way. The title comes from a quote by Jonathan Swift. 'When a true genius appears in the world, you may know him by this sign, that the dunces are all in a confederacy against him.' "

"How does one know if he's a genius or a dunce?"

"He doesn't." I took the final bite of hot dog and wiped my hands on a paper towel.

"Good answer." She shifted in her chair and leaned forward, arms on the table, hands hanging off it. "Do you think that book would have been published had Toole not committed suicide?"

"Who can say? It deserved to be published regardless."

"Ever thought of suicide as an exclamation point at the end of a creative body of work?"

"What true artist hasn't?" I went to the sink, took a last gulp of tea, and poured the rest down the drain. "But it's best if you live to see your own success. Suicide ...I don't know. It's a Hail Mary. An act of desperation after a wrong turn off the road to fame."

Thalia stood and walked across the kitchen, then hopped up on the counter. She gently swung her legs back and forth, heels bumping the cabinet door below her. "That's true. I guess if you're going to try and blow your brains out again, you'd better have something to show for it."

"I'm not going to shoot myself again." I looked out the window above the kitchen sink. A black cat was walking along the top runner of the back fence. "Too messy."

Thalia hopped down and hugged me from behind, her hands interlocking over my heart, her breasts soft and supple against my back. "What does success look like, Ches? At what point do you say, 'I've arrived'?"

"What do you mean?"

"Will you feel fulfilled if you get an agent? If you're published? Sell five hundred books? A thousand? A million? Win the Pulitzer?"

"I don't know. Maybe it's like that philosophical paradox where you can never arrive at your destination no matter how close you get."

"I've never understood people who live like their *dis*contentment can propel them toward some glorious promised land of contentment. It's like they don't even know the meaning of the word."

"I want my shiny hardcover book on the shelves of every major and minor bookstore in the nation," I said. "I want to be on the bestseller list and make enough money to live off of writing, to move away, to recede from public view so completely that I'm known only by my words."

Thalia unhooked herself from me and punched my shoulder as she walked off. "Sorry to say, dude, but if that's what it'll take to make you happy, you're *screwed*."

"Yeah. Maybe. Oh, well. There's always suicide, right?"

CHAPTER 13

The day before the two-week winter break, I stood in the maintenance area by the gym, wondering if the metal beams beneath the awning could support my weight if I were to hang myself from them. Cataloging places to kill myself was something of a hobby. It was a cloudless, sunny morning, already hot for December, and the coach and campus officer approached me.

"Chicken nuggets. G D chicken nuggets," Coach Bam-Bam said. He always initialized his curse words to avoid cussing in the presence of children. He weighed about three hundred pounds, but God forbid anyone eat anything unhealthy around him. Violators were subjected to a lecture about the evils of sugar and saturated fats. He often did this while holding a forty-two-ounce fountain drink in his left hand, hypocrisy be damned.

"Chicken nuggets?"

"Chicken. Nuggets. Some M Fers broke into the

cafeteria last night and made away with five big boxes of frozen nuggets. Who in their right G D mind would do that? It's one of the lowest grades of meat imaginable, one step up from rat pot pie or ...or effin' squirrel kabobs."

"Don't knock squirl if ya ain't neva had it," the campus officer said as he walked in. I labeled him the Creole Crackerjack. He was from Louisiana and carried a gun. No one thought the gun was a good idea, but no one was going to tell *him* that. Besides, it was district policy. In Texas, many people believe the only way to keep guns *out* of schools is to put guns *in* them.

"Did they catch them?" I said.

"No siree," Crackerjack said. "Need ya ta check tha securty camras."

He always asked me because he didn't know how to check them.

"Where'd they enter?"

"I got to go back to effin' class," Bam Bam said. "See you Bs later."

Crackerjack led me around to the courtyard outside the cafeteria. I always thought the courtyard looked like it belonged in a prison. Sometimes, as I walked through it, I imagined riots and shankings and a gaggle of tattooed white supremacists lifting weights in the corner. A window was broken by the snack bar, glass scattered on the ground. Muddy footprints ran across the '50s-era blue-green tile to the other side of the cafeteria and to the kitchen freezer behind the serving line counter, then back again. Crackerjack knelt by the glass and carefully considered the fragments.

"Da winder broken from da *outside*," he said as if

this was some grand revelation. He licked a piece of the glass and squinted as if he tasted something familiar, but couldn't quite place it.

That's when I excused myself to go check the cameras.

The perpetrators were students, a set of twins henceforth known as los Gemelos del Pollo, the chicken twins. I saw them in the grainy, pixilated footage spread over three cameras, breaking in and taking the nuggets. The two of them carefully carried each box behind the school and out of view. The alarm never went off because it didn't work. Rats chewed through the wiring sometime in the late '90s and the budget never allowed for repairs.

According to their schedule, the twins were in the gym at the time. I went over there. Bam-Bam called them over. With the two of them standing there, he waved his hand in front of me. "These aren't the droids you're looking for."

He never grew tired of making *Star Wars* jokes to the tech guy.

"We didn't do nothin' mister," Pollo One said.

"No, Señor," Pollo Two said. Pollo Two never spoke English, always relying on One to translate for him. If you didn't speak Spanish, the two of them seemed to have a Han Solo–Chewbacca dynamic.

"Come on," I said.

"¿Qué?" Pollo Two said.

"Quiere que lo sigamos," his brother translated.

They weren't identical twins. In fact, they were quite different. Pollo One was tall, Pollo Two short. Pollo Two had a chiseled chin, Pollo One had no chin at all.

One had perfect teeth, Two had teeth like an anglerfish. Two had perfect hair, One had hair like a baby chicken. One had soulful eyes, Two had eyes like a flounder. If they'd had detachable features like little Mexican potato heads, you could have rearranged them into the world's most attractive boy and something that looked like the Hunchback of Notre Dame.

"What did you do with the nuggets?" I said.

"¿Qué?"

"Él quiere saber lo que hicimos con los nuggets," One said to Two and then turned back to me. "We don't know what you're talkin' about, mister."

"I saw you on the video."

"Ya están descongelados," Two said. "No sirven para nada."

One punched Two in the upper arm. Two rubbed it and gave his brother a hurt look.

"What did you do with them?" I said.

"Can we cut a deal?"

"What am I, the DA? What did you do with them?"

"Hicimos arte con ellos."

"What did he say?"

"We used them to make some art, mister. It's the only thing that pollo is good for, anyway. It made us very sick last week. We think it's rat meat."

"Estamos enojados a causa de los nuggets."

"What kind of art?"

They led me around to the back of the school, past the dilapidated mobile home classrooms and the dumpsters and recycling bins, to the back edge of the soccer field that had muddy tire tracks in it. By "art," they meant the nuggets were arranged on the grass to say: FREE US FROM LOS TESTING. It was big enough that it might have been visible from space, or at least a low flying helicopter.

Their parents braved the Rio Grande for this? The nuggets were already beginning to thaw in the Texas December sun and the area smelled like rubbery pseudo-chicken.

"No entiendo," I said. I knew just enough Spanish to exchange mild pleasantries and know when someone was calling me an asshole.

"Siempre nos están probando. La prueba de la mañana. La prueba de la tarde. La prueba nocturna—"

"We don't like the testing so much," One said. "Beginning of year tests, middle of the year tests, six-week snapshots. And that's on top of the pop quizzes and all that other mierda."

"Watch your language."

"Sorry. But it's enough already."

Standardized testing in Texas is a revered pastime, like high school football, or Christmas. Anything produced on an assembly line must have standards—cars, hamburgers, toy robots, children—otherwise, you could end up with any damn thing. The future of America had been reduced to little multiple-choice bubbles—A, B, C, D, and E—with a one-in-five chance of guessing any one answer correctly. That's probably better odds than any one of the test taker's chances of being quantifiably successful in the system they were being groomed for.

"And you needed the nuggets to say this ...why?"

"We don't like the nuggets, either."

I wondered if all this made sense in Spanish.

"Can you keep a secret, mister?" One said.

"Yeah. Sure." A promise to keep a secret counts for nothing until the one telling the secret is of legal drinking age.

"A revolution is coming. In April, when they give us those tests, everyone is just gonna lay down their pencils and go to sleep, man. They can't fail all of us, man."

"A revolution? Neat. That should give you something to write about," Thalia said, standing behind them with a fat Cuban cigar hanging from her lips. She held up a fist. "¡Viva la Revolución!"

I didn't know she smoked.

"Mister?" One said, noticing I'd zoned out.

"What?"

"You gonna turn us in?"

"Go to class."

"¿Qué pasa con el video?"

"You're lucky the Creole Crackerjack doesn—"

"Who?"

"The Cre—the officer. You're lucky he doesn't know how to pull anything up on the video."

Watching the two scamper off, Thalia looked like she had an idea. She took another drag of the cigar and let the smoke bellow out of her mouth as if in slow motion. "¡Viva la Revolución!" she said and put the stogie back between her lips.

Is there anything more phallic than a cigar? When I think of cigars, I think of Cuba and Castro and dictators, and I don't know about the etymology of the word "dictator," but dic(k) is right there in the title.

Thalia's eyes took on the countenance of a sexual deviant and she backed away from me, unbuttoning her olive-green shirt. When she arrived at the bottom button she turned away and dropped the shirt onto the ground, leaving me to gaze at her bare back. She turned her head so I saw her confident face in profile with the cigar standing erect from her mouth.

Damn.

CHAPTER 14

Christmas.

If I succumbed to temptation and indulged in every Thalia fantasy that popped into my head, my right arm would be ten times bulkier than any other part of my body. I hadn't earned that level of familiarity. I didn't have permission. It would have been rape. To keep my mind ...er ...de-aroused, I transcribed my work in progress to the laptop.

When finished, I sat on my couch in the living room and stared up at the starry sky mural on the ceiling. My couch only had two cushions. I threw the third one out. It had blood on it, I think, or maybe cranberry juice. Either way, I didn't want it in my house.

"Other than the stain," the neighbor who gave it to me had said, "it's practically new. I'll help you get it in off the curb here if you want it."

"I haven't seen your husband around," I said. "He okay?"

"Here, grab an end," she said.

The phone was ringing again. Even on Christmas, it was ringing.

The timer rang as soon as the phone quit. My ham potpie was ready. I fetched it and brought it over to my TV tray and poured myself a glass of cider.

Perhaps it was the cider or the potpie or the fact that I tried sniffing glue for the first time in my life, but I saw my father sitting on the floor in the corner and he looked just as he had when I saw him last. His head was still ruined, split apart like the petals of some gory flower, the shotgun perched between his knees.

"Merry Christmas, boy," he said, as best he could. His lips were of no use, being so far apart from one another. It came out like, "Errrry Cisssas, ooyy."

It was the last thing he'd said to me in real life.

Perhaps this is a Dickensian visitation and he's come to warn me the ghosts of Christmas Past, Present, and Future are on their way. He was already all of that rolled into one.

"Uuu wayshing ur ayfe, oy. Uuu ot ohing ooo ow or aw ur ois uon a earff."

"I can't understand you, Dad. Don't mumble. *E-nun-ci-ate*. Isn't that what you used to say to me?"

He held the two parts of his jaw together and held his lips in place with his pinkies. "You're wasting your life, boy," he said. "You've got nothing to show for all your toils upon the earth."

Though I'd understood him fine, I shook my head and furrowed my brow to indicate I didn't.

He sighed and a bubble of blood bulged from his gaping right nasal cavity and popped. He fiddled with his teeth, pulled a few out as if they were Chiclets, and stuck them back in again as if it might help. He got frustrated and let his arms drop to his side. He always was a quitter.

He stared at me, those glassy eyes framed in bruised and swollen eyelids. I looked away toward a stack of paintings that leaned against the far wall.

"I painted a picture of Mom a while back," I told him. "Couldn't get the nose right."

He moaned, chest heaving in and out quickly.

Is he crying? Did he even have tear ducts anymore? I looked back and he wasn't there anymore. The painting I did of his final moment was just barely visible behind the one of Mom getting chemo. It's a myth that more people off themselves during the holidays. Studies have shown that there's no demonstrable increase, in fact, there's a small decrease. There *is* an increase in January, but who *doesn't* want to erase their map in January? January is shit. Dad pulled the trigger on September 8th, 2001. The funeral was on the 11th, but no one came. I guess they were too preoccupied with what happened in New York and Washington that morning. If he'd waited three more days and seen the twin towers collapse, would he have still gone through with it, or would his life have come into sharp and appreciative focus?

The phone rang again.

Thalia didn't show up on Christmas. Would she ever come back to me?

CHAPTER 15

Fucking scar. It hurt sometimes when the temperature dropped significantly as it did two days after Christmas. It also hurt under stress. Thalia was the only thing that comforted me anymore and she was still missing.

I stood in front of the bathroom mirror and held my hand over it. There I was. The man I *used* to be. The man I was before I shot myself. I was never pretty, but at least I was average before the scar. At least children didn't stare. I shot myself and now I had this hideous mark on my face and Thalia was right to wonder why I hadn't shot myself again.

Let's be honest, the whole thing *was* a cry for help. I just wanted to be heard. I had nothing to say, yet I wanted to be heard.

The scar speaks for me. It tells some that I should be pitied, some that I should be ignored, and others that I should be despised.

When the scar became unusually sensitive I'd rub numbing cream on it for relief. I was out of numbing cream. I went to McKay's Pharmacy down the street. They carried my preferred brand, Patty's Pain Paste, but their pharmacist was an asshole. An asshole in a bowtie. In the same way a pig wears lipstick or a turd wears tinsel, this asshole wore a bowtie. It seemed counterintuitive to think that *anyone* in a bow tie could be an asshole. The fact that they're wearing it suggests a healthy amount of whimsy; they're the nerd version of a good-natured hippy. However, this pharmacist, this lanky, balding shit of a man, flew in the face of all reason and good common sense.

I lived west of the pharmacy, but when Libby and I had the apartment, we lived east of it, about the same distance away. It's where I went for Vicodin after I shot myself. I had a prescription with a couple of refills, but this guy was convinced I was some kind of addict. He made a production of it every time I picked up my meds, calling the hospital, calling the doctor, quadruple verifying the legitimacy of the prescription. The second time he did that, I asked to speak to the manager only to discover he was not only the manager, but the sole proprietor. The third time he did it, I keyed his car. At least I *think* it was his car, there were only two in the parking lot and one of them was mine.

It was the only place in town that sold Patty's Pain Paste. When I find an ointment that works, no other ointment will do. The pharmacist wasn't always there, but when he was, I got the feeling he knew I was the one who keyed his car but couldn't prove it. In passive-aggressive annoyance, he followed me through the narrow, brightly lit aisles as if I might steal something and run away.

He gave me the stink eye all the way to aisle five. I could feel his look. How two people who knew nothing about each other could have such intense animosity toward one another is a mystery to me. It must be something primal in our DNA. Maybe he had some ancient caveman stirrings from deep within his soul that told him that I wanted to club him to death with a wooly mammoth's leg bone and make his cavewoman my concubine. It's strange to think that some instantaneous stream of hate could drag one into irrationality and violent, decisive action. Road rage. Voluntary manslaughter. Genocide.

A moment of red. A lifetime of black.

I took the cream to the register and set the tube on the little gray mat that's supposed to disarm whatever it is in product packaging that sets off alarms. He manned the register, standing in front of a wall of cigarettes, cigars, and chewing tobacco. "That all?"

It wasn't so much what he said, as the way he said it, like "That all, motherfucker?"

"What's your problem, man?" I said.

"Sir?"

"Don't act like you don't know what I'm talking about. I've been coming here for years and you've never been anything but a total dick to me."

"Maybe you shouldn't come back."

"Look." I took a big breath, held up the tube of cream, and pointed at it. "This is Patty's Pain Paste. I need it and you're the only motherfucker in town that sells it. Tell me some other place I can get Patty's Pain Paste and I'll never darken your door again."

"Sir, please leave."

I put the tube down and took another big breath. Back to aisle five, I grabbed all the Patty's Pain Paste I could carry. I dumped the tubes on the counter and dropped a twenty in front of him. "Keep the change."

"You still owe me fifteen ninety-four."

I wadded up another twenty and threw it at him.

He picked up the money and paused. "You want to know what I think? I think you're a coward. I know how you got that scar. Shot yourself. Read about it in the community newspaper a few years back. Well, my brother committed suicide. You don't know what it does to those left behind." His face was getting red, angry veins spidering up his neck. "It's the worst thing you can do to a family. It's the worst thing you can do to yourself. I'm a pharmacist. I fill prescriptions. I help depressed people fight against the dark every day and here you are, trying to take the easy way out. I despise selfish pricks like you. You are an affront to God Almighty." He stuck a slender digit in my face. "And you keyed my car, you son of a bitch."

I could tell he was one of those men that wasn't comfortable with bad words.

"Can't blame your brother," I said, "being related to you, it's no surprise. Ever consider that it's people like you that make people like me and your brother *want* to check out? Your whole business revolves around staying alive, but here you're faced with someone that death can't intimidate and it scares the hell out of you. Fuck you, man. Deal with it."

I scooped up my tubes of pain paste, stormed out, and then went back in. "And take off that fucking bowtie.

You don't have the personality for it."

CHAPTER 16

Shortly after I applied a generous glob of pain paste to my face, Libby called. She found my cell phone number somehow. I think maybe one of my coworkers gave it to her. A few of them have it. I answered because caller ID told me it was her and I knew she wouldn't stop calling if I didn't answer.

"Been trying to reach you," she said. "You never answer the home phone."

"Yeah. My rich social life keeps me busy."

She chuckled because she knew better.

"I sent the check last week."

"Yeah, it may come back to you. I don't live in Fort Worth anymore. I moved back here. That's why I needed to get in touch with you."

She had me fetch a pencil and paper and gave me the new address and we made meaningless small talk for a few minutes. Small talk was excruciating for me and she knew it. She wasn't doing it to be malicious, she just didn't have a smoother way of transitioning into the real purpose of her call.

"Look. I just want to let you know I'm getting married again. I wanted to be the one to tell you."

"Oh. Alright. Anyone I know?"

"Uh, yeah. Bill Anderson from Elsik High. You remember Bill?"

Do I remember Bill? He tortured me endlessly throughout high school. He sprinkled fake dandruff on my back and shoulders every day for two weeks until I finally noticed. Earned me the nickname "Head & Shoulders" for the rest of the year. He copied my answers off a math test and punched me in the kidney when we both failed. He loosened the lug nuts on the front passenger wheel of my car so that the wheel flew off at forty miles an hour about two miles from school. I crashed into a ditch.

"Vaguely," I said.

"How about you? Got anyone special?"

"I ...don't know how to answer that."

In hindsight, the fact that I got married at all is still a mystery to me. The fact that I married someone like Libby, so put together and focused, an even greater one. I'd existed in the dark throws of dysthymia as far back as I could remember, but for a brief period, roughly ages twenty to twenty-five, I emerged from that black fog and took on an air of normalcy. I don't know why. Sexual prime? Living on my own? The trauma of my father's death? I wanted what my peers wanted—career, family, religion—and to that end married Libby, a perfectly lovely, perfectly normal woman. Although we went to the same high school, we didn't actually know each other until college when we both worked at the university co-op. We took it slow, dated for a couple of years, and got married just after graduation.

She knew little of the angst-ridden, self-hating person I'd once been, knew little of the depths of despair to which I was capable and, at about twenty-six, when I regressed, she was understandably caught by surprise. I loved her. She loved the person she *thought* I was. I stole four years from her, a crime for which I always felt guilty.

She thought I was being coy. "Who is she?"

"Doesn't matter."

"Oh, come on."

"She died. She's dead."

"Oh."

"Hello?"

"I'm sorry, Ches. I—"

"It's okay. Look, I need to go."

"You're scaring me."

"I'm a scary person. You've said so yourself."

"You're in the abyss again. Like when you—"

The abyss. That's what she called it. Depression's ground floor. "When I what?"

"You know."

"Got the cheek piercing? Ventilated my face?"

"Don't put it like that."

"I'm fine, Libby. Really."

Click.

CHAPTER 17

Calli came to the house on New Year's Day. I'd been sitting on the porch with a shoe box full of rejection letters. Some rejections were from publications I'd submitted short stories to, some were from art galleries, a couple from women. The ones from the publications bothered me most. I drew one out at random. *Sci-Fan Quarterly*. A rejection of my pseudo-scholarly article defending the use of people-based food sources as seen in the 1973 film *Soylent Green*. You mean we can solve world hunger and over-population at the same time? Yes. Yes, we can. And if we make it a point to eat the criminally insane, well, that's three birds with one stone.

It was mostly written in jest, but I guess my heady, dispassionate tone was too sophisticated for the readership of *Sci-Fan Quarterly*.

Callie's car door slammed and snapped me back to the present. She drove a white Ford F-150, late '80s. It probably belonged to her dad—giant tires, gun rack, mud flaps, a pair of rubber testicles hanging from the trailer hitch. Nothing says, "I have no balls," like hanging them from the back bumper of a pickup truck. Why are men so fixated on balls anyway? I've never seen a woman hang rubber ovaries off the back of her car.

I tried to run in the house, but she'd already seen me and followed through the screen door.

"Please leave," I said.

"Hey, I thought we were friends. Did you see me on the news?"

"No. I didn't."

"They interviewed me. I was sensational." She handed me an envelope full of newspaper clippings. "In case you need them for your research or whatever."

She let the screen door flop closed and surveyed the house. She was particularly taken with the west wall of the living room, a nighttime city scene, vivid with blues, purples, silhouettes, and yellow lights. The perimeter of it was framed in black strokes like the sketch lines of an unfinished watercolor. She rubbed her fingers on it and then walked down the hall.

"These are amazing," she said. "Why bother writing? You could make a fortune painting murals."

"Painting's easy. It's not a challenge. It's not where my heart is."

"Screw that," she said.

I followed her into the bedroom. She stopped when she saw the burning monk as if afraid to step any closer. "What the hell is wrong with you?" she said.

"He needs people roasting marshmallows on sticks around him, doesn't he? It'd be more palatable that way."

She rolled her eyes and walked back into the living room.

"Hot dogs, maybe?" I called after her.

She was frozen, staring at the painting of Thalia. She hadn't noticed it when she came in.

"What the fuck?" She turned back to me, left hand on hip, right hand pointing at me. She moved her index finger in little circles to indicate the whole of my being. "You seem like a normal guy, but you're like one of those paintings. What do you call them? Where they look nice from across the room, but you get up close and they look like shit?"

"Impressionistic."

"Yeah. You're like an impressionistic painting. Normal from across the room—batshit up close. You don't even *look* like a normal person up close."

"*Must* you be here?"

"Where're the pages?"

She looked around and spotted my loose-leaf chronicles. I'd only written notes in them since I procured a computer, but she didn't know that. I tried to snatch them, but she beat me to it, grabbing them off the TV tray and knocking the tray over in the process. She spilled my apple juice. She sat on the couch, eyed the spot with the missing cushion, and then plunged into the binder. She slowed as she went, flipped backward, and then forward again. "What the hell is this?"

"It's something else, not what you're looking for."

She looked down and began pointing out the name "Thalia. Thalia. Thalia." Over and over again. "You're seriously going to tell me this isn't it?"

"Would you please leave?"

She stood up and paced, still thumbing through the chronicles. "It begins in the last hour of her life?" Flipping more pages. "She appears to you as a ...what? Ghost? This isn't about her, it's about *you,* you self-involved prick. And it's not even true. Ghosts aren't real, space cadet."

"I never said I was writing her biography."

She shook her head with furious resolve, smiling in a "can't wait to see you flayed alive," kind of way. "Daddy's going to love hearing about this."

"Tell him. I don't care."

"Oh yeah? Well maybe I wi—"

The phone rang. She tilted her head as if to say, "Well? Aren't you going to answer that?"

"I don't ever answer it," I said.

She answered it for me, listened, and said "Yeah. He's right here."

She held it out, but I grabbed it and hung up.

She was aghast. "You're so weird."

"It's bill collectors. It's always bill collectors and now you've reset the timer."

"What are you talking about?"

"They have seven years to collect and they can't garnish wages in Texas. I was waiting them out and now you've reset the timer by answering. That's another seven years."

She waved her fingers at me. "I don't even think that's a thing. Oh, I forgot something. Be right back."

The phone started ringing again. She paused, looked at it, and looked at me as if it were a crime not to answer a ringing phone. I stared at her dead-eyed and put-upon. She let it go and ran out to her car.

It occurred to me I could lock her out, but by the time I tried to shut the door, she jammed a foot in the crack and banged on it. I let her back in, thinking about those movies where the hero, forced into that very situation, would shove a shotgun through the crack and unload. That's usually for zombies, deranged killers, or Bible salesmen though, not ninety-pound annoyances in purple sweatpants.

She shoved a backpack full of library books about true crime, biographies, and Thalia's old scrapbooks and journals into my hands.

"Inspiration," she said.

"I already have inspiration."

"What. That?" she asked, pointing at the chronicles.

"I'm not a biographer," I said. "Why are you having trouble understanding this?"

"Well, you are now. What's your problem anyway? Don't you want to get published? People are interested in real life shit, ya know. Charles Manson. OJ. That fucker that dressed up like the Joker and shot up the theater that time. No one cares about ghosts that appear to whiny authors. *Dumbass*. No one who wants to get laid, anyway."

"You don't know me."

"Just write the fucking book," she said, spun around, and let the screen door clap shut as she left.

When the door was closed and she was safely out of sight, I flipped her off. Both hands shook. In the religion of fame, Calli was a zealot. You can't reason with zealots.

And shouldn't she be too bereaved to even be thinking about this nonsense? Something about it wasn't right.

CHAPTER 18

January. Back to work after the break. January is the Monday of months.

Of all the horrors of modern living, work commutes may be the worst. Even the loveliest of people become exhaust-puffing monstrosities when they're encased in two tons of steel and glass. They drive as if only one can survive, like spermatozoa attempting to fertilize the egg that is corporate America.

Hell, maybe violent road rage should be encouraged. Thin the herd.

I sat at a stoplight, waiting for the left turn signal to turn green. News radio was saying something about starving children in ...somewhere. A vagrant stood in the median holding a Styrofoam cup. He was young with a month or two's worth of beard, and wearing dirty fatigues. He looked familiar.

Is it him? De la Muerte? Leslie? Surely not. I didn't make eye contact, but tried to observe him out of the corner of my eye. If it *was* Leslie, I certainly didn't want him to know that I knew who he was. And if it wasn't him, I didn't want him to think I had spare change.

The lady in the Lexus in front of me was on the phone. A Jesus fish on her trunk lid. The light turned green and she didn't go. I honked and she flipped me off. I think the vagrant flipped me off too. The man behind me was on the phone too, and close to my back bumper. I couldn't even see his headlights, just windshield and a little hood. After we were through the intersection, he honked, cut me off, and shook his head as if in righteous indignation.

Every morning, different drivers, same insanity.

I pulled into the school parking lot and Lurch, a math teacher, held his hand out for me to stop. He rolled his finger in the air so I'd put my window down. He was on the phone but took a moment to say. "Internet's down."

I nodded and parked.

As I walked into the door, Mommy Dearest, an English teacher, was lying in ambush while talking into her Bluetooth. "Internet's down," she said and then, "Not you," to the person on the other end.

"Oh, okay. I'll check it out."

A music teacher I called Happy Trails said, "Internet's down." She was texting.

"Thanks for telling me," I said. "I'll check it out."

Captain America switched his phone from his right ear to his left, grabbed my sleeve. "Internet's down."

"Oh man, thanks for letting me know."

Thalia appeared as I passed the women's restroom, staying a step or two behind me. "Why don't you just tell them you know and to shut up already?" she said. "Have a sign made and wear it around your neck."

It'd been a while since I'd seen her. I played it cool. "I wouldn't want to ruin their satisfaction of being the first to report it."

"Did you say something?" The Mayor, an assistant principal, said. She was using her phone to take pictures of graffiti on the front of a water fountain that said, "Pencils down." Either a movement was stirring I didn't yet understand or street gangs were getting way too allegorical with their names.

"No," I said.

"I thought you did. Internet's down."

"Seriously? I'll go check it out."

I went to my office to check my email, but remembered the internet was down. On my way to the server room, I passed teachers, clerks, admins, and a few students, most of them fidgeting with one device or another.

"Look at them," Thalia said. She traced the locker-embedded walls with her fingers as if on hallowed ground. "They all talk, but no one listens. So many voices, all indistinct."

She stopped to admire a large bulletin board full of printed blog entries, short stories, and humorous Facebook exchanges. It was some sort of literacy awareness campaign the English department was doing.

I stopped and looked.

"How do you raise your voice above it all?" she said.

"Got me." I continued down to the server room at the end of the hall, a hall faintly dystopian with its drab colors and harsh light. Pseudo-political posters encouraged students to vote for this overachiever or that overachiever.

The server was unplugged. Servers don't unplug themselves. The day they do, we're all screwed. That's some *Terminator* Skynet shit right there. I left it unplugged and sat down on a step stool to jot down some ideas in my abbreviated loose-leaf chronicles.

"Mister Computer Man?"

"Holy fuck," I said with a start, jumping to my feet. I thought I was alone. I turned around to find five students standing against the far wall. They all wore hoodies with bandanas tied around the bottoms of their faces. Sinister in the dim single light of the room. I thought two of them might have been those chicken twins.

"What the hell are you doing in here?" I asked, genuinely concerned I might have some of those little *Village of the Damned* fuckers on my hands.

"We need your help," the shortest one said. Judging by the voice, I thought maybe it was a girl, but at that age, who can tell?

"You're not supposed to be in he—" I thought about what the short one said. "Help with what?"

"The Pencils Down movement. You made the school website, didn't you? We want you to make *us* a website."

"Why would I do that?"

"You have the expertise. And the motivation."

"What motivation?"

The tallest one held up a phone and played a video. There I was, talking to myself and stealing Ribbeshaw's laptop. "Little bastards and your cell phones."

"Watch your language. We're just kids."

"Just kids, huh? You cease to be kids with your first attempt at blackmail, as far as I'm concerned. Jesus, when I was your age I was still eating my own boogers.

You've already turned to organized crime."

"Build us the website and no one has to see this." They handed me a packet of information about their "movement" and then scuttled out one by one.

I sat back down on the step stool.

"They unplugged the server to get you in here," Thalia said.

"It would seem."

"Clever. Well, are you going to plug it back in?"

"Eventually. I'd like my coworkers to think it was something complicated that took time to repair."

"Those kids sure don't like testing," she said.

"If they succeed in getting the whole student body to refuse to take standardized tests, there isn't a person on this campus who wouldn't secretly applaud them for it. And why shouldn't they? The state is manufacturing kids to a set standard based on a misguided conviction that they must all go to college, climb the corporate ladder, become ravenous consumers, conscientious voters, ardent worshippers—to be the very embodiment of the American dream. Whatever that is."

"To be everything you're not," she said as if some grand revelation had occurred to her. She tapped the server as if it might start up. "Why would someone who, up until a few weeks ago didn't even own a computer, get into this line of work?"

"My father owned his own computer and appliance fix-it shop. I worked for him in the summers growing up. I hated it, but this kind of work is second nature to me. Machines make sense in a way people never do. The shop went under after he died. I just fell into this job. An old customer of my dad's was a teacher here. Probably felt sorry for me. The teacher got stabbed by a parent and decided to retire."

She sat with her back to mine, a tight fit on the little stool. "I always had this fantasy of making out in a school supply closet," she said. "Like in *The Breakfast Club*."

We turned our heads to the side and we were cheek to cheek. I could almost feel her breath, warm, her cheek, so soft. I closed my eyes and remembered she wasn't really there.

I plugged the server back in and watched all those gleaming green lights blink on, flickering like a Christmas tree. I watched them awhile. All that information flowing in and out. None of it any more valuable than the electronic ones and zeros it consisted of.

On the way back to my office, another assistant principal, The Hemorrhoid, caught me by the arm—*oh God, oh God, please don't touch me*—and handed me a packet of paper. "Can you scan this and send it to me in a PDF?"

"Yeah, sure. What is it?"

She made air quotations. "A manifesto."

Turns out, that anti-testing cabal taped two pieces of anti-testing propaganda to the front door of the school overnight. They also included them on a flash drive baked into an Easy-Bake cupcake covertly placed on my desk. Almost choked on the damn thing.

The first page was addressed to the adults:

Pencils Down Manifesto

We, the members of Pencils Down, believe that a teacher's certification, issued by the state, should include an implicit trust on the part of the state to rely on its professionally trained and vetted educators to accurately assess their own students. Unfortunately, standardized testing has supplanted that trust as the primary measure of a student's progress toward arbitrary and biased educational benchmarks. No other professional occupation is judged in this manner—not doctors, not lawyers, and certainly not politicians. The idea that a politician's fitness to remain in office be solely dependent on the actions and attitudes of their constituents would send them running for the hills.

At best, standardized tests measure students against a fundamentally flawed, rote-based set of standards as opposed to more meaningful ones. In short, our educational system prizes Pavlov's dog-like students who regurgitate answers with only the most cursory of considerations to the questions themselves. At worst, standardized tests reveal nothing but a student's proficiency at taking standardized tests.

Real life problems cannot be solved with canned, over simplistic answers. It's the difference between knowing which lever to pull and being able to disassemble and reassemble the parts of the lever to ever more practical, efficient, and creative uses.

It is the assertion of Pencils Down that these tests are created by people who are, in large part, not educators nor are they capable of anticipating the complexities of any individual student, classroom, or school. In addition, we believe the state has sold its students' souls to the lowest bidder, a corporate interest whose only concern is the bottom line. Testing is big business, but at what point do we decide as a society that education should transcend any and all monetary benefits?

In observance of these deeply held convictions,

Pencils Down asks students statewide to refuse the end-of-grade test. Only through unified, decisive action will changes be made. Our administrators can punish some of us, but they can't punish all *of us.*

Stand with us and when those answer documents are handed out on April 26th, encourage your students to *put their pencils down!*

The second page was addressed to their fellow middle schoolers, and in red crayon said:

TESTING IS BULSHIT. JUST SAY NO!

No middle school kid wrote that first one, they had to have had help. Still, it *was* printed on pink paper with a scary font and an angry emoticon in the corner. Not to mention the fact that it smelled like strawberry lip balm.

In spite of the aesthetic, they had me convinced.

CHAPTER 19

Maybe I was trying to make the best of a bad situation, but I managed to generate plenty of motivation to do the anti-testing website. Testing was as much a hassle to me as it was to the kids. I always had bathroom duty, only one kid allowed in at a time so they can't talk about the test. You can only watch pre-teen boys piss themselves so many times before you lose your innocence. I longed to see the student body stick it to the state, the superintendent, the school board, and all their addle-brained cronies. For abnormals like me, a standardized test was an early mile marker on a journey to abject marginalization. By whose standards were we judged? We're nuanced, complex beings, not mathematical problems to be solved and demonstrated on a chalkboard.

That Friday, I walked the streets of a nice neighborhood looking for an unsecured wireless connection because I didn't have internet at home. I sat in the bushes outside a two-story red brick on Misty Canal and piggybacked their network. Their network was called "Our_Happy_Home." Sickos.

HTML code. I didn't know what "HTML" stood for, couldn't be bothered to look it up, but I knew the language. The Bible has Greek and Hebrew, the internet has HTML. And like Biblical Greek and Hebrew, HTML propagates bullshit millions believe without question.

```
<!DOCTYPE html>
<html>
<body>
<h1>Obey.</h1>
```

<p> Jesus loves you. The aliens have landed. Government can solve your problems. Lose weight fast. It's not your fault. Jesus never existed. There are no aliens. Government solves nothing. You're beautiful the way you are. It's all your fault.</p>

```
</body>
</html>
```

If the internet says it, it must be true.

A week later, after sneaking out for two or three hours a night, I had an attractive website called pencilsdown365. net dedicated to the anti-testing revolution. Things like pencilsdown.com, putyourfuckingpencilsdown.edu, and shoveapencilupyourass.org were already taken. The website had all the information—test dates, subject areas, objectives—as well as a passionate plea for students to refuse to take state tests. Only problem was, how would I get middle schoolers to take an interest? After years of deleting rogue photos off school computers, I knew one thing that would draw them in: For boys, tits, and lots of them. For girls, pictures of whatever all-male teeny bopper group was fashionable at the time.

In exchange for digital signatures, they'd get access to the good stuff. A symbolic gesture, but with the web counter of signees constantly going up, it could be a psychological boon to the cause.

After I took it live, I sat there in the bushes, back against the wall of the house, admiring my work.

"The website looks good," Thalia said. "The porn might get you into trouble, but it's a nice touch." She sat on an electrical box to my left and watched me, head tilted.

"Just tits and ass. That's not really *porn*. Is it?"

I closed the laptop, stood up, and brushed the mulch off my pants.

"Well, no one is ever going to see it if you don't advertise," she said.

Thalia had been a master of guerilla marketing. It had certainly worked on me.

I went home and dressed up like a ninja—black sweatpants on my head, right leg wrapped above my eyes, left wrapped below them. I drove over to the school, spray painted the web address on the sidewalk out front, and then ran like hell.

CHAPTER 20

Ms. Santi, also known as Squeaky, was a first year reading teacher. She sat next to me in the uncomfortable row of plastic chairs outside the principal's office, quietly weeping.

I leaned over to her and tried to lighten the mood. "What are you in for?"

She folded a tissue in half, and wiped her nose., "To discuss my teacher evaluation. You?"

I shrugged.

The principal had a student in his office and we could hear them through the door. His secretary was drinking a diet soda that I suspected had rum in it. She kept shooting breath freshener into her mouth after every other sip.

Squeaky was trying to collect herself. I fetched another tissue from the end table and gave it to her.

"Thanks," she said.

"Sure."

"Sorry."

"It's okay."

She blew her nose.

All first-year teachers cry uncontrollably in fits and starts. It stems from the uncomfortable transition from believing their greatest enemy is ignorance to realizing their greatest enemy might well be the mother of allergy-prone Sally Frankel whose single greatest concern regarding her daughter's education is that she never, ever, eat a peanut.

Squeaky blew her nose again. "Mister Hemingway says you're writing a book."

"Yeah."

"Me too."

I crossed my legs and gave her a patronizing nod. "Writing's tough. Hard to cut through all the clutter. Internet. Social media. Stuff like that."

"Well, what kind of platform do you have?" she asked. "Traditional website? Blog?"

"Neither."

"Oh, you *have* to have a writer's blog. All the writer's publications say so. My favorite e-zine listed it as one of the top ten most important things an unpublished author can do for themselves."

"I don't have anything to blog about yet."

She wiped the mascara off her cheeks and blinked away some dampness. "They say we authors need to build a fan base so we have an audience. Ya know ...once the book comes out. *If* it comes out."

She seemed like she had a lot riding on this. I did too, I suppose, and what she said made sense. Maybe she was serious about this writing business, after all.

"We can exchange manuscripts, sometime," I said. "If you want."

"That sounds nice."

The principal's door opened and the student emerged, smiling as if he'd successfully swayed the meeting his way. "What are we gonna do next time you feel the urge to hit someone?" Mr. Johnson said to him.

"Walk away and find the nearest adult," the boy said. He had a black eye and his shirt was torn and bloody.

Principal Johnson had a way with kids. I didn't have a nickname for him. It seemed disrespectful. Maybe I was soured by the fact that the more mature eighth-graders already referred to him as "Mister Cock" or "P. Cock" sometimes, an unoriginal play on the euphemistic nature of his name.

He called me in. He generally didn't keep the lights on in his office, preferring the natural light from the window instead. His furniture was surprisingly modern. I guessed he wanted it to have a light and airy, non-intimidating look. He wore his dark brown suit and backup spectacles, the ones with scratches on them. He always looked frightened, though, his nerves ground to nubs by meddling school officials, psychotic parents, and teachers who seemed to be one twitch away from trying to shove a marker up his ass. His hair stood on end from running his hands through it, back to front. Though embarrassed for him, I decided not to point out the condition of his hair. Seemed rude.

He reached out for a little desktop Zen garden in front of him, working the sand with a tiny rake. Photos of anti-testing graffiti lay on the credenza behind him. I sat down and waited for him to get to it.

"Whatever happened with the nugget thing?" he said.

"Come again?"

"The nugget thing. The theft and vandalism. Happened right before the holidays?"

"Oh, yeah, right."

He was just now addressing this?

"That's when all this anti-testing propaganda began to appear," he continued. "Did you get a chance to review the footage? It was those twins, wasn't it? The weird ones."

"Well, I had my suspicions," I said, "but those videos are so grainy. You can never be sure."

He nodded with defeat. "And then there was the manifesto. Judging by that, they have adult help, probably one of these opt-out parents. And the website address painted on the front sidewalk yesterday morning when I arrived. It was someone from this school, I just know it. They're encouraging the student body to conduct a strike during testing. I'm sure you've seen this graffiti everywhere."

"Uh. Yes, sir. I have."

He raked the sand a little harder just thinking about it.

"Do you think you can figure out who created the website?" he said.

"It's not those twins?"

"No, no. The website's all in English."

"I can try."

"We can't have students sit out on testing," he said. He broke the rake. Startled, he put his hand to his chin, trying to keep calm, assessing the damage. He looked up at me like a beggar. "Our whole lives depend on those test results. Our bonuses. Our raises. Our school ratings. Our job performance assessments. The student's chances of positive high school and college placement."

"Oh, yes sir. Our test scores were pretty good last year. I got a decent bonus on account of it and I'm not even a classroom teacher. Trust me, I know how important testing is."

"See what you can do to find out who's behind this. If we can stop their leader, we can stop the whole movement. Make an example out of them."

"I'll do my best, sir."

"Thank you. You've always been one of the best members of our team here."

He said that to everybody. "I appreciate you saying so, sir."

He pulled a straw out of a discarded latte cup and began working the Zen garden with it, sand sticking to the end.

"Oh, and one more thing," he said.

"Yes?"

"Mister Ribbeshaw lost his laptop somewhere. Don't know when. He's foggy on the details."

"I'll file the paperwork, sir." I stood up, gave him a reassuring nod, and walked over to the door.

As I left, he called Squeaky in. She slinked by and closed the door, looking frightened.

\#

Back at home, Thalia sat on her knees in front of the laptop, reading aloud an excerpt from my unfinished book. Hearing it read back to me helped the editing process.

She looked up over the monitor at me, face illuminated in light blue. "So, do you think I'm a figment of your imagination or a ghost?"

I hated the question. Either way, it made her seem less real. "I don't know. One answer makes me crazy and the other makes me wrong about the afterlife."

She nodded and proceeded to read the rest to herself. "What do you think?"

"It's wonderful, but still needs something."

I wanted to run my fingers through her hair, to hold her head to my chest so she could listen to my heartbeat. If there was one.

"What do you think it needs?" I said.

"I don't know. A few flashbacks to fill in her background. A dream sequence maybe."

"Nah. Dream sequences are for hacks," I said.

#

I had a dream.

I was in a diner, sitting across from the burning monk who, in spite of the flames, wasn't consumed by them. He was calm, poised, and didn't even seem to know he was burning. He took a sip from his teacup, placed it on the table in front of him, and nibbled on his cinnamon-raisin bagel.

Everything was in grainy black and white. The two of us sat there staring at each other a long while.

A waitress waddled by with a coffee pot, ignoring my empty cup. If asses were sandbags, hers could've stopped a storm surge. I watched her walk down to the table on the end, her hips dipping and rising like a west Texas oil pump—right side up, left side down, left side up, right side down.

The monk put his hand to his mouth, coughed, and looked out the window. People walked by outside and didn't seem to notice him even though he sat amid a raging inferno. I looked around the diner at the other patrons eating their food and laughing and carrying on. Nothing.

The monk pulled out a cigarette and lit it with a match. I thought it was funny under the circumstances. He held the cigarette between his fingers casually, elbows on the table, and blew out a stream of smoke. The flames engulfing him crackled and whipped every time someone opened the door.

I leaned against the window and put my legs up on the seat, my left arm extended over the back of the booth. He offered a cigarette, but I waved it away. He rubbed the back of his head. As if thinking something through, he turned to look over his shoulder at the door, back at me, and then out of the window again. He took another drag and smoke spurted out of his nose in black micro-plumes. He took another sip of tea and we stared at each other awhile again.

I nodded.

He nodded.

A man on the other side of the window was dry humping a woman and she pushed him away laughing. They ran off around the corner. The kid in the booth behind me shot me with his plastic gun. His mother made no effort to stop him.

"No one cares," I said to the monk.

"Humph. You're one to talk, you self-centered prick," he replied.

When I woke up, I wrote it all down.

Meaningless bullshit, sure, but if I'm going to get up in the middle of the night to jot it down, it's going in the fucking book.

CHAPTER 21

Pencilsdown365.net was a huge success. At first. Students whispered about it in the halls. The web address appeared on lockers and bathroom stalls everywhere. The momentum was strong, and the rumor was that the tide of revolution had spread to other campuses, other cities even.

Site traffic doubled in the first couple of days, then tripled, quadrupled, and whatever's after a quadruple. An epidemic of risqué images culled from my site ran rampant on smartphones and netbooks and even a few teachers' computers. The Facebook page amassed over 1,500 likes.

I felt like a God—little g—or at least some sort of cyber-messiah. I was the subversive, the radical, the conscientious objector. It fueled my desire to write, but siphoned away time to do so as I concentrated on posting increasingly inflammatory rhetoric about standardized tests. A job worth doing is a job worth doing right.

Especially if you've been strong-armed into doing it.

The wicked little student cabal that birthed the idea was pleased with my work. One of them slipped a 3x5 notecard under my office door with a happy emoticon sticker that said: Job Well Done. I was flattered in a cool-kids-like-me kind of way. I reviewed security footage from the hall outside my office and found the culprit. A small, bespectacled girl looked both ways, dropped the card on the floor, and slid it under my door with her right foot. She wore red Converse All Stars. I didn't recognize her and couldn't raise suspicion by asking around. As with Leslie de la Muerte, I didn't know what I'd do with her if I caught her, anyway.

Alas, the nudity and other pirated content proved fatal when school administrators made a successful plea to the web hosting company to have it removed. They sought charges against the owner of the website but realized its creator probably wasn't Che Guevara, the name I used to register the free site.

It didn't matter. It had served its purpose and the buzz continued in the halls, whispered amongst students titillated by disorder.

The school district's network administrators were able to figure out the computer used to create it was Ribbeshaw's, but no one knew who actually had it. I changed the laptop's inventory status from missing to stolen and filed the appropriate paperwork. They made me look into it further. My investigation began and ended with a half-assed inquiry with Mr. Ribbeshaw.

He sat in his Corvette across the street, smoking.

"Hey computer dude, how's it hanging?" he said as I approached.

I wanted to see if I could put an end to that question. "It doesn't hang." I pointed at the scar on my face. "I was shot twice. Here and . . ." I directed his eyes down.

"Oh damn, man. Sorry," he said. He took a drag and then looked as if something had occurred to him. "Wait . . .I thought you shot yourself. Not that it's any of my business."

"You really think I'd shoot my own dick off?"

"Good point. How'd it happen? If you don't mind my asking."

I looked up over the roof of his car with an introspective glint in my eyes. "Jealous lover," I said.

"Damn." He nodded as if to say, "There, but for the grace of God, go I."

"Can I bum one of those off you?" I said, nodding my head at the pack of cigarettes on the console next to him.

"Yeah. I didn't know you smoked." He handed me one. I leaned in and he lit it for me.

I didn't smoke.

Don't cough, don't cough—

I coughed in his face with tremendous force. He leaned away, afraid I might get something on him. I collected myself and continued, "Do you remember where you saw your laptop last?"

"Your secret's safe with me, man," he said, looking at my crotch. He was probably wondering about the smallish bulge and if I wore a prosthetic of some sort. I bet he wouldn't ask me how it's hanging anymore. I nodded a thank you and bellowed out a clumsy cloud of smoke.

"Let's see," he said, "I had it getting out of my car, but I don't remember ever making it into the building with it. Now that I think about it—"

"Fair enough," I said. "Thanks for your time."

I flicked the cigarette into a storm drain and walked across the street to go back inside. The spray-painted web address was still visible on the sidewalk, though faded due to repeated power washings.

#

I went to my office, a dusty place, poorly lit and filled with dead equipment on floor to ceiling metal shelves. My desk was a piece of plywood sitting atop two stacks of gutted CPUs. I sat on a student chair that was retired from circulation when a kid drew a voluptuous pair of tits on the back of it with a Sharpie. I had spools of wire mounted on peg boards and jars of tiny screws and bins of USB cables. Complicated schematics of random machines I pulled off the internet were taped to all visible patches of wall. Shelves were piled high with derelict DVD drives and hard drives and broken mice and keyboards. None of that was necessary, but I found that the more disorienting an office is, the quicker people want to leave it.

I searched lists of author do's and don'ts, and they all agreed. I needed a writer's platform. Couldn't write in a vacuum. If I could spark interest in a silly anti-testing website, I could generate interest in my writing. Got to be careful, though. Can't offer porn or anything like that. Or maybe I could. No. I shouldn't. Got to keep it classy. People love classy authors. Publishing is a classy business. Isn't it? Sometimes it isn't. Not even close.

Just create the blog, I concluded. The rest will fall into place.

I sat back with my hands behind my head, wondering

what I might call it. I thought of all sorts of creative names, but they were all taken. I settled on *Writes for Attention* because maybe that was as honest a name as any.

"You're selling your soul to the devil," Thalia said. She was lying on her back on the only empty shelf in the room, the one I took naps on sometimes.

"That's a bit extreme, don't you think?" I said.

"Humph."

"I have to put my name out there."

She swung her legs around and sat up. "Excuse the corporate lingo, but your name is your brand. What kind of author do you want to be?"

"A ...published one."

"Do you want to regularly share your innermost thoughts with the general public?"

"Not as such, no."

"Do you want to continuously interact with people on the internet?"

"Like I want a hole in my head. Well ...*another* hole in my head."

She stood and hovered over me. "Do you want to be dark and mysterious?"

"Dark and mysterious is good."

She put her mouth close to my ear. "Do you want to be a *conformist?*"

"God, no. There's nothing worse."

"Do this blog"—she said 'blog' as if she were vomiting—"and you'll be an ant, crawling out of your hole to join an endless procession of other ants. *Everyone* has a blog. It's intellectual masturbation."

"I like to mastur—"

She scrunched up her face cautioning me not to complete that thought. She squatted next to me. Some of her hair rested on my arm, soft like the tattered end of a silk tapestry. Her breath was warm. She looked up at me, those eyes like dark jewels in the dim computer light. "You're still considering it. Why?"

I looked at my computer and pointed at the screen. "Because *Writer's Digest* says so."

"Fine." She smiled. "Do your blog if you want. Satiate your curiosity. Nothing will come of it. You'll see."

Her breath smelled like cinnamon. She radiated phantom heat. I leaned into her, but she was gone.

I'd get to the blog, but first, I needed to make some progress finding de la Muerte. I fished the address I'd gotten from his room out of my wallet.

Band Practice @ Don's. 514 Rutherglen. Last Thursday of every month

CHAPTER 22

514 Rutherglen was a lone house at the back of a cul-de-sac in an unfinished neighborhood. It was the last Thursday of January and I sat on a public bench on the other side of a few vacant lots with a clear view of the house. Finally, I saw Leslie's bandmates stumble into the garage, one by one, instruments in hand. They drove cars all beat to hell and had tattoos and long hair and a wobbly way of walking that displayed their hair's free-flowing, side-to-side sway. Leslie wasn't among them.

Thalia sat next to me on the bench. "Now what?"

"You think they know where he is?"

She smirked. "You gonna go ask?"

"I could go ask."

"What if they sacrifice you to the Devil?"

"No one really does that stuff. Do they?"

She shrugged. She had no idea.

"Seems like the Devil would be choosier than that."

As the sun began its slow bow for the day, a spastic

death metal drumbeat barreled across the field and assaulted my ears. Then came the angry guitars and blood-curdling growls of their new lead singer. I liked rock and roll, but this was aural warfare. I tried banging my head to death metal once. I got dizzy and had to lay down.

Thalia had a pained expression on her face with her fingers in her ears. "You should wait 'til they stop playing."

I didn't have the heart to tell her the Zombie Cowgirls weren't much better. Behind me and across the street, an old man walking his dog passed by, adjusting his hearing aid and mumbling something about long-haired sons of bitches and every Goddamn week. A mother cupped her daughter's ears and walked her into a house. Dogs howled. Cats fled.

A squad car showed up about forty-five minutes later and shut it down. The band members stayed in the garage and though the music didn't start up again, I could hear them, rowdy and good-humored, inside.

"Now's your chance," Thalia said.

I ordered a couple of large pizzas and had them delivered to the park and then I carried them to the garage's side door and knocked. A stocky fellow with lip rings and a bushy beard opened the door. He gave me a puzzled stare, eyed the pizza with voracious intensity, gave me another puzzled stare, and then smiled.

"Hi," I said. "Love your music. Figured you guys would be hungry after a jam session like that."

The guy pointed at me with a look of sudden recognition. "Jeff. Hey, guys, it's Jeff."

I had no idea who Jeff was.

"Jeff, get your ass in here, man," someone yelled from inside as the guy at the door stood aside to let me pass. I expected the garage to smell like weed but it mostly just smelled like gasoline from the lawnmower in the corner.

The drummer, spinning side to side on his stool said, "You lost weight dude. And cut your hair."

"And shaved," I added, guessing these people didn't know what Jeff looked like any more than I did.

"Yeah, shaved. You look, I dunno ...respectable."

I didn't know what they were high on, but whatever it was, it was primo shit. I set the pizzas down on top of a four-foot-tall Marshall amp. "Dig in, fellas."

They made a run at the pizza like starving dogs. One of them pushed me out of the way.

I looked around. "Say, where's Johnny?"

"Damn dude, you haven't heard?" The man who'd answered looked like Satan would, if Satan was a low-priced porn star.

"I've ...been in jail," I said.

"Oh yeah. Public indecency, right? No man, Johnny shot his old lady. Been on the run ever since. Rotgut there is fillin' in for 'im." He pointed at a six-foot-three mountain of a man so hairy, I could only describe him as forested.

"No shit?"

"No shit."

"That's a shame. I met this guy, record producer, who says he saw you guys play. Wants to maybe make a deal, but he seemed dead set on talking to Johnny in particular."

Porn Satan put his hand over his open, overly

excited mouth. "Damn. He must've saw us play at Crazy One Eyed Bill's last year. Nah man, I don't know where Johnny is. He was plugging some new chick, but I never met her."

The drummer piped up. "So what if some fuckin' producer wants to talk to Johnny. Johnny's goin' to jail, fellas. Not some fuckin' record studio."

The guy by the door chomped loudly. "Yeah, but Johnny's white and an entertainer. Add a record deal and they'll work somethin' out for us."

"Stupid," the drummer said.

The room erupted into vigorous debate that quickly drifted into a discussion on when their dealer was going to show up and who had the money to pay him. It was as if I became invisible. I started to leave when Porn Satan came over and leaned into me. "Hey, I saw Johnny about a week ago."

"Really?"

"Yeah, man. Didn't talk to him 'cause he was with someone, but I saw him go into this house on …Roseglen? Roselawn? Rose somethin'. He had a suitcase. The house was yellow and it had one of those half-circle driveways you don't have to back out of."

"You're *sure* it was him?"

"As sure as that poodle is sitting on the washing machine over there."

There was no poodle. There *was* a washing machine, though.

"You remember what neighborhood?"

"Nah."

"Part of town?"

He thought about it. "Nah."

"Nearby landmark?"

"Yeah, man. A Valero gas station was, like, three or four blocks down."

"There's a Valero on every corner."

"Oh. Right."

"Well, thanks. I'll tell Johnny 'hi' for you if I see him."

"Cool, bro."

That little tidbit of information turned out to be a gust of wind blowing me toward my very first felony.

CHAPTER 23

Some people think greeting card companies invented Valentine's Day, but it actually began as a pagan festival in ancient Rome. Drunken, naked men skinned goats and slapped drunken, naked women with their bloody pelts and they even had a kind of fuck-buddy lottery where they drew names from a jar and paired up; couples for festival-long merriment of the slippery phallic kind. Now *that* was a Valentine's Day I could get behind. In fact, I'd be *guaranteed* to get behind and lots of it. What ever happened to the debauched, orgiastic celebrations of old, anyway?

On second thought, I couldn't imagine anything more horrifying.

Calli caught up to me on Valentine's Day at Full o' Beans, my coffee shop around the corner. She must have spotted me through the window on her way to my house. The coffee shop had free internet and I was working on my new blog while occasionally making book notes in my loose-leaf chronicles.

She wore Thalia's coat, only she'd patched the holes. That coat was all I could see as she sat across from me. The bottom of her face was framed in the poofy collar the way Thalia's had been. I wanted to wrest it from her; she wasn't worthy to wear it. Seeing her vaguely Thalia-esque face there was like a ruined version of something exquisite—like a Corvette after a head-on collision.

She smiled, taking pleasure in my visible disgust.

"Happy Valentine's Day," she said.

"Is that today?"

"You know it is. You act like you don't care, but you do."

"Shouldn't you be out on a date or a street corner or something?"

"Cute. You've got a computer now, I see," she said. I'd affixed a skull and crossbones skin to it as a disguise. She tilted her head, noticed a thin, rectangular protrusion and peeled the corner back until she could read the property tag beneath it. "You work at that school over on 40th? That's the one with all the weird vandalism, right? I read about it in the paper."

I swatted her hand away, still fuming over the coat.

"Who's Ribbeshaw?"

I'd forgotten his name was written on the back edge of it. She snatched my loose-leaf chronicles off the table. "Why are you still writing in this?"

She flipped through the notes, shaking her head. "Still with this bullshit?"

"Leave. Me. *Alone*," I said.

"I know you're obsessed with her, you creep. I saw that puppy dog look in your eyes at the funeral. You were smitten. You're going to write her biography for me. It's a matter of principle now. Have you even looked at the stuff I gave you?"

"No. I haven't."

She tried to grab the computer away from me, but I held on to it and we engaged in a tug of war. The manager of the shop was eyeing me. He'd warned me about hanging around there and was in no mood to have his patience tried. I let go and shrunk in my seat.

I watched her click and read and scroll and read and click some more. "Ho-leeee-shit," she said after a minute or two. "You're the one who created that website the news was talking about. The one offering porn to kids."

"Keep your voice down," I said. "Not porn, *per se*. Tits and ass. Just tits and ass. And it's not like they don't already look at it. You can type ...type ...*Oprah Winfrey* in a search engine and it'll return pictures of some big-boned naked black chick with Oprah's face photoshopped on it. It's like getting in trouble for handing a kid a pecan when he's already standing under a pecan tree."

I pulled the computer back over to me.

"Methinks you'd get fired if your boss knew about this," she said in a tauntingly playful way.

God, I wanted to throw my hot coffee in her face. "Do your worst," I said.

"Don't think I won't."

I closed the lid to the laptop and cradled it in my arms looking down at the floor and rocking. I couldn't let her get me fired. I needed the income. "What do you want?" I said.

"You know what I want. Write her biography, but you're going to tell it from my perspective. Imagine me on the *Today Show*, being interviewed. That's what I want to happen. Use that thought for inspiration. Think about it—the last man to see her alive just happens to be a writer who befriends her sister at the funeral and together they write a biography about her. You can't make this stuff up. How can it lose?"

"You're a nut case."

"*I'm* a nut case?"

I sat there frustrated and ashamed that I was even considering giving in to her blackmail. "Okay," I said, "we'll have to meet regularly. I need you to tell me—"

"Uh-uh. Just make something up. You'd better make me look good, too. I gave you all that stuff last time we met. Go through it. You'll come up with something. Now I gotta take a shit in the worst way. Watch my coat?" She trotted off to the bathroom.

As soon as the door closed behind her, I tucked the coat under my arm, searched for prying eyes, and then hurried away.

CHAPTER 24

After my encounter with Calli, I went to the grocery store because I am an emotional eater.

Few public spaces make me feel more anxious than grocery stores—narrow aisles, tall shelves, carts with wobbly wheels, cryogenic food sections with glass doors that fog up when you open them. I'd been watching the lobsters in the seafood section, partly because it was an open space that gave me a breather and partly because I wondered if they would battle to the death if I reached into the tank and removed the rubber bands around their claws. They were so docile, so resigned to their fate. I wanted to see one of them do something crazy like shear the eyestalks off its nearest neighbor or burst through the glass, spill onto the floor, and make a run for it—little legs pumping, women screaming.

Through the aquarium glass, squatty and distorted, I saw the girl from the surveillance video, the one who slipped the notecard under my door, standing by the ground sirloin with her mother. I recognized her red

Converse All Stars. She was a mousy thing, smaller than most of the other kids, slouched over, glasses too big for her face. I knew it was her as soon as she locked eyes with me, face betraying fearful recognition. She looked at her mother and then the floor, trying to pretend I wasn't there.

I followed them at a distance, slightly conflicted about the moral implications of stalking a thirteen-year-old girl regardless of the fact that she was blackmailing me. As her mother searched for the perfect loaf of bread, the girl looked at me out of the corner of her eye, pulled her phone out of her back pocket a couple of inches, and then slid it back in. A warning. Threatening to expose my theft video. It was *definitely* her.

I paid for my weeks' worth of frozen potpies, went outside, and stood by the centipede of conjoined shopping baskets, waiting to spot her in the checkout line through the window. There she was. Her mother was texting. She leaned in, said something, mom nodded, and she came out to meet me.

"Okay. You know who I am," she said, standing too close and looking up at me at a severe angle. "It doesn't change anything."

"I did what you wanted. Destroy the video."

She pushed her glasses up. "I would, but there are other parties involved. They took a vote. The video stays in our possession. Each member has a copy. Sorry."

"Dammit."

"Language. If it's any consolation, you did a wonderful job with the website, although I really didn't like the pornography. The male members of the movement outvoted me when I suggested we have you remove it."

Her manner of speech had a child prodigy sophistication to it.

"Male members? Those chicken twins?"

She rolled her eyes, disappointed that I'd figured out two more identities. "I knew those two were going to be a liability. Cousins on my mother's side. They live with us. Dad's always telling me to include them in everything."

Her mom was at the register now, the cashier scanning and bagging, scanning and bagging. I looked back down at the girl. "What do you guys hope to accomplish, anyway?"

She pushed her glasses up again. "We just want kids to know they have more power than they think they do. If enough of us demand change, they'll listen."

"Who wrote the manifesto?"

"I did."

"Bullshit."

"Language. And I *did*." She scrunched up her face the way people do when they're going to come clean. "With a little help from an online message board full of civil lawyers who helped me spice up the wording. Under the guise of helping an innocent little girl with her social studies homework."

Inside the store, mom was loading the bags into the cart. "What now?" I said.

"I don't know."

I sighed with resignation. "What's your name, anyway?"

She looked as if she was calculating the risk of divulging that information, and realized I could just look her up in the school database anyway. "Elvira Moon."

"That's some name."

"You'll see it embossed on the cover of a book one day. See you around, Mister Computer Man. Thanks again." She scuttled over to the door and met her mom at the threshold.

I was frustrated and more than concerned. I couldn't lose my job. Not now. I went back inside the store to buy cigarettes and a lighter. I always heard smoking calmed the nerves. Not as much as a bullet to the head, but still.

A pervert in line in front of me had ten boxes of condoms. He dumped them out of his arms onto the conveyor belt and leered at the teenage cashier as if to suggest she didn't want to miss out on the party. A party, I assumed, that would end with her in chains in a basement.

Was there any honor left among us?

"Sir," I spoke in earnest, "Those are snuggies, for the man of extra small proportions. Kudos to you for standing up and being proud of it. Why, I think the short hung should have parades, just like the gays do, and come out to their parents and everything."

I patted him on the shoulder. He was confused and more than a little embarrassed. The girl laughed until he walked away, leaving his purchases behind. She rang up my cigarettes, still chuckling. That made me feel a little better.

CHAPTER 25

Days went by and my blog wasn't doing well. The net traffic statistics didn't lie. I closed the laptop's lid and set it aside.

A cigarette hung loosely from my lips, smoke rising and spooling in the golden morning light passing through the window. The house smelled stale, smoke already entrenched in the carpet and upholstery.

The backpack Calli gave me leaned against the wall. Above it, Thalia's coat hung from a nail. Sometimes, I liked to sniff it and rub its sleeves on my cheek. I stared at the backpack.

Open it?

The backpack could hold the answers to a more complete understanding of Thalia, but I didn't want that. Not really. I *needed* the mystery. I needed not to know, to supply my own answers the way religious people and conspiracy theorists do. I needed *my* version of Thalia.

I left the backpack there.

Thalia appeared next to it with a wicked smile upon

her lips. "What are you scared of? Don't you want to know the *real* me?"

"You're already all I need to know."

"Awww. Sweet. It's nice to know I left a lasting impression. But aren't you at all concerned about authenticity?"

I wanted to take her right there on the floor just to reaffirm the fact that she was mine.

"I want to know you as you were in that one perfect moment I met you. This version of you doesn't get headaches or need to go to the dentist. This version of you isn't a slob. Your shit doesn't stink. You can't really hurt me."

She grew teary-eyed. Because she was moved? Insulted?

"Shit." I extinguished the cigarette and crept over to the backpack on my knees, knocking over a stack of books along the way. The phone rang again.

I opened the flap of the backpack and saw an 8x10 glossy of her, probably sixteen, seventeen. She wore a yellow sweater. Brown hair. Bad teeth. She sat on a stool in front of a cheap, photo studio background, one with autumn trees and a lake and a grand, white country house with smoke billowing out of the chimney.

I slipped it back in and vowed to never again open that infernal bag.

I looked at the time on my phone. 8:43 a.m. I had my monthly appointment with Dr. Norman at 9:00. I could use the help.

\#

"I think I'm psychotically depressed," I said, sitting on Dr. Norman's ugly golden ochre couch. I'd already been there awhile, filling out a questionnaire with emotionally intrusive questions—

1. In the last two weeks, I've thought about suicide:
a. not at all
b. 1–5 times
c. 5–10 times
d. constantly.

2. I find it hard to talk about my feelings:
a. not true
b. sometimes true
c. true

—shit like that.

"I see someone's been reading about depression on the internet again." He wore a turquoise dress shirt with no tie and the sleeves rolled up.

"I have all the symptoms."

"What have I told you about self-diagnosing?"

"Don't."

"You have neither the training nor the objectivity to assess your own state of mind. Regardless of what you might think, I do more than just tick off boxes on a list of symptoms. When you first came here, you were convinced you were bipolar. Then it was cyclothymia. Hyper-empathy. Narcissism. And let's not forget my favorite, schizophrenia."

"You agreed with me about narcissism. And I was just fucking with you when I said I thought I was schizophrenic."

"Yeah. Sure, you were, Ches. You have dysthymia."

Dysthymia. I knew the description. "Chronic but *mild* depression—mild is a very deceptive word in this context by the way—with an increased risk of major depressive episodes."

"That's right. Like the episode that first brought us together."

"Did you know more than three million people are diagnosed with dysthymia per year?"

"Sounds about right. Too common for you? You wish you had something more exotic?"

I didn't answer.

"Trust me, you ought to be glad you don't have something more severe."

"Why don't they roll all the kinds of depression into one thing?" I asked. "Call it Depressive Personality Disorder or something like that. Psychopathy and sociopathy are called Antisocial Personality Disorder now. Asperger's and autism are Autism Spectrum Disorder." Something occurred to me. "What if someone had all three? DPD, APD, *and* ASD. Would he, like, murder a pre-ordained number of people, cut them up, organize their body parts in little piles according to size, then hang himself with such mathematical precision that the coroner lets him dangle longer than normal just to bask in the mechanical beauty of it?"

Dr. Norman stared at me, disapproving. "Anyway," he said, "What is it that has you thinking about all this?"

"For starters, I've been seeing Thalia for the past couple of months."

"Do you believe she's really there? Do you think other people can see her?"

"Yeah, no. I'm not sure. What difference does it

make?"

"It's the difference between having an imaginary friend and a genuine hallucination."

"A hallucination. She's a hallucination."

"No, she's not."

"Ghost?"

He shrugged. "Beyond my expertise."

"There's a lot of pressure on me right now."

"Like what?"

"I'm being extorted by Thalia's sister, blackmailed by these weird kids at work, Libby's getting married to this asshole from high school, I'm trying to write this book. Almost finished with it."

"Blackmail? Extortion?"

"And grandiose thinking. Fantasizing about being famous. I got in a fight with Thalia's dad a while back. Oh, and I got into it with that pharmacist, the one who called you all those times to check my prescriptions."

He pinched the bridge of his nose as if deciding whether I was full of shit or legitimately crazy. I was afraid he might accidentally thumb his artificial eye out, but when he looked back up, it was still firmly ensconced in its socket.

"There's a lot to unpack here," he said. "We're almost out of time. I have a ten o'clock. I want to meet with you every week for the foreseeable future. Here." He handed me a prescription. "Get back on your meds."

I snatched the prescription. "I can't go back to McKay's pharmacy."

"Then don't. There are hundreds of pharmacies in the city."

"I'll try."

He took a chastising tone. *"Ches."*

"I'll try."

I wasn't going to try shit. I was hoping he'd prescribe me something that would make me see bright spinning colors, unicorns with tits, and talking DayGlo salamanders, but it was for eighty milligrams of fluoxetine. As usual.

I wonder if he regrets not putting me on something more substantial?

CHAPTER 26

March 6th. I slipped into the school's copy room and printed what I had of my manuscript in 12-point Times New Roman with one-inch margins all around. I gave it to Hemi and a week later, we met in the teacher's lounge.

"First off," he said, and leaned forward, whispering, "did you really steal Jack's computer?" He was referring to Mr. Ribbeshaw. "Because if you did, that's funny as hell. Guy's a dick."

I hadn't even thought about the ramifications of showing my story to a coworker. "Nah, I made that up."

He looked disappointed.

"What did you think of the rest?" I asked.

"Man, dude, I don't get it," he said, sliding my manuscript across the lounge table at me.

"I'm not done, of course, only about hal—"

"I don't think it's salvageable. Not as a proper book at least."

He cracked open the soda I bought him and took

a sip. The break room smelled like burned popcorn. I inadvertently put my finger in a dried blob of gum on the bottom of my chair. I had the sudden urge to pick it off and drop it in his soda while he wasn't looking.

"What do you mean 'Not as a proper book?' "

"Where're you going with this? What's your point? This isn't much more than a personal diary. Hell, it's not even a *good* diary. You've gotta raise the stakes. Life and death, man. Your non-fiction certainly reads like fiction so you might as well make some stuff up. Beyond petty theft, I mean. Sex and violence always works. I gotta be honest, you're just not that interesting. Your life thus far works only as, I don't know, a cautionary tale?"

What do you know, you balding circus monkey?

"And your dialog lacks ...lacks sizzle, ya know."

"Sizzle?"

"Yeah. I'm sitting on the porch swing in the backyard last night and I overhear the couple next door. The lady says, 'Whadja get me for my birthday, Johnny?'—she had a trashy accent, but I couldn't place it, maybe New Jersey or Chicago—and Johnny says, 'I got you lemons, bitch, now go make me some lemonade.' Ha. He actually said that and I thought, now that guy's got sizzle," Hemi chuckled just thinking about it and then his face straightened. "Yeah, your characters don't have sizzle."

"Sizzle."

He shrugged. "Don't feel bad. And don't give up, either. They say almost all first books are unprintable. Even the masters had misses, man. Michael Chabon's *Fountain City*. Abandoned 1,500 pages in. Stephen King never published *The House on Value Street*. Hell, Evelyn Waugh burned his manuscript of *The Temple at*

Thatch and then tried to kill himself. But to be fair, a dude named Evelyn might have had other issues in the mix."

I sighed and slumped in my chair, properly deflated.

"Hey, you asked for honest feedback," Hemi added. "Someone else might feel differently."

I was pouring my life into those pages, the ignorant swine. It was a work of genius.

Wasn't it?

What if it wasn't?

But then again, what if Hemi was too stupid to know genius when he saw it? He never finished a novel of his own. How could a failed writer give *me* advice?

"You're right," I said. "I did. I should have some more pages for you to look at soon."

He made a lemon-squeeze face and eked out an indecisive groan. "I don't really have time right now with spring break and testing coming up and all. Do you have anyone else who can look at it?"

Before I could answer, he pulled a paper from a stack of student work he'd set on the table between us. "Now, this girl is going to be a hell of a writer. Best I've seen in all my years of teaching. Does these great character descriptio—"

"What's her name?"

"Elvira Moon," he said, beaming. "Isn't that great? What a great name for a writer."

"Yeah. I guess it's pretty good."

I indulged in another Thalia-kills-Hemi fantasy, one involving a turkey baster, and then grabbed my manuscript and left him sitting there looking smugly perplexed at my reaction.

On my way out, I bumped into Squeaky. She looked happy, not crying like the last time I spoke to her. She handed me her manuscript. "I was hoping maybe you could check it out and see what you think."

I took it and looked at the title—*A Kiss Before Living*—what did that even mean?

"Yeah, okay," I said. *I don't have time for this.*

"Is that yours?" she asked, looking down at my manuscript.

"Yeah. First half, anyway."

"Can I read it?"

Are you really interested or do you feel obligated now? "Sure. Knock yourself out." Hemi walked out into the hallway about that time. "*Some* people say it sucks," I added. Hemi smirked, shook his head, and rounded the corner.

That afternoon, I slashed his tires because I thought it would make my story more interesting.

CHAPTER 27

I was lying on my back with Thalia in the grass at the park down the street that following Sunday. Our feet pointed opposite directions and her head was right next to mine and upside down. A cloud floated above us that looked like Miss Piggy.

Despite Thalia's usual allure, a grandiose daydream stole me from the moment and I sat on a stage next to Oprah Winfrey in front of a live studio audience. Oprah came out of retirement just for me. The daydream went like this:

"How does it feel to win the Pulitzer twenty years in a row?" she asks.

"It's not about the awards, Oprah, it's about making a *difference*."

Wild Applause. I stand up and do a jig, just to get the crowd going. Women hyperventilate and collapse. Men do too.

Oprah waits for calm. "What was it like in those early

days when you were just starting out?"

I get teary eyed and have to look away to compose myself. Finally, I turn back. "It was hard. *Really* hard." A single tear rolls down my cheek and I wipe it away as she hands me a tissue. "I lived in a refrigerator box under the bridge, surviving mainly off a diet of nutria, mosquitoes, and motor oil. I wrote with a paper clip that I'd stick in my forearm—I used blood for ink in those days—and I'd write on the backs of real estate signs I pilfered from yards in the surrounding neighborhoods. Nobody cared about me, not even my family or friends. Hell, the other under-the-bridge folk wouldn't even read my stuff. And believe me, they had *nothing* better to do."

I pull out a cigarette rolled in a hundred-dollar bill and lit it. They don't allow smoking on the set but make an exception for me. I take a long drag and reflect on my life, tapping ash out on the shiny, hardwood floor. I blow a little smoke in Oprah's face and though it makes her cough, she finds it delightfully charming.

"How did you finally get noticed?"

"I accosted literary agents as they drove by." I chuckle. "I'd jump on their hoods and throw beer cans at them, screaming about the book, and shoving manuscripts through their sunroofs. I got pepper sprayed and arrested so many times, I lost count." Everyone laughs and I nod to encourage them. "Yeah, yeah. But ya know, word got around—the agents talk amongst themselves and one of them finally took the time to read it. The rest is history, so to speak."

That would show 'em. Hemi, Libby, Dr. Norman, and the rest.

Another cloud, this one shaped like a cow and kissed

with golden evening light, brought me back to reality. My daydreams always spun out of control like that. The requisite downward spiral of assumed imminent failure took hold as it so often does when my narcissistic dreams soar too high.

"I'm having doubts," I said. Thalia's face was close, hair tickling my temple.

"About what?"

"The book."

She turned her head slightly in my direction. "Oh. I thought you were happy with it."

"Am I able to really put this story into a *reader's* mind?"

"It's too subjective. You can't know what your readers experience as they read your work."

"I feel like there's something missing."

"Well, the various threads aren't finished, yet. One big one comes to mind."

"Leslie—John de la Muerte—Olenbacher III."

Thalia turned on her side and pecked me on the cheek. "You'll sort it out."

Even though I was only about thirty-five thousand words into my book—that's novella territory—I fully expected its conclusion to be written shortly after the events of March 24th, the day I decided to avenge Thalia's death. My plan had all the makings of a satisfying conclusion to the series of events described herein. I would lurk in the shadows, stalking my prey through the cold, hard city streets, waiting for the perfect time to reveal myself, gun in hand, and exact bloody revenge on my nemesis, Leslie, the villain of this tragic tale.

\#

A yellow house on Rosesomething with a half-circle driveway. That's all I'd gotten from Leslie's old bandmate. Ever since that night, I'd been looking for the house. First, I did an internet search of all street names and made a list of ones with "rose" in the name. Then I looked them up on a map and arranged them most likely to least likely according to parts of town. Finally, I did street level virtual tours down each one.

Rose Meadow. It was on Rose Meadow. Yellow house. Half-circle driveway. Valero down the street. I ran searches for the address, but couldn't find anything of use, nor how this house connected to Leslie.

I drove to the house on a Friday evening and sat in my car, staring at the place for three hours, waiting for anyone to come out or go in. My gun was in the glove compartment. It was almost dark when I saw him. He passed under the porch light, walked down three steps, and got into a minivan.

Captain Ahab had found his white whale.

I followed the homicidal piece of shit down the street and around the corner to a drugstore on Finmont. My heart was thumping, hands shaking. He parked in the second spot to the end, a conveniently dark place between the fluorescent cast of the store windows and the orange halo of the streetlight. I parked by the dumpster behind the store.

"You sure you know what you're doing?" Thalia asked as I pulled the gun out of the glove compartment. She was in the backseat, leaning forward, hugging the headrest of the passenger seat in front of her.

"It's like the night I shot myself. Just do it. Quick. Don't think."

"Look how that turned out."

I shrugged.

"I don't like guns."

"They're not so bad." I admired the weight of it, the way it fit cleanly in my hand. "I can think of at least two justifiable reasons for having one right off the top of my head."

"And they are?"

"Suicide. *Everyone* should have access to an expeditious death."

"And again, I have to bring up your failure at said expeditious death. What's the second? Home defense?"

"No. That's bullshit. It's like living in a rickety glass bubble under water that could collapse in on itself at any moment just to avoid the remote possibility of a house fire."

"Okay. What's the second?"

"Snakes."

"*Snakes.*"

"Nasty creatures. One time, Libby and I had a picnic under some low-hanging trees on the bank of the Colorado River, up near La Grange, when this Goddamn three-foot water moccasin fell out of the tree and landed with this sick, dull *smack* right across a plate of brisket. I've never wanted to decisively kill something so fast in my life. Fucker had to go, but I had nothing to kill it with. White-mouthed and hissing. I told Libby picnics were bad news, but *no,* she wanted a romantic day in the country. I ended up running like hell to the car and never looked back, but what I needed was a *shotgun.* Point and shoot. No aim, just pull the trigger and behold a bloody bloom of meat and bone. Did you know some snakes can bite up to an hour after decapitation? An hour. No body. Just a *head. Hell* no." I aimed the gun at nothing in particular. "An apocalypse on them all, I say."

At first, she looked at me as if I'd farted, but then she smiled. "Look at you, all full of nervous energy."

"I guess."

"What if you get caught? You've made sure you're on that detective's radar with your probes into my murder. It's not such a great leap to finger you for it."

She had a point. Still, Leslie had to pay. If *I* found him, the cops should have found him a long time ago. They probably weren't even looking.

I stepped out of the car, tucked the gun in the front of my jeans, and waited around the corner of the store, out of sight. He came out after twenty minutes, fumbling with his car keys while managing four shopping bags. This was it. My big chance. I moved out of the shadows, gun in hand, and took aim.

POP!

It's like the trigger pulled itself, I wasn't even cognizant of it. Leslie winced and dropped his bags. I'd missed, shattering the rear window of an SUV on the other side of the parking lot.

He held his hands up submissively. I got a good look at his face and, while the resemblance was striking, it wasn't him.

I lowered the gun, apologized for the attempted murder, and ran back to the car. I raced out of the alley and took a left. Maybe he wouldn't see what I was driving. The street lights rolled over me like the tread of a moving tank. A cop car was up ahead. I took a right through a neighborhood and wove through the narrow streets to the next major road.

When I got home, I ran straight to the restroom and threw up.

"You actually pulled the trigger," Thalia said, standing behind me as I leaned over the commode.

"No shit."

"You really would have killed him for me."

I nodded, took a strip of toilet paper, wiped my mouth, flushed, and then sat on the floor with my back against the tub. "Yeah." I chortled. "Yeah, I guess I would have."

She caressed my face with the back of her fingers and looked into my eyes, her irises darting from right to left. I leaned in for a kiss, but she pulled back. "You've got puke on your chin."

"Shit." I unfurled some more toilet paper and wiped it off.

Thalia started to giggle, her shoulders quickly shaking up and down as she held her hand over her mouth.

"What?"

"You really are the worst shot I've ever seen."

I hung my head, arms draped over my knees, and laughed. Leslie was out of reach. I had no other leads. My book's big finish had fizzled. All I could do was laugh—that is, until the fear of a potentially immanent arrest sucked all the kooky fun out of the situation.

CHAPTER 28

The following week, after coming to terms with my new identity as an attempted murderer, I found Elvira Moon sitting in the cafeteria nibbling on a PB&J and looking around sheepishly for someone, anyone, to be nice to her. It was at that moment that I first suspected social rejects probably ran the Pencils Down movement. I surmised they started this grand rebellion to lead the very ones who'd turned their backs on them. That endeared them to me.

I dodged a couple of errant peas flung from the next table and sat down across from her. She scooped her lunchbox towards herself as if I might steal it. She stared at me, chewing.

"Hi," I said.

"Nice to see you again," she said, left cheek pooched out with sandwich.

I saw she had a book on the seat next to her, but I couldn't see the title.

"Whatcha readin'?"

She swallowed and looked down, back at me, and then picked it up to display the cover.

Twilight. Doesn't bode well.

"Good?" I said.

"Drivel. I'm just reading it to learn how *not* to write."

Kid had promise.

"I should show you some of my writing."

She rolled her eyes. "I've heard about your writing."

"What? How?"

"Mister Hemingway."

"He talks about my writing in class?"

"Used you as an example once. He put an excerpt of some of it on the board and made us find the grammatical errors. There were sixteen. I was the only one in my class who found them all. Everyone else missed that you used 'your' instead of 'you're' and that you ended a sentence with a preposition."

"That preposition rule is passé," I said, attempting to recover at least a little dignity. "It's okay to end a sentence with a preposition these days."

"Not the way you did it," she said.

"Okay. You passed."

"Passed what?"

"Mister Hemingway says you're one of the best writing students he's ever had. I had to see it for myself."

She blushed. "He does?"

"Well, sure. And if you wrote even twenty-five percent of that manifesto, I'm moderately impressed too. Do any freelancing?"

"What's that?"

"It's where someone pays you to write something for

them. Like articles or ...or biographies maybe."

"Not really."

She had a funny voice, a little voice. Most kids do, I guess.

"I need someone to ghostwrite a biography for me. I scratched your back, now you scratch mine."

"Scratch your back? Look, mister. I'm not going to go to your van for candy."

"Funny. Look, I made that website for you and your little group. Now you do this for me."

"I don't know. I'm only thirteen. What do I know about writing a biography?"

"Did you know Shakespeare was four when he wrote Hamlet?"

"Really?"

"No, of course not. But the point is, you believed me for a second and I believe you believe you can do this."

"And if I don't, you'll tell everyone about my involvement with Pencils Down?"

This is what it'd come to. Blackmailing children. "Yeah."

"But then I'll just show them your video."

"Well then, we'll just go down together."

She stared at me blankly.

"Look, I'll sweeten the deal," I said. "What would it cost me?"

"I like books and my mom can't afford many."

"If I keep you stocked up on books, you'll write it for me?"

"Sure. I guess."

"How fast can you write? I need to start getting pages for this thing pretty fast."

"I could maybe do a couple pages a night. Who's the biography about? Johnny Depp? Please say it's Johnny Depp. I wrote a paper about him in fourth grade."

"No one gives a shit about Edward Scissorhands anymore."

"Language."

"Sorry. Look, this is about someone I knew. Someone very important. She died. I'll bring you all the information I have and you can get started, okay?"

She twisted her mouth and rubbed her chin, giving it skeptical consideration. "Okay," she said. "I'll make a list of the books I want."

"Fair enough. Now you can't sign your name to it, okay? That's just part of the deal, so don't go thinking you can sue me for the rights later or something. And when in doubt, just make something up."

"Okay."

"Oh, and your subject has a sister named Calli. Tell it from Calli's perspective."

"I don't know anything about this Calli person."

"Let's see." I thought about it a moment. "She's like the ugly sister the boogeyman keeps in his attic."

"That'll be a hard sell, don't you think?"

"I suppose so. I suppose so. You know what artistic license is?"

"Yeah, I guess."

"Well, there you go. As long as it's flattering, she'll never know the difference. I'll get the materials to you by tomorrow and expect some pages the day after that."

We shook on it. Her hand was like a doll's hand only not plastic.

"Thank you, Elvira Moon," I said.

"You're welcome, strange computer man."

\#

Two girls got into a fight after school, shoving, punching, pulling hair, and finally writhing on the ground as they attempted to sit on top of each other and get in a few more unprotected blows to the face. They were like rabid dogs. I'd spotted the crowd outside under the awning by the gym and shoved my way through the makeshift ring of knuckleheaded spectators, half of whom were recording it on their phones. I managed to pull one of them off the other as they jawed at each other using colorful derivatives of "fuck" and "bitch" previously unknown to me. I had to grab one's wrist and pry her fingers off the other one's hair to get a clean break between them. A female teacher busted in and pulled one to the side, a relief for me, as male adults grabbing female students, even fighting ones, can easily turn into accusations of inappropriate groping.

Girl fights were the worst. Relentless, emotional, violent, and lacking the unspoken code of honor observed by boys—no sucker punches, no shots to the balls, no biting, no hair pulling. Clumps of hair were on the ground. As the school officer hauled the girls away, an assistant principal started confiscating the phones of the little ingrates who'd filmed it.

As per district procedure, I went to our police officer's office and sat down to write a statement about what I saw and what I did to stop it. My hands weren't shaking. I was calm. Notable because I'd had a lifelong aversion to violence that always left me trembling for hours anytime I witnessed acts of such vehemence.

I remembered very little about high school, but I

remembered the fights. I remembered Nicolai Johnson sidled up behind Ty Ford as he sat in the cafeteria and smashed his face into the table. Broke his nose. Got blood on me. Jenny Marquez slapped Tiffany Brown on the back of the head as they were getting off the bus and a nasty exchange of blows happened right there on the bus's steps, Tiffany pinned Jenny in the narrow exit and pounded her in the chest while Jenny held her arms up over her face. A guy I didn't know walked down the hall between 3rd and 4th period when three boys rushed out of the crowd and pounced on him from behind, the way a wave crashes over rocks. Bill Feldman was punched in the face for bumping into a gangbanger from Southwind. You could follow a trail of drizzling blood all the way from the courtyard, down the main hall, and into the clinic. Feldman was lucky. It could have been much, much worse. Charlie Awolowo was an amicable enough guy, always nice to me, and I was shocked when I saw him sucker punch a teacher and commence beating an underclassman half his size, culminating in a body slam that left the smaller boy unconscious. Bo Nguyen wore shiny black shoes with chrome tips that came to a dull point and he occasionally used them to get a couple of free kicks in on fights he didn't have anything to do with. He said he just did it for kicks. Ha ha, very funny, motherfucker. Juanita Villalobos damn near scratched Samantha Smith's eyes right out of her head at the back of the bus while we were on a field trip to the zoo. They tore each other's clothes to ribbons and clawed at the exposed flesh. That was the first time I saw real live tits.

Each of these moments was a mild form of trauma that left me queasy, unfocused, and shaking. Sick to my stomach. No appetite. And judging by the excitement of the crowds that gathered around these brawls and their subsequent reenactments and embellished retellings, I knew I was alone in that reaction. I took it as a sign that I was meant for peace, to live a life of nonviolence.

When I saw the girl fight break out after school, the fact that it didn't faze me was a sign that maybe I'd turned an appalling corner. In the months leading up to that day, I'd punched a man. Knocked him out. I got into a verbal altercation with a pharmacist. I tried to *kill* someone. Was I becoming accustomed to brutality? Just how far was I willing to go? Was I stumbling into the animalistic urges of the masses? God, I hoped not. For me, to be "normal" was a fate worse than hell.

\#

My blog doubled in hits. It'd gone from half a visit per day to a full visit per day. One of the visitors even left a comment. It was about purchasing discount shoes online. If I avoided raw numbers and described the growth in percentages, I could spin it into quite the blogging success story.

"OMG! Yay, me."

We may have computers, internet, printers, and word processors, none of which the great writers of old had access to, but those guys never had to screw around with social media.

If you ask me, *they* had the better deal.

\#

I already owned most of the books on Elvira Moon's list, the rest I found at the second-hand bookstore for an average of a $1.99 each.

I met her by the flagpole after school, the books

stacked in four plastic grocery bags. I set them down in front of her and she pulled a few out, checking to make sure everything was there.

"Used?" she said.

"What's wrong with used? No pages missing or anything."

"No offense, creepy computer man, but you're a cheap bastard."

"You have the pages or not?"

She handed me a binder. I flipped through it, saw that it looked pretty good, and nodded. She grasped the floppy handles of all four bags and struggled to pick them up.

"Nuh-uh," I said. "One bag now, the rest a little as you go. You'll get the final bag when you hand me the final draft. Which bag do you want first?"

She looked through them.

"This one," she said.

"Then that's the *last* one you'll get."

She scowled and kicked me in the shin. It hurt so badly my vision went white. "Oww!" I kneeled down to rub it. "You need incentive to finish. It's just good business."

"This time next week," she said, pointing at me. "I'll give you another section." She grabbed one of the other bags and went away, limping under its weight.

Given all that happened, I'm still not sure if enlisting Miss Moon was a good idea.

CHAPTER 29

Calli finally caught up to me. In order to avoid her, I'd started parking on the street behind my house, jumping the fence, and entering through the back door. She intercepted me as I swung my left leg over the old wood slats on my way into the yard.

She sat on an old refrigerator that was nestled in a patch of ragweed in the shadow of a dying crepe myrtle. My laptop and loose-leaf chronicles were in her lap and she wore Thalia's coat over her white sundress even though it was hot as hell out. Obviously, she'd been inside. She was doing something new with her hair. It was blue and curly and reminded me of pocket lint. Sweat was beading on her forehead and I could only imagine how bad she must have smelled. Fortunately, I was upwind.

"You're trespassing," I said.

"Where're the pages I asked for? I don't see them here."

"How did you get in my house?"

She nodded toward a broken window on the back porch.

"You broke my window?"

"I didn't. Mikey did."

I felt a presence behind me, saw a shadow creep up. I turned to see Mikey, a freakishly tall, lanky fellow with a thick neck, slight shoulders, and a bowl cut. Against the blinding light of the sun, he looked like a penis standing erect in the middle of my yard.

He popped me in the nose. It wasn't a hard hit, but involuntary tears welled up in my eyes. I stumbled back and faced Calli again. As absurd as it was, she seemed to be the more reasonable of the two.

"That's Mikey," Calli said. "He used to date Thalia when they were in third grade."

"Third grade?" I said, looking back at him. "Jesus."

Mikey came around to a more suitable viewing light. Still looked like a penis, but more like one of those big donkey dicks that would be comical if it wasn't so intimidating.

"I think you two should leave or I'll call the police and report you for breaking and entering." They knew I was about to do no such thing.

"Where're the pages?"

"They're right here," I said and handed her a satchel with Elvira Moon's work. I hadn't even read it yet.

She considered the satchel a moment and then grabbed it from me. Mikey watched her open it and then squinted at me as if trying to explode my head with the power of his mind. The thought of it made me want to giggle, amused at the thought of ejaculatory brainwaves crushing my skull. I kept it together to avoid another nose bump.

Calli read, Mikey stared, I waited. She sat back down on the refrigerator as she skimmed it, nodding.

"This is good," she said. "*Really* good. We might actually be onto something here."

"Really?" I said.

"Don't you think?"

"Uh. Yeah. Sure, I guess. It's not my genre. I'm only writing it 'cause I like you."

"Asshole."

The Dick chuckled. He obviously had a thing for her. Why wouldn't he? She was, after all, a cunt.

"Oh my God, this is so much better than that other stuff you were writing."

"No," I said, incredulous. "Not better. *Different.*"

"No. Better. *Way* better. I mean, I can't even believe this is written by the same person better. It's really good."

"Okay," I said. "Whatever you say."

A thirteen-year-old girl can write better than I can.

Calli looked up from the pages and smiled. "Come on, man," she said. "Why so glum? I'm paying you a compliment here. I'm sorry, but this," she held it up for emphasis, "is your calling, not that other stuff. The other stuff is just—"

"Well, if you don't mind, I've got somewhere to be."

"Where do you have to be?"

"Inside. I need to be inside. You've got your pages, more are on the way, let's not force ourselves to endure each other, and Mikey here, any longer than we have to."

"You're such a freak," she said as she came over to

me and shoved my things into my chest. Mikey chuckled again and the two of them left, cutting through the house to get to the street.

"I want that coat back," I called after her.

"Up yours," she called back.

CHAPTER 30

The night before testing. April 25th. Ready or not, all grade levels were running face first into academia's show of shows. I was antsy, sitting in the corner, staring at the burning monk and pondering my book revisions. My cigarette was burned down to a nub. I stamped it out and lit a new one. Pondering my book almost always led to pondering ways to procrastinate writing it. "The school needs a Pencils Down refresher. The buzz has waned," I said.

"So, what?" Thalia said.

She sat on the bed, dressed like a schoolgirl—plaid skirt, short sleeve button down, black tie. Her knees were together, hands resting on the edge of the bed, pushing her shoulders up above her jaw line.

"Haven't you always wanted to see a real live revolution?" I asked. The room was smoky, like a bar.

She laughed, slouched over, and then straightened up again. "This isn't a revolution," she said. "This is one step up from a food fight."

"You don't understand how important testing is to these people. If the kids put their pencils down and refuse to take it, if word gets out they're doing this, if it becomes a trend, it ...it could—"

"It could what? Change things?"

"Maybe."

"That's really all this is, isn't it? You just want to shake things up. You have no control over anything in your life and here you've found one small thing that maybe you can help change. You're lost."

Her knee highs were white silk and I could almost feel the stretch of them, the tautness over her calves, the way they would wrinkle between my fingers if I were to pull them down over her china doll feet—

"You really think they'll do it?" she said.

—to cup my hand beneath the gently calloused sole of her foot like Prince Charming, to run my fingers up the soft inside of her leg—

"Well?"

—Tracing up and up, her skin warm to the touch.

I shook it off. Couldn't disrespect her memory like that. It didn't feel consensual, either.

"I don't know," I said, palms sweaty. "Seems like the momentum waned after they took the site down. It's been a while."

She leaned forward, resting her elbows on her knees. She twisted her mouth to the right, deep in thought. "Maybe they do need one last push," she said.

The phone rang again. Neither of us flinched.

#

Midnight. I parked a block away and walked to the school, dressed like a ninja. Though I had keys to the building, I entered the same cafeteria window the twins smashed on their chicken run. It had a piece of plywood over the hole that was easy to punch in. I knew no alarm would go off. The mask ensured that even if someone other than me looked at the video footage, they wouldn't know who they were looking at.

The halls were dark. Pale orange light poured through the windows at pleasant angles, from the street lamps outside. The halls smelled like bleach and lemon-scented floor cleaner.

Thalia walked backward in front of me, dressed like a cheerleader. "This is exciting."

"What the hell am I doing here?"

She turned back around and walked next to me. "You're an outlaw." She pointed at a bank of lockers. "Here's good."

I spray painted, PENCILS DOWN: IF YOU ALL FAIL, NONE OF YOU FAIL, diagonally across them.

She did a handstand and walked on her palms for a few feet, skirt flipped up around her stomach. Red underwear. When she was upright again, she asked me my favorite kind of music.

"I like everything. Except maybe jazz and country."

She pointed at another bank of lockers.

As I spray painted, REFUSE THE TEST! as large as it would fit in the area.

"Jazz? Really?"

"I feel like I'm supposed to like it, ya know. Like, *obligated*. But I just don't. There's too much going on. I find it disorienting."

"Fair enough. Favorite book?"

"Tough one." I was walking around the corner,

entering the cafeteria. "*Where the Wild Things Are*, I guess."

"That's kind of heartbreaking."

She made finger guns at the cafeteria tables with both hands. She fired, blew the smoke out of her index finger barrels, and holstered them. I spray painted the tables.

"Let's see, favorite TV show?"

"Don't watch much TV. Why is it heartbreaking?"

"What?"

"Why is it heartbreaking that I like *Where the Wild Things Are*?"

"*Where the Wild Things Are* was an angry, lonely kind of story. It's sad. You're kind of an angry, lonely kind of guy."

"I never thought of it that way. I liked the fact that this kid got lost in his own imagination. Anyway, I try not to be angry. Can't help the loneliness."

She turned my attention to a cinderblock wall between the boy's and girl's restrooms.

REFUSE THE TEST! The paint fumes were acute and intoxicating, wafting through the halls, making me lightheaded.

A little further down, Thalia patted the elevator doors. "Let's see. Favorite graphic novel?"

I tried to paint a broken pencil on the elevator, but my hands were shaking, partly out of fear and partly because my hands were tired. I made the eraser too big and the pencil ended up looking like a crooked dick.

I faced Thalia. "Easy. *V for Vendetta*."

"Lovely," she said, looking at the elevator. She pointed at a door across the hall. "What's in there?"

"Supply closet."

"Oh. Let's have a look."

I opened the closet and found the school's cache of No. 2 pencils stacked high in little boxes of forty-eight. As I snatched boxes off the shelves, she asked me my favorite movie.

"*Taxi Driver.*"

"Huh. Figures."

I scattered thousands of pencils in the school entry hall. It sounded like it was raining sticks.

"Did I already ask about TV?"

"Yeah. But now that I think about it, I guess I'd have to say *Alf.*"

"*Alf? ALF?*"

"Well, yeah. That furry little fucker was funny."

"Maybe if you were twelve."

"I was—"

Motion.

A flashlight bounced in the windows across the courtyard, rounded the corner, coming my way. I panicked, froze, and looked back and forth, unable to decide where, or *if*, I should run. The neighbors must have heard something.

It was the Creole Crackerjack. I knew him by the jangle of his keys. What was he doing there at that time of night?

I had to get out quick. That crazy bastard would shoot me for sure. The front entrance had those convenient fire release bars that made it easy to slam a door open in a full run. Thalia was there, waving me through.

The door alarm went off as I left—a shrill, ear-splitting thing that must have frightened the officer as much as me. I looked back and saw the flashlight rolling sideways. He'd slipped and fell on the pencils. He fired his gun wildly a few times. A bullet pierced the window, and I swear I felt the wind of it pass my face.

Crazy fuck.

I pissed myself a little.

Another shot. It grazed me on the upper arm and I felt a burning sensation, but not much more. He *was* shooting at me.

I ran around the corner and ducked into some bushes. He crashed out of the door and ran right by. As soon as he was out of sight, I ran the other way to the back of the school, jumped the hedges on the other side of the soccer field, and made it to my car.

As soon as I was in the driver's seat, door closed, engine running, I began to laugh and slap the steering wheel.

My arm was bleeding and starting to hurt, but nothing life threatening.

Thalia was there, laughing too. She swung her right leg over my lap and straddled me, her thighs strong, waist firm.

And then she wasn't there.

\#

When I got home, I cleaned my wound with a rag soaked in warm water and dabbed hydrogen peroxide on it with little cotton balls and then wrapped it in gauze. I was glad it wasn't a direct hit, one where the bullet was lodged in my arm. I had a Tarantino-esque vision of pouring whiskey over an oozing wound, biting down on a stick while digging the bullet out with a pair of needle-nose pliers, dropping the slug in a metal dish with a satisfying *clunk,* and then sewing it up with a toothpick and mint-flavored dental floss.

Because that's what criminals who've been shot do, right? Hospitals have to call the police for gunshot victims. Can't go there. Don't know any seedy veterinarians or mob docs who get paid under the table. What the hell's so bad about an unextracted bullet anyway? Avoiding TSA metal detectors? Lead poisoning? Hell if I know. I smell Hollywood bullshit.

Yep. Better that I was only grazed.

Still restless.

My hands shook as the last remaining drops of adrenaline circled my brain drain. I couldn't sleep. I called Libby, but her machine picked up. In unison, she and her new fiancé said, "We're not home right now, please leave a message." I hung up.

I called the number Dr. Norman had given me for emergencies. "H—Hello?" he said, after several rings. It was the "hello" of someone who'd been asleep.

"Sorry, wrong number."

I called the police station and asked to speak to Detective Kuklinski. I asked him if he'd caught Thalia's killer yet and he said no and told me to stop fucking calling him.

I fetched the laptop and opened my blog's admin page. Nothing new.

The blog was an unmitigated disaster. I did have four followers, but they each had blogs of their own and I suspected they were only following me in an effort to guilt me into following them. Selfish bastards—as if I really gave a damn about ice fishing in Milwaukee or the best sushi spots in New Orleans.

Day after day, post after post, no one cared.

They simply weren't listening.

Perhaps voicing my frustration over a lack of readership came off as despicable and self-loathing. My rant on the benefits of assisted suicide for the homeless didn't go over well, either. Soon, I'd have no readers at all.

I decided a blog is psychological junk mail. You construct a well-worded exposition on something, polish it up, send it out to the World Wide Web, only to have it seen, promptly crumpled up, and tossed in the recycle bin of other people's brains. I might as well have stood on the roof and shouted anything that popped into my head or camped out on the front lawn and cornered my neighbors, subjecting them to baby pictures and shitty art and "Chopsticks" quality music I created on my phone. Between the neighbors, the arresting officer, the judge, and fellow inmates, I'd have caught more attention than I ever would with that blog.

I closed the laptop lid and abandoned the blog like a derelict tractor in the middle of a cornfield, left to rust until the end of time.

Never did get to sleep that night.

#

Superintendent Truss surveyed the damage at the school the next morning with an entourage of lackeys behind him. He wore a neatly pressed gray suit with a deep red tie and a district logo pin on his lapel. He was a tall man, intimidating in presence, with hair like a gray Chia Pet. He never spoke as far as I could tell, not to commoners at least, unless a camera was pointed at him.

You can always tell how high up the chain of command

someone is by his general-type A assholery. Other powerful assholes don't even notice. Just one big circle jerk. This particular asshole, Superintendent Truss, was placed in his position by a board full of assholes who were elected into their positions by even more assholes. It'd been so long since Truss had boots on the ground on a real campus, he'd succumbed to the modern public perception of education—a complete fantasy. You know the one—angelic children quietly facing forward while an unfulfilled dragon of a teacher attempts to crush their fragile spirits by any means necessary. As such, he'd instituted a barrage of district standards that turned the screws on teachers while making sad little victims out of juvenile delinquents and noble heroes out of emotionally and/or physically abusive parents. At the end of the day, no matter what, everything is the teacher's fault. Parents and administrators are almost universally absolved of responsibility.

Shouldn't be surprised. It's not uncommon for horrible people to rise to the top. In any overly-litigious society, it's easier to promote than to fire. Firing takes too long, requires too much paperwork, and leads to uncomfortable confrontations. Danny can't get along with his coworkers because he's an asshole? Make Danny a manager. No one likes managers anyway. Can't seem to stop Susie from dressing like a ten-dollar whore for work? Make her chief of sales. Nothing sells like a low-cut halter top and miniskirt. People who are truly skilled at their jobs can expect to stay right where they are. Why mess with a good thing?

The custodians had already picked up the pencils before the students darkened the door. They did their best to clean up the graffiti or to drape paper over it, but it was futile. It had been hard to assess my work when I did it, the halls so dark and all. It looked okay considering, but there were a few misspellings that irked me. The poor handwriting would be an annoyance to the English teachers. The upshot was it would be hard for anyone to imagine an adult could have done it.

The Creole Crackerjack stood in front of the bullet-riddled window as if trying to hide it. His holster was empty. I could only assume he'd been relieved of his sidearm. He watched me, narrow-eyed. With suspicion?

The superintendent leaned over and whispered something in Principal Johnson's ear, something not meant for mere mortals, and then left. The principal came over to me. "Check the cameras after testing, but we need you on bathroom duty first. Only one kid at a time, remember." His voice was shaking and his hair was more disheveled than usual, poking out as if maybe he'd been licked against the grain by a cow. He turned to the administrative staff and spoke in a yelling whisper. "We're finished if these children don't take these tests. Finished. All of us."

He'd be working at the central administration building by the end of next week, I guessed. Superintendent over bus routes or something like that.

The bell rang and the kids came in, laughing and pointing at all the glorious rhetoric.

Would they heed the call?

I sat outside the boy's bathroom in a little student desk. The boys did their pee-pee dances and laughed at one another, and whispered, and pushed, and shoved, eyeing me in anticipation of a rebuke that would never come. Testing hadn't even begun yet.

God, I hated bathroom duty.

The brain of the average middle school boy is grossly underdeveloped. I imagined their skulls filled with copious amounts of gelatinous fluid in which a baseball-sized mass floated, tethered to a loosely knit spool of nerves as if it were a balloon. It would drift left and right, up and down, back and forth with every convoluted, spastic movement of the child, beating against the sides, bruised and waiting for the day it might occupy the whole of the cavity around it and produce original thoughts of a nonsexual nature for a change.

The test coordinator, a woman who spoke like Tommy Lee Jones with a lisp, came on the intercom and doled out directions. After the preparations were complete, testing was officially started. My fellow adults acted as if nothing had happened, as if we weren't on the brink of a revolution.

Were we?

Everything was quiet, as it always was during testing. I looked up and down the gray, locker-lined hall. One kid was getting a drink of water, another shuffled down the corridor, late and twirling a pass around his finger. I leaned forward to see if I could hear anything, but there was nothing. I leaned back, resigned to failure.

A door to my right opened. Ratbeak poked her head out and looked both ways, clearly concerned. To my left, another door, Cat Piss this time. Then Hemi down at the other end followed by Snitwit, Mountain Manny, Dildolores, Cheech, Chong, and Loopilicious Lucy . . .

CHAPTER 31

One by one, the doors opened. The administrators started going room to room and I heard arguing coming up the stairwell from somewhere downstairs. It was Principal Johnson and one of the assistant principals. A swell of reserved chatter floated out of the classrooms and into the halls as testing came to a screeching halt.

Roughly sixty-five percent of the student body refused the test outright. Another ten to fifteen percent were culled through threats of violence from abstaining peers. The holdouts were separated from the herd and taken to the cafeteria where, rumor had it, Elvira Moon, mousy as she was, stood on a table and chastised them for their cowardice. She was dragged off the table by one of the coaches and sent to the office. Ultimately, testing was canceled for the day. The administrators were frantic, teachers showed restrained jubilance, students defiant.

I dashed into my office at about noon and made an anonymous call to the news stations and told them what was happening. Their vans were there by the dismissal bell, sitting just off campus.

I bumped into Squeaky as I pushed my way through the unusually subdued gaggles of children. She grabbed my arm and pulled me aside.

I don't like to be touched.

"Did you get a chance to read my manuscript?" she said.

"No, not yet," I said and pulled away.

"Some of us are going to Tío's at five," she called after me. "Meet us? I've read yours."

I stopped and turned. She just got interesting. Plus, it was the first time anyone at work had asked me to eat with them since I proclaimed to hate soul food at the Black History Luncheon. "Yeah, okay," I said. "I'll try to make it." I hated social gatherings, but I wanted to hear what she thought.

As I was getting into my car, a reporter from Channel 11 stopped me to ask if I'd answer some questions.

If I'm going to be a famous author, I'd better get used to the cameras. Soon, the world will lap up Thalia's story like thirsty dogs.

"Sure," I said.

"Do you work here?"

"No."

She looked down at the picture ID I wore on a green lanyard around my neck, the one with the school logo and the picture of me looking caught by surprise and wild-haired.

"Oh, *here*," I said, "I didn't realize you meant here. I

uh, what do you want?"

"What can you tell me about what happened today?"

"The little bastar—students. They pulled a Pencils Down job for the test. Refused to take it. It's *their* future, and they're not taking into consideration how it affects the rest of us, but that's kids these days, ya know, selfish, mean-spirited, over-sexed, and ...and hyperactive for the most part—something in the water here at the school, I suspect, or maybe those chicken nuggets we serve in the cafeteria. That stuff is made of rat, I think. And the water is recycled, tied to the toilet and dish-water pipes so I'm sure that really messes with their heads, and—"

The lady was horrified, I could see it in her eyes. I tended to ramble incoherently under pressure.

"Yeah, okay," I said. "Get what you needed?"

Before she could answer, I ducked into my car and drove away. It occurred to me I could probably be fired for talking to the media. It was against district policy.

\#

Tío's Texas Taquería was a Tex-Mex joint like most Tex-Mex joints. Neon beer signs, Tejano blaring on the juke, salt shakers made out of Corona bottles. The smell of the place alone could give an old man heartburn. It was loud, gaudy, excessive in every respect, and promised to be fabulously delicious.

"Over here," Hemi said. Squeaky didn't tell me *he* was coming. He sat on the end, Squeaky on the opposite side, and ten or so others were there, talking about the events of the day.

As I sat down, Hemi said, "Hey, look." He was pointing at the TV behind the bar. The news was on with closed captions and there I was, heavily edited and sanitized for public consumption. They had my name and occupation wrong. "Cheese Sims, Janitor" is what it read under my face. I was surprised they didn't air everything I said—that could have been a story in itself. They probably hadn't taken me seriously. No one ever does. My hair was askew, the light unflattering. My scar made me look like the Joker.

Teachers on either side of me clapped and patted me on the shoulder.

I don't like to be touched.

"We're going to be the ones who pay for this testing insanity," Hemi said. "We can forget our performance bonuses."

"In the long run, this might be for the best. These kids have power none of *us* do," the art teacher at the end of the table said.

They should fail every kid who sits out without parental consent. Hell, even *with* parental consent, they should fail. We *all* take tests. It's part of life. What are these kids gonna do when they have to take the SATs? Other college entrance exams? Refuse? Cry foul? It just doesn't work that way," The math teacher said.

"See, I'm on the fence about this," Hemi said. "It's easy for you to say that, your subject area is about as objective as it gets, but with literature, history, it's not so simple. There's always something left to be said. Multiple choice just doesn't cover it. What do you think, Ches?"

"I don't know," I said. "I'm not a teacher." I didn't want to go hard one way or the other. Didn't want them to think I was agreeing because I was involved in Pencil's Down or disagreeing to cover my involvement. "I will say this. Soon, you will all be replaced by robots."

They laughed. Don't know why, I was serious. They *will* be replaced. The teacher of the future is a flat screen monitor. This is the beginning of the end.

They all began talking over one another. I turned to Squeaky. Before I could say anything, one of the coaches—not sure which one on account of they all look alike—grabbed my upper arm and pulled me over.

"Did you see that game the other night?"

"Oh yeah," I said, no idea what he was talking about. "I couldn't believe that one play when the guy—"

"Oh, yeah. A. Maze. Ing."

I turned back to Squeaky, but the Spanish teacher, who had hair like the Liberty Bell, got my attention. "I'm looking into buying a computer for my daughter since she'll be going off to college soon and—"

"Go down to Best Computer Deals Superstore over on 59," I said. "Tell what's his name—John. Tell John I sent you. He'll help you out. Give you a discount and everything." I didn't know any John, but money said there was one around there somewhere, the size of that place. This is why I didn't make a habit of socializing with coworkers. Not that I socialized with anyone.

I turned back to Squeaky, very casual-like, and got her attention. I dipped a chip in the salsa bowl in front of me and ate it, crunching and choking a little. The salsa had kick. "You were saying you had a chance to look at my manuscript?" I asked.

"Yes. It's really interesting. Unique, I mean. There were parts of it I enjoyed. Like how you wove this testing business into it. And the attempted murder was kind of intense—"

All code for, "It not only sucks. It blows, too." She didn't understand she was reading non-fiction at all.

She pulled my manuscript out of her handbag with all kinds of ungraded student work and started flipping through it. "How much value do you place on the symbolic? What does Thalia's ghost-like presence *really* mean?"

"I suppose it means that either there's life beyond the grave or I'm one crazy son of a bitch."

"Hey, you found a new reader?" Hemi said, breaking his conversational trajectory. He'd been fussing about some turd who slashed his tires. "That's great, man."

Squeaky turned to him. "You've read it too? What did you think?"

"It's all over the place. He might cobble together a decent short story out of it. What he really needs is some writing lessons and a *very* patient editor."

"Yeah, I think so too," Squeaky said, emboldened by the second opinion. Critics are like pack animals.

"I didn't particularly like the main character," Hemi said, smiling at me knowingly.

Squeaky agreed. "And the part about the attempted suicide made me queasy."

"You're writing a book, Ches?" The Spanish teacher asked.

"Yeah. Trying."

Hemi grabbed the manuscript. "Oh shit, guys, listen to this," he said, addressing the table. He found the part he wanted to read. "Yeah, here we go," he read an admittedly grotesque part that was ultimately edited out for legal reasons. "I mean, *shit*," he said when he was finished. He pointed at me. "He can't be right in the head."

The others at the table looked disgusted and made comments about losing their appetites and that it certainly wasn't the kind of thing they'd read.

I tried to redeem myself. "He didn't read it in context."

Hemi shook his head. "The context doesn't help here. Believe me."

It was all downhill from there. I tuned them out. The negatives drowned out what few kindnesses they offered.

I told myself I wouldn't react this way. Their critiques are nonspecific and impossible to work with. Yes. That's the problem. They are simple-minded.

"Well, this has been fun," I said, "but I've got somewhere to be at five thirty so . . ."

I stood and they protested. Hemi, with no uncertain amount of venom, announced to the table that I was too sensitive to make it as a writer.

I should have shoved my napkin-silverware roll down his throat and set it on fire.

I'd ordered a crispy cheese puff, a guacamole salad, and some cheese enchiladas. I wasn't going to stick around for them and I sure as hell wasn't going to pay for them.

CHAPTER 32

A second day of testing. Day two was 8th grade social studies, 7th grade reading, and 6th grade reading. The students opted out again. The news that evening said other schools in the area were participating. Somehow, the administrators managed to round up the Pencils Down crew and isolate them in the office like the little political dissidents they were. How did they find them all? I was pretty sure it wasn't Elvira Moon who told them. That little girl wouldn't tell them jack shit. Those chicken twins were probably the culprits, the stool pigeons.

I imagined little Elvira sitting on a booster seat in a high-backed executive chair in front of a mahogany desk, smoking a fat Cuban cigar and ordering her cronies to fit those twins for concrete shoes and drop them off the I-45 causeway on the way to Galveston Island.

Was knowledge of my involvement in the Pencils Down scheme imminent? Even if the twins didn't squeal, all an admin had to do was recover one phone with that damn laptop theft video on it. Everything else would fall into place and I'd be out on my ass.

Still, it felt good to win at something for a change.

But what had I really accomplished? Getting a bunch of preteen assholes to act like assholes?

Somehow, it was beneath me, but then again, could anything be beneath me?

\#

It was lunchtime on the third day of testing—7th grade social studies, 6th grade math—and still not a pencil had been lifted. I sat at a little student desk on the second floor, watching the bathrooms, frustrated they wouldn't let me proofread my manuscript while I sat there. I'd printed a fresh copy of it that morning, but testing regulations said no reading.

A poster was taped to the wall across from me touting the importance of voting in spite of the fact that none of our students were old enough to vote. I wasn't sure why they weren't allowed to vote. Maybe SpongeBob SquarePants was exactly who we needed in the Oval Office.

We were seven months shy of a train wreck of an election. Americans vote like they shop for cars. This one is pro-life, that one is pro-choice. This one thinks you've got to break some eggs to make an omelet, that one thinks all eggs are precious. This one has interesting hair, that one doesn't even have a dick. Such binary thinking leads to righteous indignation, and righteous indignation blazes right past reasoned discourse on its way to the apocalypse.

As such, I never voted. Not even once. Fuck 'em.

The Creole Crackerjack ascended the stairs on my right. I knew it was him by the chatter of his police radio and the squishy leather sound his belt made when he walked.

"Mista Smith," he said. He didn't look happy.

"Yeah?"

"Need ya to come with me."

As I stood he grabbed my upper arm right where he'd grazed me three nights before. I winced and he pulled his hand away. He looked at me as if he was doing math in his head and then poked me on the arm again. I winced again and called him an asshole. Bathroom line students giggled.

"It *was* you, the otha night," he said as if he hadn't believed it before, but had to face the indisputable truth now.

I pled the fifth and followed him downstairs. Principal Johnson was there, waiting. He held a clear Ziploc Freezer Bag with phones and a copy of the Pencils Down manifesto in it. Elvira Moon looked apologetically out at me through the main office windows.

The principal twisted his mouth as he gathered words to express how disappointed he was in me, but his phone dinged and distracted him. He reached into his suit pocket and pulled it out, holding a finger up to tell us to wait a moment.

That was my chance. I elbowed the officer in the gut, ran down the hall, and out into the parking lot. I needed to get rid of the laptop—it was evidence. They'd be serving me with a search warrant soon, I suspected. I was surprised to find no one pursued me. It would only be a matter of seconds—

The latest draft of my manuscript.

I raced back in and took the hall to the left. No one saw me. I burst into my office and grabbed the draft off the printer. It was the most complete one I'd have once the laptop was disposed of. I didn't trust the door. I climbed up my shelves and wiggled out of the thin, high mounted window. Once I dropped to the ground, I squatted and looked both ways. Still no one. Either I was really good at evading capture, or no one gave a damn.

I scampered back out to my car and raced home. I think I ran over a squirrel. No one gave chase, but I couldn't let my guard down. That's how they get you.

At home, I ran to the back room, grabbed the laptop, and carried it back out to the car. I took a long drive to the north side of town, minding the traffic laws so I wouldn't call attention to myself. I found one of those old-money neighborhoods and prowled the streets awhile. Finally, I found three Mexicans feeding tree limbs to a wood chipper. I waited until they walked around the side of the house and then I climbed out of my car and tossed the laptop in. The grinding noise was grotesque, bits of plastic and metal blowing out of the shoot and jangling into the metal dumpster. There was sparks and smoke and it smelled like an electrical fire.

I looked up and one of the Mexicans was standing there staring at me. He didn't care, as long as it wasn't a body. I slipped him a five and drove home. I didn't go inside. Instead, I crawled into the treehouse next door and waited, watching for the police until I fell asleep.

#

The police didn't show while I napped in the treehouse, the lazy bastards, not as far as I knew anyway.

Not that I was complaining.

"What are you going to do now?" Thalia said. She wore army fatigues—tight ones, with a zipper down the front.

"I don't know. I wonder if it's safe to go in." I scanned the street. It was evening and almost dark. "They could be staking out the house."

She laughed. "Yeah, like they don't have anything better to do than stake out a middle-school computer tech. You'll almost certainly get fired, but arrested?"

I ticked the obvious violations off with my fingers. "Breaking and entering. Vandalism. Theft. Contributing to the delinquency of minors."

She rolled her eyes. "Yeah, maybe, but they're not combing the city looking for you right now, I can tell you that much."

"You don't know." I sat with my back to the wall, knees up, arms wrapped around them. "I needed that job."

"It's just a—"

"Hey," someone yelled from down below. I peeked out and saw the neighbor standing there. He was a well-dressed man, average in every way, tight haircut, no kids, in spite of the tree house.

"Get the hell out of there," he said.

He was a serial murderer, I was sure of it. The tree house was bait, the bodies buried below the garage.

I climbed out.

"I'm going to call the police if I catch you in there one more time," he said, clearly uncomfortable with open confrontation. Probably saved all that pent-up rage for his victims.

"Sorry," I said and jumped the fence back into my own yard.

I kept the lights off and planted myself by the front window, keeping the gun in my lap, delusional to the point of thinking I might be ballsy enough to engage in a shoot-out.

The phone rang.

"Look on the bright side, more time to write," Thalia said.

I nodded and watched her twist her left pigtail. She crossed her legs, arched her back, and slowly began to unzip the front of her fatigues revealing silky white skin and the subtle curve of her inner right breast, ripe for the plucking. The quiet rustle of the fabric—

A car door slammed outside.

Calli and Mikey, two peas in a toxic pod, were coming up the sidewalk. I tucked the gun in the back of my waistband like they do in the movies and then hid behind the door. Calli banged on it with an inappropriate amount of thunder and fury.

"We know you're in there, weirdo. We saw you in the window."

"Leave me alone."

"Open the Goddamn door. I want my pages."

"There are no pages. Our deal is finished. I got fired. The school already knows everythi—"

Mikey kicked the door in, hurling me across the room. His presence filled the splintered frame with Calli peeking around him. I rolled on my side and pulled the gun out, pointing it at them and shaking.

It was terrifying pointing a gun at another human being—uncertain, thrilling—the steel heavy in my hand.

"You broke my door, you fuckwit."

"Oh, shit," Calli said.

They knew just enough about me to know I might be capable of anything.

Mikey stood there with his big dumb hands out in front of him.

"Don't you make a move. You twitch, I twitch. Got it?" I said, pointing the gun up at them from the floor. "I've shot at people before. Now, get the hell out of here and don't ever come back or I'll shoot you in the face." They seemed hesitant, but began to back away. "I said don't move." I was shaking the gun at them like a nervous bank robber from one of those old fifties crime flicks. "If you don't leave right now, I'll shoot you in the face," I continued. "You won't even have a face left, just a hole where your brains were. If they were ever there to begin with. If they were, they wouldn't be there anymore. Because I shot you in the face."

They weren't moving, just staring at me with pissed-themselves-eyes. In retrospect, I may have sent mixed messages.

I stood up and backed them out onto the porch.

"Now here's the deal," I said. "I lost my job today, I think. Your blackmail game is over, I destroyed the laptop and my connection to your precious pages is cut off. My ghostwriter is unavailable because if I go near her, I'll probably get shot. Or at least arrested."

"What are you talking about?" Calli said, feeling brave, getting squinty.

"Shut up, bitch," I said. It felt good to call her that aloud and to her face. Even the most feminist of men have just enough misogyny in them to want to call a woman a *bitch* or a *cunt* at least once in their lives. I assume every woman has a comparable longing that involves dicks and scissors. "You heard me. I was having a *thirteen-year-old girl* write your dumb book. You're so stupid you couldn't even tell. But none of that matters now because this deal is through. Got it?"

I gave Mikey the stink eye and twitched him back down the sidewalk. Calli stood out in front of him.

"I'm telling Daddy," she said with one defiant hand on her hip.

"Go on," I said. "Go on and tell Daddy. I've got some lead for him too."

They went back to her truck, climbed in, and drove away. Mikey was looking back at me and I thought I saw him shoot me with a finger gun through the back window.

The thought of this thing escalating scared me, but what was done was done.

#

Later that night, I laid in wait on the roof—the side facing the backyard—certain Thalia's father would be along soon to square everything up. I was on my back, watching the clouds roll by. Even on clear nights, you couldn't see the stars in the city, just a murky black-orange soup with a few pinpricks of light in it. Who needs stars anyway? Show-offs.

I taught myself how to blow smoke rings.

The shingles were still hot from the afternoon sun. The gun rested on the steep slope of the roof, ready to slide down into the gutter at the slightest nudge. I should have been writing but I was too distracted.

Was I losing touch with reality? Was I ever in touch

with it to begin with?

A warm wind blew. The trees rattled. The streetlights seemed to go on forever.

Another car door behind me.

Here we go.

I rolled on my belly, grabbed the gun, and crawled to the ridge to peek over.

"Principal Johnson?" I called down. He was standing there in a suit with no tie, holding a cardboard box.

He jumped back, startled when he heard me. "What the—What are you doing up there?"

"I come up here to unwind sometimes."

"I guess you've got plenty of unwinding to do."

I nodded.

"I tried to call, but there was no answer."

"I never answer the phone."

"I don't blame you. Nothing good ever comes of it. Why don't you come down here, so we can talk?"

"We can talk fine like this, if it's all the same to you." I feared the police might be using him as bait.

"Yes, well. I suppose we can. I brought your things."

"Thanks."

"I guess you understand what this means."

"Yeah. I guess I do."

"You aren't allowed back on campus and I need your keys."

I felt my pockets and realized I didn't have them. I had to think where I'd left them. "I think they're on the floor by the door. My cell phone's there too. I guess you'll want that as well, since the district pays for it."

"Yes. Uh ... You don't currently have a door." Fucking Mikey.

"Oh, yeah. Right. Can you just go in and get them? Just take the school ones off the ring. Leave my stuff inside."

He was hesitant, looking from me to the door, but finally complied. A few moments later, he was standing back in the same place, fiddling with the keys.

"I'm not sure I understand what you were trying to accomplish," he said. "There's a warrant out for your arrest. I'll almost certainly be fired. As will the rest of the administrative staff. You, Ms. Moon, and the rest created one hell of a problem for state testing." I could hear him kicking at the roots growing over the edge of the sidewalk. "I never liked testing, but I wasn't willing to lose my job over it." He started to cry.

"I'm sorry," I said, and I was. We never really understand the full ramifications of anything we do until we've already done it.

He slumped into his car and left. I'd been at that job for seven years and was oddly upset.

Another chapter closed.

#

Sobered by Principal Johnson's visit, I used the fence to climb down off the roof and stood in the middle of the yard with my eyes closed. I was trying to take in the feel and sound of the moment, but the sound of the moment was the *chk-chk* of a shotgun. The feel of the moment was warm, wet, and yellow. The gate on the far side of the house was open. I turned to see Thalia's father in the shadows, pointing it at me.

"Don't you move, you son of a bitch," Calli's dad said. "Get on in the house."

"What is it about pointing a gun at someone that

makes us contradict oursel—"

"Shut up, smartass. Get in the house."

I turned slowly, hands up, and walked to the back door.

"Pull a gun on *my* girl," he said, "there ain't no place on earth you can go to get away from me. Your donkey's in a ditch now."

I used to find hayseed riffs charming.

We entered through the back door. He was pressing the gun into the small of my back. It felt like a pipe.

"Turn on the lights," he said.

I did.

"Jesus Jumpin' Mary Jane. What the hell is wrong with you?"

"In general? Or has something specific caught your eye?"

"The painting, man. You're a few pickles short of a barrel."

He was looking at the burning monk. "Don't worry, everyone has that reaction."

"You jack off to it or somethin'?"

"No. Well, once." Why did I tell him that? "I've been meaning to paint some people roasting hot dogs or something like that. I think it'll soften the impa—"

"Shut up, man. Just shut up. Let's go on in the front."

I walked with my hands up and stopped in the middle of the living room. I turned my head just enough to see he was examining the paintings there, too. His gun drifted away from my back. A duffle bag sat on the milk-crate coffee table. The only existing draft of my manuscript and my cigarettes were inside it. My loose-leaf chronicles were on the table next to it. The gun was tucked in my pants, beneath my shirt.

The phone rang. He jumped and looked over at it. I shoved him and the gun went off, shooting a hole in the ceiling. I grabbed the duffle bag and ran into the coat closet despite the wide-open front door only six feet to the right of it. Panic is a funny thing.

As soon as the door was shut, I sunk to the floor, back against the wall, and yelled, "I've got my gun in here. You'd better leave or I'll start shooting."

"Well maybe I'll start shooting, too," he said.

"It'll be justified." Not that it would matter to him. I fumbled in the dark and felt for the handle of the gun. Once I had it, I held it out in front of me.

"Get your ass out here," he yelled.

"Not only no, but *hell* no."

He tried to sound calmer. "Get your ass out here."

"Screw you, man."

"Goddammit," he muttered.

He shot through the door, aiming high, probably at my head. The blast made me jump. Splinters showered down on me and thin beams of light shone through the pepper holes in the wood. I could see his face through them. He held the gun up again and I started firing with my eyes closed, gun kicking furiously.

Silence for a moment. The smell of smoke was acute and frightening.

The living room window shattered and a fire glow appeared under the door and through the buckshot holes. I kicked the door open. Calli's dad was on the floor, bleeding, writhing. I wasn't sure if he was bleeding because I shot him or because of the broken glass. The carpet was on fire. Mikey stepped in through the broken window, another Molotov cocktail in hand.

"Oh shit," he said when he saw Calli's dad. As he squatted next to him, the unlit Molotov rolled from his left hand and into the fire. The white cloth hanging out of the end ignited, the glass burst, and the fire consumed the couch and crawled up the walls. Mikey screamed as his pant leg flared up. He tried to beat the fire out, but he had gas on him and the fire spread up his body and onto the bleeding man at his feet.

Those two did *not* have a clear plan of attack in mind.

I crawled out of the closet. It was unbearably hot and the fire was too close. My loose-leaf chronicles were burning on the table, pages brown and curling. All those notes. All those short stories. All gone. I ran outside, duffle bag around my shoulder. At least I still had my manuscript.

Calli's pickup sat out front, engine still running, with Calli standing outside it, shocked to see I was the one who came running out of the house. We stared at each other for an instant and then the slow terror of what had happened seized her. She ran past me to the doorway, fire billowing out of it like an angry demon. She backed away and dropped to her knees. I pointed the gun at her small frame and then let it fall to my side, hoping maybe a spark would ignite her greasy hair.

She did this to herself.

She'd probably blackmail someone to write a book about it.

I jumped in my car and sped away, clueless as to where to go or what to do next. All I knew was that I didn't want to be around people. I wanted solitude. A chance to think. I headed southwest to the outskirts of town, the quickest route possible—west on Berryman, northwest through the unnamed backstreet behind Ferguson shopping center, southwest on the feeder, merged onto Highway 59—expecting a police chase that never materialized.

I exited the freeway and went east on Highway 257 until I found an old dirt road that led to a clearing with access to a bayou. I parked and stumbled out of the car. A full moon floated above quick drifting clouds. Swamp moss hung from lazy trees and blew in the wind. Unseen creatures splashed in the water, probably turtles or alligators, maybe snakes, the vile things. There were so many mosquitoes I feared I might breathe some of them into my lungs and get bitten from the inside. The whole area smelled like a septic tank. I lit a cigarette and wondered if the lighter might cause an explosion.

I sized up my car and then the bayou. It'd probably fit.

CHAPTER 33

"Why are you here?" Thalia said. She was standing on a tree trunk lying on its side, protruding from the mud. Like a gymnast, she had her arms out for balance.

"They'll be looking for me. Got to get rid of the car. And the gun. I'll grow a beard to change my appearance. Isn't that what they do? Get rid of the evidence and grow a beard?"

"Isn't that what *who* does?"

"You know. People in situations like this. In books and movies and such."

She shrugged. "Well, they'll definitely be looking for you *now*. The principal said you've got a warrant out."

I opened the trunk, stopped, and looked over at her. She was luminescent in the night light. Short plaid skirt. White T-shirt tied in a knot over her stomach. Her pigtails wiggled back and forth. I thought I might like to see her hop in the water and emerge from it slowly, the white shirt see-through, hugging her firm chest—

"Has it occurred to you," she said, "that your story is writing itself now?"

"Yeah, sort of. Starting to feel like a character in my own book."

I hung the cigarette loosely between my lips, tossed the gun in the trunk, and shifted the car into neutral. With the driver's side door open, I put one hand on the wheel and the other on the door jamb and pushed until gravity took hold and pulled the car down the bank and into the bayou with a disappointing splash. Unfortunately, at its deepest, the bayou only covered the top of the front wheelbase. I stood there expecting it to sink, but it didn't. It just planted itself more firmly in the sludge at the bottom.

"Damn," she said.

"Damn," I concurred, cigarette still hanging loose. "Thought it was deeper."

"Well, that's that."

"Oh, shit, my manuscript." I slushed out into the bayou as if to save a drowning fawn and found the binder still sitting on the driver's seat. "Guess it's a good thing the car didn't sink."

Thalia watched as I shook excess water off my pant legs like a cat just getting out of a bath. "You may be the worst criminal in the history of bad criminals."

I nodded and took a drag of the cigarette before flicking it at the quarter-sunk car. "Yep. Well, let's go."

#

I walked back to the highway and hitchhiked. I wanted to hitchhike anywhere else in the galaxy, but I settled for a ride back to town in a Toyota Tercel with a missing front fender.

The Tercel pulled off onto the shoulder, exhaust pipe oozing white smoke that diffused the red light of its one working taillight. I thought it might be a bad idea to get into a car with only one taillight, cops notice things like that, but I couldn't be sure anyone else would pick me up.

The door handle didn't work so the driver leaned over and let me in. She was a big woman, but I couldn't see much in the way of detail because it was too dark and the dome light hadn't come on. I knew I was no danger to her, but she had a tough disposition, and I wasn't entirely sure she wasn't a danger to me.

"Thanks," I said.

"Rough night?" she said. She had a voice like Nick Nolte.

I was muddy, ash in my hair, wet pants, and was clinging to the manuscript as if it was my sole possession in the world. That was the moment it occurred to me that, other than my clothes, it *was* my sole possession in the world.

"You have no idea," I said. "I'm surprised you stopped. They always say not to pick up hitchhikers."

"You don't look like much of a threat, if you don't mind me saying. What are you doing out here?"

"Ditching a car to evade police. I'm wanted for all kinds of shit."

She laughed until she had a coughing fit. It was a wet, nasty cough and I turned my face toward the window to avoid breathing in whatever she was expelling.

"How 'bout you?" I said, once she'd gotten herself under control.

"On my way home from a signing."

"Signing?"

"Book signing at this little mom and pop shop in Victoria."

"You a writer?"

"Yeah."

"Me too."

"Small world," she said, but intoned it wasn't.

"Sort of a writer anyway."

"Either you write or you don't," she said.

"There is no try," I added, but I don't think she got the reference.

We rode along awhile and said nothing. Signs of civilization were appearing again—a gas station, a dry cleaner, an adult bookstore.

"You published?" she asked.

"No. You?"

"What do you think I was signing? Love letters written on personalized stationery?"

"Right." *Dumb.* "How many?"

"Love letters?" she said, and laughed and coughed again. "Thirteen novels. Even had one on the *New York Times* bestseller list for four weeks back in '85. Called *Love's Lost Charms.* Ever hear of it?"

"No. Sorry. Is it romance? I don't care for romance."

"No, no. It was a gay werewolf story set during the Renaissance with a slight sci-fi twist there at the end. A genre bender before it was all the rage. First in an unfinished series."

A real-life published author. I marveled. And a bestseller, no less. Must be a sign.

I looked at the deplorable condition of her car and

thought maybe she was teasing me. It smelled like cigarettes masked by a cardboard air freshener hanging from the rearview mirror. The freshener was supposed to make the car smell new, but it didn't. I looked in the backseat and there was a half-empty box of *Love's Lost Charms* sitting on the floorboard.

"Do you mind?" I said.

"Knock yourself out."

I took out one of the books. We were passing under streetlights and it grew dim, then bright, dim, then bright. The book was paperback and its cover confirmed it was indeed a *New York Times* bestseller.

"It's not in print anymore," she said, "but I still have a lot of copies in my garage. You can take one if you want. It's pre-signed."

The car backfired and I jumped. The glove compartment fell open and I tried to make it close again, but the duct tape that held it shut had lost too much sticky to be of any further use. I just let it hang open on top of my knees.

"Did you lose everything to gambling?" I said. "Were you taken for everything in a pyramid scheme or something? Drugs? Was it drugs and fast living?"

"What the hell are you talking about?"

"You're a published author. What's with the car?"

"Hah. That's cute. He's under the impression that authors make money," she said, to no one in particular.

"Don't get me wrong, writing's not about the money," I said, "but it's nice to think you might be able to make a living at it."

"It *is* nice to think that. Some people can. Just not you or me."

"I had a friend. She asked me why I write. Why do *you* write?"

"For the fame, mostly."

"Ah," I said.

She pushed in the lighter and looked over at me. "Mind if I smoke?"

She fumbled with a carton of cigarettes.

"No. Can I join you?" I helped her fish one out.

"Sure."

The lighter popped out and she lit up. I pushed it in again and waited for it to pop back out, but it didn't.

"Hmph," she said, and shrugged. I tried to light mine with my lighter, but it wasn't working either. I settled for secondhand.

We crossed that mysterious border from country to city. The highway became a freeway, humping over cross streets, the buildings grew larger, ambient light grew brighter.

"What are you writing?" she said.

"It's a kind of autobiography, I guess. It's about the creative process mostly. About society in general, too. I have a love-hate relationship with the whole thing."

"That's natural."

"Actually, I feel quite lost."

She coughed again and I was certain a piece of phlegm landed on me, but I couldn't figure out where.

"I'm going to drop you off at the next exit," she said. "I trust you can find your way from there?"

"Yeah." It was only one exit past the one I would have taken if I'd been going home.

She pulled into a grocery store parking lot, a dark one with graffiti gang tags on the front.

"Thanks for the company," she said, as she stopped horizontally across two spots.

"Thanks for the ride. And the book," I said, holding it up. I got out and looked back at her. She was older than I imagined and looked like she wanted something for her trouble. I didn't have any cash. She saw it in my eyes, waved me off, and drove away, leaving me in a cloud of exhaust.

#

That night, I slept behind a dumpster. It wasn't too bad, but I woke up with a man squatting at my feet, staring at me. He wore tattered army fatigues, holey boots, and I swore I saw a ferret nesting in his beard. "You're in my spot," he said.

"Sorry." I got the hell out of there.

Luckily, I still had my wallet. I went inside the store, withdrew the $500 maximum at the ATM for a wretched $3 fee, and approached the counter to ask for change for the phone. The cashier made me buy a pack of gum to get it.

I went outside and looked for the payphones. There weren't any. I walked down the street. I still didn't find any. I went around the block and continued to not find any. When did we, as a society, get rid of payphones? Cell phones are ruining everything. They're just glorified servant bells for the common man.

At least it was a nice day—not too hot, gentle breeze, partly cloudy.

I found a gas station, asked to use their phone, bought another pack of gum, and called the one person I knew would come.

Libby.

CHAPTER 34

Libby pulled to the curb in her sky-blue VW Beetle and beeped the horn. It was a bad idea to call her, but good ideas had gotten me nowhere. I climbed in, buckled my seatbelt, and gave her a quick smile as if this whole thing were perfectly normal.

I'd talked to her, but hadn't seen her in several years. She'd cut her hair short—boy short—and was wearing designer red-rimmed glasses and a brown pantsuit. She had a Bluetooth behind her ear, GPS on the dash, and a smartphone in the cup holder next to her grande latte. The car smelled new.

I guess she decided to "reinvent" herself after our divorce. Anything to get my stink off her.

She stared at me. "Well, out with it."

I nodded cordially. "How've you been?"

"Fine. And you?" She was being sarcastic.

"Been better. Been better."

"I'm sorry to hear that. Things'll pick up, I'm sure."

"Oh sure. They always do. Did you get the check last month?"

"Uh. Yeah."

"I lost my job, you know, it might be a while before you get another one. Say, when's the wedding?"

She closed her eyes and took a big breath. I felt the cabin pressure of the car lower a little from it. She put the car in park, cut the engine, and turned to me.

"What's going on, Ches?" She erupted.

"Well, I still have some money in savings. You don't have to get all bent out of shape about it."

"I'm not talking about that. I don't care about that. The police are looking for you, been calling everyone. Apparently, your house burned down? They found two dead bodies there, neither of them you, obviously."

"Oh, shit. They died?"

"Uh, yeah. Who the hell were they?"

"It was one of those home invasion deals. Whole thing just went south."

"Home invasion."

"Yeah. Crazy, right?"

"And you didn't wait for the police."

"Didn't want to mess with the paperwork."

"*Come on,* Ches. Your aunt called me this morning. Says she hasn't been able to reach you in years. Same with your grandmother, Charles, Freddy, Marisela. No one. The police contacted them thinking you might seek shelter in Ohio."

"Ha. They don't know my family too well. I'd rather go to prison."

"Don't be an idiot. Now, after all that, you call *me* to come pick you up in a part of town that can only be described as this city's unwiped ass."

"Does Jesus know you talk like that?"

"Don't test me."

"I do appreciate it," I said.

She closed her eyes as if trying to will her level of stress to lower. It wouldn't work. I had that effect on her.

"You interrupted my prayer time," she said. Libby had turned to the Lord a few years prior and somehow that obligated her to help me even when she didn't want to. To be fair, I guess she wasn't one of those bat-shit crazy Christians, yet, but I judge all religions by their radicals just to be safe. Hope for the best, prepare for the worst, right? Little Johnny Jesus might be tossing me a Bible, but I'd better tuck and roll in case it's a grenade. Or should that be the other way around?

"I've hit a bad patch," I said.

Tears welled up in her eyes. She wiped her cheek. "Your whole life's been a bad patch."

"There was you. For a while."

She hung her head. "I know you think I left you because you shot yourself, but I—"

"I know. I get it. I was taking you down with me. Had you stayed, it would've been out of fear that I might hurt myself again. You would have been an emotional hostage."

"It wouldn't have been—"

I held up my hand to stop her. "Do you have any of my old clothes?"

"No."

She wiped her eyes again. Crying makes me uncomfortable.

"I just need a place to get cleaned up. Regroup."

She nodded, sniffling, then started the car and put it in drive.

"What's that?" she said, indicating my manuscript.

"New writing project."

I could actually feel her eyes roll, as if the very shift of them sent small waves of negative energy to my side of the car.

"Still with that?" she said.

As depression spun me down during marriage, writing became a sort of mistress to me. We fought about that more than money or the prospect of having kids or my lack of emotional intimacy.

"I'm glad to see our separation hasn't made you *more* supportive of my creative endeavors. That would just be confusing."

"You're *not* creative. You only think you are."

That one hurt. "Fuck you," I said. You can't unsay *fuck you* so I gave it a twist of emotional appeal. "You *never* supported me."

"Fuck me? Fuck *you*, Ches. You're too sensitive. You can't take criticism. You're *not* the next big thing. You've got to let it go. It's *literally* killing you. You're so desperate for validation. You need something— anything—to confirm your *genius*, but no matter how much validation you get from others, it'll never be enough. Your desperation bleeds through everything you write. *Like* me, *love* me, *worship* me. Please."

BAND-AIDs were peeling off, bandages coming unspooled, sutures popping. "I'm sorry I called you," I said.

"Don't be sorry. Look, I'm taking you to see Dr. Norman and get you back on your meds. Then the police so you can get all this straightened out."

That wasn't an option. I reached for the door handle, flung it open, and rolled out onto the grassy median. I skidded to a stop. My elbow was scraped raw where it rubbed against the inside of the curb. Her VW came to a screeching halt. She jumped out.

"Oh my God, you nut job. Get back in the car. Please. Just get back in. You need help. Let me help you."

Her voice faded as I walked away, masked by the passing traffic. I didn't look back. Not even once.

\#

Perhaps it was cosmic providence that I ditched a mere half mile from a secondhand store called New Life Apparel. I bought some clothes, changed in the bathroom, and cleaned myself up in the sink. I also bought an old burlap backpack to keep my manuscript in and settled for some penny loafers because that was all they had in my size. They didn't go with the outfit, but were pretty comfortable.

As he counted my change, the clerk said, "Did you see that guy outside? The one painting the mural on the wall?"

"No. Guess I came in from the other direction."

"My boss hired him to paint something that reflects the community. It's shit, man. Incomprehensible shit. Mister Francini's gonna be pissed when he gets back from Tahiti. That painting reflects this community about as much as my balls reflect Marilyn Monroe's tits."

I was confused by what he said until I actually *saw* the painting. The artist was one of those white, middle-class Rastafarian wannabes with matted dreadlocks— the kind you wouldn't touch without tweezers and latex gloves. I watched him work, rattling his spray cans, fumbling with stencils, rubbing details on the wall with his fingers.

God, he was awful. *Really* awful.

The wall was painted black, the mural was various shades of hot pink. Chubby skeletons wielded disproportionately small guns that shot bubbles and a bug-eyed Jesus rode a Teenage Mutant Ninja Turtle— not sexually, but rather like a horse. For the life of me, I couldn't figure out what it was supposed to mean.

He painted with conviction and purpose and had a look in his eyes I thought I recognized.

He turned toward me, held up a fist. "Right on, brother."

My God. He really believes he's creating something of value.

I knew if I'd taken the time to inquire, he almost certainly could have explained every bit of it. I might have even bought into its message as if brainwashed into some mad cult, but the meaning should already be there—on the surface. Or at least *under* it.

Right?

Ah, I thought, but what about great works of modern art where no readily apparent meaning presents itself? Is this any less meaningful than any of that? Just because Jesus Christ is riding a Teenage Mutant Ninja Turtle, doesn't give me the right to dismiss it. Does it? Perhaps he's saying something about ...about the over commercialization of religion or maybe the childishness of the horrors of modern society? I know. He's making a statement about the brainwashing of America's children into accepting the horrors of the modern world by making them seem somehow—playful?

Eh. I had nothin'.

I took comfort in the idea that if I could extract a few drops of meaning from this Technicolor nightmare, this wall vomit, then anyone could take meaning out of even my worst day's scribblings.

Did others think *my* writing, like this dreadlocked dweeb's art, was the work of a madman? *Was* I mad?

When Hemi and Squeaky read my manuscript, were they thinking, "Wow, this guy's mental. I'd better throw him a compliment or he might peel me and wear my skin while pleasuring himself in a basin of Vaseline."

I made a mental note to expand on the man in the basin of Vaseline. It had the makings of an interesting character.

I wasn't too far from Dr. Norman's office.

If ever I needed a priest for the modern world, it was now.

#

A five-mile walk to his office. I would have hailed a cab, but Texans don't hail cabs. We call them and wait thirty minutes for them to show. I had the time and money, but not the phone or inclination. I didn't understand the bus routes enough to attempt that gauntlet. I needed the exercise anyway.

Dr. Norman was just leaving his three-story office building when I arrived. It was only noon. He wore a red sweat suit that made him look like a kickball with legs.

"Hey there," he said, standing by his car. "I was wondering if I'd ever see you again."

"Yeah. Sorry. Looks like you're on your way out."

"Headed to the gym. I'll be out the rest of the day. I

have an opening tomorrow morning, first thing. Can you come back?"

"Fine, fine."

"What's that?" he said.

"The manuscript I've been working on," I said.

"You brought it with you? Want me to take a look? Give you a little constructive feedback."

I handed it to him. A psychological analysis might not be a bad thing.

"It's my only copy," I said.

"I'll be careful with it. See you tomorrow."

He got in his car and drove away as I watched.

A vending machine was inside his building. I went in and bought a can of soda and some potato chips for dinner.

I decided I'd spend the night in the woods out back. An overpass was nearby and a drought-stricken bayou ran under it with shopping carts and beer bottles lying about. The whole area smelled like exhaust fumes and piss. A steady cacophony of horns, sirens, and revving trucks kept me company. Blackberries were in the brush here and there. I ate a few until I found one with a little white worm in it. Lost my appetite after that.

What I wouldn't have done for something to read. Fortunately, I had my signed copy of *Love's Lost Charms* in the backpack. Three pages into it I found myself still longing for something to read. How the hell did it end up on the *Times* bestseller list? Were people stupider in the '80s? Was there a drought of good literature? Damn. I'd lost my whole library. I should have shot Calli in the back for that alone.

I tried to build a fire that night by rubbing two sticks

together but apparently, there's more to it than that. I also tried discarded pieces of roofing shingles thinking the rough texture might get a good bit of friction going, but they crumbled in my hands.

Another dream about the burning monk that night, under the city half-light that stole through the trees. I remembered nothing except these words:

Burning Monk: "If your life were a novel, what chapter would you be in?"

Me: "Right now, life has a penultimate feel to it."

CHAPTER 35

"What's going on with you?" Dr. Norman said the next morning as we sat down in his office—him on his throne, me on his couch. My manuscript sat beside him on the end table and I knew I'd only half-hear anything he said until I knew what he thought. After that, I wouldn't hear anything at all. I shouldn't have given it to him.

"Lost my job. Lost the house," I said.

"*How?*" He seemed genuinely concerned.

I considered answering, but knew we'd spend the rest of the hour discussing it. "I don't want to talk about it."

"You want to talk about this," he said and patted the manuscript.

"That's my whole life now. It's all I have left."

"You're investing far too much in this one thing."

"How bad is it? Am I crazy?"

"How bad do *you* think it is? How crazy do *you* think you are?"

I laughed. Typical.

He stared, waiting for an answer.

"I lack objectivity," I said. "I remember the first time I met Libby. I couldn't get her out of my head. She could do no wrong. She was perfect. When I thought about her, it was as if she was flawless, bright, and shining in a halo of yellow light. Her voice, her laugh, the way she tilted her head as she listened. All those perfect moments were like placeholder photos in a picture frame.

"In time, the yellow light became the luminescence of a cheap light bulb, and her voice was like a thousand splinters in the palm of my hand and her laugh was *at* me, not with me. She only tilted her head to accentuate just how wrong I always was. And she had a wart. A big one. On her inner thigh. I spent far too much time wondering if it bothered her when she walked. Drove me crazy thinking about that wart. All the time, thinking about it."

"You think things would have been any different if, what was her name—Thalia?—had survived and you'd been able to have a relationship with her?"

"Thalia. She *is* different."

"Is?"

I shook my head and waved my fingers as if pulling some sleight of hand on him. A Jedi mind trick. "You're getting off subject. My point is that it's the same with my writing. Infatuation turns to loathing. I usually end up hating everything I love." *Except Thalia.*

"Well, what I read of your book isn't *that* bad. I see nothing to loathe here," he said, taking the manuscript into his lap. I made note of the fact he accentuated the word "that," as in, "It's bad, but not *that* bad."

"Do you see any meaning in it?"

"As your psychiatrist, I find all the stuff about suicide insightful. It's almost as if you view suicide as an act of control. An act of power. A way to circumvent your own impuissance."

"What's that mean?"

"Suicide as an act of control is like a child who gets mad and takes his toys home."

"No. Impuissance. What's it mean?"

"It's a kind of weakness. An inability to stand up for yourself."

"Oh. Yep. That's me alright. Historically speaking, at least."

"The demon *inside* you is greater than any demon *outside* of you. There's a twisted comfort in that. No one can hurt you any more than you're willing to hurt yourself. You'll be damned if the world is going to control your fate."

"I'm beyond suicide now. I survived. I'm in the ashes, ready to rise. That manuscript right there is my ticket to the sun."

"These are delusions of grandeur," he said.

Stunned silence. He'd never taken that tone with me.

"I'm sorry, but they are. You have to own that. You're self-destructing. Don't you see that? I mean, by what measure of success do you judge yourself? Is there a magic number of books sold? Readers? Awards? Positive reviews? Even if you have some specific goal in mind, will it *ever* be enough?"

Pussy that I was, tears welled up in my eyes. He was right, the fucker. My desire for success, however undefined it was, was probably insatiable.

He noticed I was upset, had mercy and relented. Leaning back and crossing his legs. "What kind of feedback have you gotten so far?"

I shrugged. "Not good."

"Do you trust other people's input?"

I thought about it as I collected myself. Voice cracking, "I once joined an online forum and submitted a short story I'd written for critique. I got good comments, bad comments, crazy comments, mean-spirited comments. I didn't trust the nice comments, I resented the ugly ones. It's a mess. It occurred to me that most of these people don't know any more about the craft than I do and no matter what I submit, they will always have something to criticize. By that fact alone, it can never be perfect. It can never be finished. It's madness. Pure madness. It's like that philosophical paradox where you can never arrive at your destination because no matter how close you get, you're still only halfway there."

"The dichotomy paradox."

"Yeah. That." *Know it all.*

He had a look of extraordinary concern on his face, his posture stiff, yet regal. I imagined him in graduate school, sitting in a class of students seated in front of full-body mirrors where they did nothing but practice those sorts of poses.

"Out of curiosity," I continued, "I copied a really beautiful excerpt from a novel that won the Pulitzer, one that wasn't too well known. What was the name of that book?" I rubbed my head as if to conjure it, but I couldn't remember. "Anyway, I posted this excerpt and no one even realized the source. I got three rather harsh critiques and the rest were only lukewarm. I did the same for a passage out of a Cormac McCarthy book, *Blood Meridian,* and got five rather strongly worded admonitions to learn the proper use of punctuation. Quotation marks, in particular. One of the critiques just said, and I quote, 'and ...and ...and learn to use a fucking comma, moron.' Cormac McCarthy. One of the greatest American authors of all time, for Christ's sake."

I sat back, resigned. "It seems to me that getting published is like having your work become concrete. No longer fluid. It's validated. On the published side of the fence, inconsistencies become *ironies.* Confused phrasing becomes *difficult, yet rewarding prose.* Frustrating sparseness becomes *artful obscurity.* Deficiencies are imbued with meaning and purpose. It's Goddamn madness."

"You're being dramatic."

"Maybe." *Definitely.*

"You write to connect, yet you don't feel that's possible?"

"Before she died, Thalia said that artists don't create art to connect. They create art to ask one central question: 'What the fuck is wrong with you?' And you know what? She was right. *Successful* art leaves its audience saying, 'Yeah. What the fuck *is* wrong with me?' But what if it's just *these* readers that don't get it? Is it possible the problem is with the audience and not the art?"

"You can tell yourself that. If it makes you feel better."

Smartass. My mind was clouded with a million contradictory thoughts. "I can't tell if my readers don't understand brilliance when they see it, or if it's because I simply am not brilliant. I suspect the latter. Fear the latter. There are just so many other voices out there and they are all the same to me and I *cannot* be like them."

"Sure you don't suspect the former?"

Ouch. "I couldn't be so presumptuous."

He scanned me with his one good eye for a moment from beneath his bushy eyebrows. "Perhaps your greatest fear is that you *are* like them."

I nodded. Maybe. Probably. Yes.

"Is that really so bad?" he asked. "To be normal?"

I balked at the question. "Is it really so bad? It's the worst thing imaginable. How can I comment on the outward imperfections of a box if I'm *inside* it?"

"Then how can you hope to relate? To be relatable? Maybe the central question of *successful* art isn't, as you so eloquently put it, 'What the fuck is wrong with *you?*' Maybe it's 'What the fuck is wrong with *us?*' It may be that it's your stubborn refusal to adapt, to find common ground with your audience that keeps you in this mental prison of yours."

He shrugged and stared at me a long while, allowing it to sink in, probably hoping it might take root.

"What happened to your job? To your house?" he asked after a long pause.

Ugh. "Do you have yesterday's paper?"

He frowned and rose to fetch it from a small basket next to his desk. He handed it to me and I perused it. Surely, there would be mention of it somewhere. There it was. Page six. I was glad to see my picture wasn't there, but my name was, along with my involvement in the testing business and the connection to Thalia and the bodies in my burned-out house and my subsequent escape to God-knows-where. Hell, they'd already found the car and the gun in the trunk.

Hey, I'm almost in print now, I thought sourly and handed Dr. Norman the paper.

He read it, folded it in half, and tossed it on the floor. He sucked a bit of something from his teeth and watched me for a while. "You should probably get back on the meds."

"What did you really think of the book? Overall?" I asked. "It's not finished, you know."

"You should probably get back on the meds," he repeated.

I never saw him again after that. As a rule, homeless people don't tend to have psychiatrists.

CHAPTER 36

The prospect of being homeless curiously excited me. It was the ultimate "up yours" to the American dream, to the clock punchers with their meetings and self-evaluations and to the world of mobile phones and internet and all the devalued relationships that come with them.

For the first time in my life, I felt free.

I followed the bayou that ran behind Dr. Norman's building, pondering no particular destination. It was a nice day, a little hot, decent breeze. The cicadas were singing. The winding bayou with all its tributaries cut low through the city like a last bastion of unclaimed nature, concrete bridges passing over it, *clunkity-clunk* of cars echoing beneath them. Patches of brush along either side were cut back and well managed in some places, wild in others.

"Free as the wind blows," Thalia said. She walked a few steps behind me, hopping over tires and poking the occasional turtle or snake with a stick.

"I'm a vagabond. Home is where I lay my head."

"No more morning commutes," she said.

"No more paychecks."

"No more insufferable tasks arbitrarily assigned to you by insufferable people."

"No more paychecks."

"All the time in the world to write."

"But very little to write with."

I found a pack of imitation Twinkies on the ground. Only one was eaten and the one that remained looked fresh, no ants or anything. I began to eat it.

Thalia stopped and watched me. "You don't have to start eating garbage just yet."

"Never pass on a meal, I figure."

The creamy filling burst on my tongue and was delicious.

"You think that water is safe to drink?" I asked, mouth full.

The water was brown with garbage floating in it, a fine layer of gnats swarming just above.

Thalia crossed her arms and lifted an eyebrow.

"I'm kidding," I said, and laughed.

She disappeared as I remembered how lonely I was.

Oddly, I wasn't too far from the school, maybe four hundred yards. Students liked to skip class and hide along the banks, particularly in a drainage pipe that was big enough to sit in. I spotted the pipe across the bayou from me. I knew I was close.

I heard giggling beyond the bushes to my right.

I peeked through. Hemi was there, pants halfway down the crack of his ass, with his student, Rosalita Montez, pressed up against a tree, still clothed, fortunately. He was sucking on her neck.

"Oh man, Hemi," I said. "You're old enough to be her teacher."

He yelped and turned, wild-eyed and searching for my voice. His eyes locked on me. Rosalita had that *Home Alone* look of utter surprise.

"Jesus, you scared the hell out of me," he said. "Look, man ...look, man . . ." He pulled up his pants and held them in place with his left hand while holding his right hand out as if cautioning me not to jump to conclusions. "The cops are looking for you. Came to the campus and everything. Now, listen, you don't talk about this, I won't talk about seeing you here, alright?"

Rosalita sat on the ground, pulled her knees into her, and wrapped her arms around them. She was crying. I wasn't sure if it was because I caught them or because of what Hemi was trying to do to her.

"I've gotten a lot more done on my manuscript since you last saw it," I said.

Thalia appeared just behind him. "Bash his head in."

I pulled the manuscript out of my backpack and held it out to him. He looked at Rosalita and then back at me, buttoned, and rubbed his chin. Finally, he took hold of it as if he was scared not to, but I didn't let go.

"Lose it, and I'll kill you," I said and then let him pull it from between my fingers.

"Yeah, right. Killer." He said 'killer' as if it was utterly absurd. "So ...what? You want me to read it again?"

"Yeah. The story's grown some since you saw it last. It's a helluva lot better now."

He looked back at Rosalita. I thought he might cry. "You're nuts, you know that?"

"Didn't you tell me you interned at a publishing house once? Interned with an editor?"

He hung his head and nodded. "Yeah."

"Give me the full editorial treatment so I can start revisions."

He looked confused. "What?"

"The full treatment. It's expensive and I can't spare the money to have it done. Not now."

"Or you'll tell?" he asked and directed my gaze to Rosalita.

"Huh? Oh yeah, right."

"Drown him. Drown him in the bayou," Thalia said.

"How long will you give me?"

"Say ...tomorrow?"

"That's not enou—"

"About this time tomorrow?"

He nodded again and turned to Rosalita. She was freakishly overdeveloped, held back a grade most likely, old enough to know how to get in trouble, but not old enough to know how to get out of it. "Go home."

She looked up, mascara running down her cheeks, and nodded.

"Don't say anything about this to anyone," he said to her.

She nodded again.

"Not any of your little hoodrat friends."

"Okay." She stood and scampered off like a frightened deer.

Hemi started to walk away, but turned back. "I love her."

"We can't always have the ones we love," I said.

He studied my face awhile and then walked away,

tucking my manuscript under his left arm the way one might when they're about to go read on the shitter.

"He doesn't deserve to live," Thalia said. She sat perched on a low hanging branch.

"I should take to killing all pedophiles now? Do you have any idea how much ammo I'd need to kill every pedophile in Texas?"

"She's so young."

"She's probably marrying age in many cultures."

"Those cultures don't keep their kids cocooned in childhood like we do here in the States. She's not mentally prepared for this. She can't be more than fourteen."

"She might be fifteen."

"She's naïve and rebellious and he's taking advantage of it."

"We'll call in a tip after I get my manuscript back."

She watched the dejected man walk across the soccer field on the other side of the tree line. Incendiary gleam in her eyes.

#

I followed the bayou down a ways and found an unopened can of corn in a discarded grocery bag. I shoved the corn in my pocket. It bulged and swung back and forth as I walked down a nonexistent path through brush and bramble. As evening approached, the sky turned gold and the shadows grew long. I was hungry. I pulled out the can of corn and stared at it. It was the good stuff, name brand, Green Giant.

There must be a way to open this without a can opener.

I laid the can on a rock, held it down with my foot, and wedged a stick under the lip on the edge. I tried to push the top off, but the stick broke and I fell down.

Homeless people are always eating out of cans in the movies. You can't tell me they all carry can openers around with them. They must get these things open somehow.

"Just go buy some food," Thalia said.

"I have to conserve money. It has to stretch for, like, the rest of my life."

"Then go buy a can opener."

Hmm. "No. No. Can't spare a dime."

I wiggled a heavy chunk of asphalt out of the mud and hit the can with it. It dented but didn't crack open.

Jesus Christ, if monkeys can go to space, I can get this Goddamn can of corn open.

I threw the can at the concrete column of the overpass twenty yards upstream. No luck. Didn't help that I had the throwing arm of a thirteen-year-old.

"You ain't been homeless long," a raspy voice from a shadowy recess under the overpass said.

I tried not to show how startled I was. I may have let out a small yelp before mustering a pseudo-steely gaze at the interloper.

"I was born on these streets," I said. "My mom had me at the corner of Main and 51st and nourished me with a bottle of crack. A little LSD to calm my nerves."

The trollish man came into the light and walked up to me. "Main and 51st? No such place exists. Not here, at least." The rest of what I'd said seemed plausible, I supposed. The old man was clean-shaven, more or less— as clean-shaven as the homeless get—but he had wiry nose hairs hanging below his nostrils that looked as if they were trying to escape the mottled mess that was the brain inside his skull. I couldn't turn away.

"You lookin' at ma' whiskers, ain't ya?"

"No. No," I said and casually moved my eyes to his brown wool cap and back to the whiskers and down to his tattered black T-shirt and back to the whiskers and then to his dirty tan pants—tan is a poor choice for the unwashed—and back to the whiskers.

He pointed at them. "They's what keeps me balanced. If I didn't have 'em, I wouldn't be able to walk. I'd fall over."

"You mean like a cat? That thing about their whiskers is an old wives' tale, isn't it?"

He looked down at his feet to think about it and then looked back at me, narrow-eyed. "What's this got to do with cats?"

"Never mind."

"Okay. Now you'll never make it out here 'thout a can opener."

He pulled one out of his pocket and handed it to me.

"Thanks. I'm starving."

"Mmm-hmm."

I opened the can, sniffed its contents, and poured about a third of it into my mouth.

"Name's Jed," he said.

"As in Clampett?" I said, mouth full.

He squinted and leaned over. "Come again?"

"Never mind."

"Startin' to see why yer homeless." He tapped his temple. "Ain't quite right up here, is ye?"

I downed another hefty mouthful of corn, keeping him firmly in my gaze. I worried he might lunge at me for the rest of it.

"Don't worry," he said. "I'll show ya the ropes. Take ya down to our village jus' over yonder." He pointed somewhere further down the bayou.

"Your village?"

"Oh yeah. It's real nice. Most of the people is nice. Accommodations is nice."

I poured the rest of the corn into my mouth and shook the can to make sure I had every kernel. "How far is this village of yours?"

"Ova yonder."

"How far is a 'yonder'?"

He studied me a moment. "Why don't you jus' folla me?"

I looked both ways to see if there was a more preferable direction. There wasn't.

CHAPTER 37

Jed took me to a shantytown that stood amongst a lightly wooded, triangular shaped plot of land. The bayou was to the northeast, an overpass to the north, the backside of a strip mall to the east. Ramshackle tents jittered in the breeze, tarps hung from trees, metal siding attached to crooked logs creaked and rattled. The smell of cheap hamburgers from a fast food joint upwind of us overpowered a faint odor of garbage. Some shady characters were out, one reclining against an old washing machine, a couple spooning in a patch of dirt, a gaggle of three standing around an oil drum, smoking.

I pulled out a cigarette and lit it. Jed turned to me. "This is a non-smoking village, sir. You'll have to put that out. Might catch the weeds on fire, or some cardboard somewhere."

"What about them?" I said and nodded at the three amigos puffing away.

"What about who?" he said.

"Them. The guys smoking."

"They ain't smokin.' It's cold out. It's the ...the ... what's the word ...condescension—"

"Condensation. The word is condensation, but it's April. It's like ninety-five degrees. Oh, Christ. Never mind."

"You like them words. Never mind. Ain't-gots-no-mind's more like it."

I shook my head and snuffed the cigarette out. He motioned me to follow. We approached a little box shaped hovel that had four water-stained particleboard walls, a shower curtain for a door, and a ceiling made out of shrink wrap and chicken wire.

Before we entered, Jed turned. "You can stay here with me and Frisky Phil."

"Frisky Phil?"

"He's away on business. Be back tomorra."

"How frisky is he?"

"Ya don't sleep nekkid, does ye?"

"No."

"Not very."

He pulled back the shower curtain and held out an open hand as if introducing me to Xanadu. Two sleeping bags were inside, one on each side, and a narrow strip of canvas in the middle that might have once been the jumping surface for a trampoline. It smelled like mothballs.

"Me," Jed said, pointing at the bag on the right. "Frisky," he said, pointing at the one on the left. "You," pointing at the space in the middle.

"Well, okay. Not bad. I guess."

He smiled as if to say, "Hey, you might be okay after

all."

I'm going to be the meat in a hobo sandwich.

"Hell no, it's not bad," he said. "This here is how 'mericans do homeless." He laughed with pride and held his belly.

I spent that night trying not to go to sleep before Jed, but the man simply did not sleep. He just laid there staring at a pinecone.

Tomorrow, I'd go meet Hemi.

\#

I found Hemi the next day in the same place I'd seen he and Rosalita the day before. It was evening and though the sky was overcast, no rain was on the horizon. He had dark circles under his eyes and was wearing the same clothes he'd been wearing yesterday.

"You look awful," I said.

"*I* look awful. Look at you. I stayed up all damn night and called in sick trying to get this done in the time you so graciously gave me to complete it."

"You got it?"

"Yeah, yeah. Right here."

He handed me the manuscript. I took it and sat down with my back against a tree. A rusty carburetor was half buried in the dirt next to me. If you looked hard enough along the banks of the bayou, you could probably piece together a whole engine.

"I made notes in red on separate sheets of paper," he said. "I couldn't always read your writing on those last twenty something pages written in longhand. Look, man, does this square us? You won't say anything about Rosie?"

"Sit down," I said. Both put-out and nervous, he put

his hands in his pockets, let out a sigh, and rocked back and forth on his heels. Finally, he sat down with one knee up and the other leg folded under it.

I looked through his notes. Exclamation points were everywhere, preceded by every kind of positive adjective he could think of. He'd peppered it with glowing editorial comments and made only minor corrections. He was only telling me what he thought I wanted to hear. He was only concerned with his precious Rosalita and staying out of prison, even at the expense of his literary integrity.

Maybe if I puff him up, he'll leave us alone, he must have thought. I closed the binder and set it aside.

"So, you liked it?" I said. I picked up a stick and scratched at the dirt around the carburetor, absently trying to dig it out.

"It's much better now. You've really improved it. I think you're on to something."

"I didn't make many changes to the parts you already read."

"Really? Maybe it reads different now that I'm seeing the big picture."

"You're full of shit," I said.

"What?" He looked genuinely hurt. Scared even.

"You're full of shit and you think if you tell me what I want to hear, I won't tell."

"Look," he said.

I held up a hand to caution him against continuing the charade. He deflated and looked down at his hands.

"I can't go to prison," he said. His thinning hair danced in the evening breeze. He looked up at me. "Fine. Have it your way. My opinion of it hasn't changed, but I'm only one guy. I don't like stuff that comes off as too preachy or philosophical and I don't like this transgressive, woe-is-me-white-boy-self-destructs bullshit. Some people like that sort of thing, but I don't. I'm an English teacher. I teach units on Orwell's *1984*. I *hate* that book. I'm not supposed to, but I do. And I hate *Fahrenheit 451*, *Animal Farm*, *Slaughterhouse Five* —I could go on and on. The point is, these are classics by most people's standards, but not by *my* standards. I like thrillers, and mysteries, and comedies, stuff I don't have to think too much about. This just isn't my thing."

"Are you saying you think what I've written is comparable to something Orwell might have written?"

He forgot his precarious position and laughed. "God, no. As much as I hate the books I just mentioned, I'd gladly read any one of them if given the choice to read yours instead. Your book is like a cheap, crappy knockoff." His face stiffened and he shook his head. "I'm sorry. All I'm saying is that it's just me. One man's opinion, so who cares? The only thing that matters is that you're writing the book you want to write. Write for yourself, first. Don't worry about anyone else."

"That's bullshit. People tell themselves that so they can sleep at night. It's the honey they take to get the bitter pill of failure to go down a little easier."

By now, I'd dug the carburetor out enough and I could jiggle it back and forth. I crossed my legs and slumped over, still jiggling it.

"It's not bullshit," he said. Almost pleading. "It's not."

"What's it worth if I write something no one wants to read?"

"If a tree falls in the woods and no one's there to hear it . . ." he said. I thought I saw tears in his eyes. "I can't go to prison."

He can think of nothing but himself. His posture mirrored my own. Or was I mirroring him?

Loathsome, disgusting creature.

I pulled the carburetor free. I wanted to punch him, but this heavy thing was in my hand. I hurled it at his face with complete absence of forethought. The rusty machine part cracked his forehead with a heavy *thunk* and he fell back, hitting his head a second time on a rock. His legs contorted and swayed side to side. His right arm lifted, then dropped. He groaned and then his body jolted into a seizure until he went still about fifteen seconds later, eyes open.

CHAPTER 38

"Oh, shit." I looked around to make sure no one was watching. Leaning in. Speaking quietly. "Hemi?" He wasn't breathing. I dropped to my knees and shook him. "Hemi?"

Thalia appeared over us, gawking. She looked just like she did in that portrait I'd seen of her, the one Calli brought over in the backpack. So young. So innocent. "He's gone." She gazed at me in horror. "You killed him." As she backed away, she tripped, fell, and scuttled backward like a crab. She rolled onto all fours, weakly rose to her feet, and ran away without looking back.

Good. It was better that way. This was an emergent side of me no one should have to see.

I stood up and looked down at Hemi. A piece of scalp hung loosely from his forehead which had collected bits of dirt and grass on the sticky underside of it during in the seizure.

"You son of a bitch," I said. "You son of a—"

I paced a few times, anger building.

"Couldn't kill *myself* on purpose but I go and kill *you* by accident. Bet you think this is funny." There was so much blood. He threatened to be my creative undoing, my anti-muse. Now the bastard would be my physical undoing too. I picked up the carburetor and hit him again, and then again. Two concussive blows, powerful under the weight of the machine part. What difference did it make? I needed his dead eyes to stop looking at me.

Overcome with rage, I resumed hitting him, angrier with every strike.

"I hate you. I hate all of you," I said with the venomous hiss of a snake, the bluster of an angry dog. "For asking me to *bow* to *you*." Striking him. Striking him. "To entertain you as if I'm a court jester. You should bow to *me*." Still striking. "Your admiration is my riches. Self-worth by itself is poverty. I *hate* you, you fuck. You greedy, self-absorbed piece of shit."

And then I stopped—breathing heavy, mind a swirling cauldron of alarms. The tantrum faded, my vision shifting from shades of red to muted colors tainted yellow, blurry around the edges. I let the carburetor slide out of my right hand and fall to the ground with a thud. Alternating currents of guilt and titillation flowed through me.

What was left of Hemi's head was like a ruby red grapefruit smashed on the roadway. One dislodged eye continued to peer at me like a dead fish, accusing me.

The critic is dead.

CHAPTER 39

"Rise and shine, ya crazy son of a bitch."

Hemi. Leaning over me, sun against his back, head in shadow, stitched together like the world's ugliest soccer ball. As soon as my eyes focused, he evaporated like smoke.

I was still by the bayou, but the body was gone. Drag marks had been kicked over with dirt in a half-assed attempt to cover them up. The blood was covered too, the carburetor gone.

I was confused. My head hurt. Terror. Not as much for what I'd done, but for fear of being found out. Where's the body? Did he survive and crawl away? Couldn't have. Not after what I did to him. Maybe it was a nightmare. Something caused by an undigested bit of beef.

Dried blood was under my nails, caked on my cuticles.

"You did the world a service, my friend," someone said.

I sat up and turned to see who it was. A tall lanky black man stood there. He had gray hair with a few black streaks in it and a bushy beard. Olive green pants and a shirt that might have been red once, but was now pink. He held my manuscript beneath his right arm and had a dirty black rag in his hand that he was using to clean between the fingers of his other hand.

"What?"

"You did the world a service. Come on, we'd better go before someone comes along."

I struggled to my feet and approached him. "Where's—"

He held out his hand to stop me. "We can talk as we go, but we shouldn't stay here. Someone will see us."

I ignored him, ran down to the bayou, and dipped my hand in the filthy water to clean the blood off. I scrubbed and scrubbed muttering, "Out, damned spot. Out." Hemi's freakish face looked up at me from beneath the water and smiled maniacally. I fell backward.

The stranger watched thoughtfully, almost sympathetically and then began to walk away. I followed him like a hungry kitten hoping for a saucer of milk. He had me at a disadvantage and knew it. "Are you from that village over yonder?" I asked.

"Yes. We call it Malpaís."

"Malpaís?"

"Well, *I* call it that."

"Like from *Brave New World*? The savage reservation?"

"You're a literary man, I see."

"Yeah, for sure. A writer, in fact. You're holding my life's greatest work there, under your arm." I kept seeing

Hemi's dead face in my mind and had to shake my head to clear it away as if my brain were an Etch A Sketch. "What happened to ...uh ...?"

"Don't worry. I took care of the body. I buried it. No one will ever see his face again."

The body, he said. As if it was any old thing.

"I was hoping it was a nightmare. A fever dream. A bit of psychosis. Why would you do that for me? Hide the ...ya know."

"I saw that man many times over the years with his young girls. Doing his business with them along the bayou. A man like that doesn't deserve to live. You did what I only dreamed of."

"There was more than one girl?"

"Oh, yes. Many."

"Did you ever try to stop him?"

"No. Some of the men in Malpaís liked to watch in secret. They never would have stood for it if I'd tried to intervene. Sometimes you have to go along to get along, as they say. Don't tell them what you've done. They'll be angry."

"Hadn't planned on it."

He turned and handed me the manuscript. His dark hands were like roughly hewn stone. "What's it about?"

"It's about my life these past few months."

"Sounds self-involved," he said.

"Yeah, well. Maybe it does, but you shouldn't judge it before you've read it. You *can* read, can't you?"

"Just because I'm homeless doesn't mean I'm illiterate. In fact, I used to be a literary agent."

"What? *Really?*"

"Sure. I represented a couple of authors who wrote

self-help books geared toward masochists. I thought it was daring and edgy at the time. Unfortunately, according to market research, masochists aren't interested in self-help literature."

"I'd have thought differently."

"I know, right?"

"That's it? Did you represent anyone else?"

"I was only in the business for a few months before I was let go. The industry is changing. Has changed."

"What did you do before that?"

"I owned my own taco truck. The health department shut me down for excessively high carbon monoxide levels in the meat."

"Carbon monoxide?" I muttered. I could see Malpaís up ahead. It was beginning to get dark.

"Would you care to read my story?" I said.

"I'd love to."

"What's your name?"

"Phil."

"Phil? As in 'frisky'?"

"I don't care for that nickname, but I am the same."

"Sorry. About the nickname. I think Jed means for us to be roomies for the time being."

Phil stopped and faced me. "Do you sleep naked?" he asked, almost happy.

"No. No. And I might have gonorrhea." I lied.

"Pity."

He resumed, but I grabbed his arm to stop him. "Say, is it safe in Malpaís?"

He turned back. "Safe?"

"Yeah. Are there crazies there?"

"Not many." He resumed his stride. "The *real* crazies

live in the palatial estates of River Oaks. Did you know there are a higher percentage of psychopaths among surgeons than in any other field?"

"What? Is that true?"

"Read it somewhere."

"If I get my appendix removed, the guy who removes it might eat it later?"

"I suppose so. Yes."

"That's messed up."

#

If Phil told Jed what I'd done, Jed didn't let on. I washed again before I went to sleep and he gave me a change of clothes that weren't necessarily clean, but didn't have brain matter on them.

I felt Hemi's blood on me no matter what I did. "Out, damned spot," I kept muttering. His blood was parasitical, like a virus. It made me itch. He probably had Ebola.

That wasn't fair. Disparaging him like that. In spite of everything, he'd been a friend. I wept quietly until I fell asleep and dreamed.

I was back in the mall food court, sitting across from Thalia. Her face was downcast. I longed to be alone with her, to kiss those full lips and fade into darkness with her, but Leslie stood close with his gun, watching me and smiling.

Mikey was at the next table over and Calli stood behind him with her hands on his shoulders. He looked like Freddy Krueger and smoke drifted off him in gentle spools. Thalia's dad sat across from Mikey, burn wounds infected and oozing with pus. He was naked. I didn't know why. Hemi, face a tapestry of stitched flesh, sat at the table on the other side. The unburning monk sat across from him. My dad, with his gunshot-split head, sat at the table behind us all, watching with dangling slug eyes.

My manuscript sat in the middle of the table.

Thalia wouldn't look at me. Suddenly, I found myself outside her front door. She was on the other side. I could see her hair through the peephole. I banged with my fist, but she refused to answer. Instead, Hemi appeared and put his arm around my shoulders.

"Thalia wants to take a break," he said. "See other people. But don't worry, *I'm* here for you, bud."

Hemi, my anti-muse obviously planned to stay awhile.

\#

A newspaper landing on my face woke me the next morning.

"Front page." Phil said, grinning.

I sat up and fumbled with it, black print rubbing off on my fingers. The headline read:

Body of Local Teacher Found Beaten to Death, Police Suspect Foul Play

"The editor that oversaw this headline should be shot," I said, still in that haze between sleep and wakefulness. And then it occurred me—"*Hemi*?"

"You're famous."

"Famous? They're looking for me?"

"Of course."

I stood and went outside to make sure no one was listening. I went back in, leaned into him, and whispered, "You said you took care of it."

"I did."

"You said you buried the body."

"I did. But the hole I found wasn't very big and it didn't quite fit. A bit of him was ...protruding."

He was smiling like a proud parent.

"*Protruding*?"

"Just his legs," he said, reassuringly. He gripped my upper arms and repeated, "Just his legs."

"You buried him at an *angle*?"

"Head first."

"Head fi— Is that what you meant when you said no one would see his face anymore?"

"No. Did you see what you did to him? He didn't have a face. Without a face and only legs sticking out of the ground, how was I supposed to know someone would recognize him?"

I thought to argue, to articulate the finer points of modern forensics, but what would have been the point? My heart was ripping through my chest. I sat down in the corner, read the article, and then threw the paper down, disgusted.

"What's wrong?" Phil said.

"I'm going to prison."

"No, you're not. You can stay here with us. No one will find you here. You must grow a beard. Grow a beard and stay here and finish your revisions. You'll be fine. You'll see."

He handed me the manuscript as if it might make me feel better to hold it.

It did.

"I read it," he said.

"You did?"

"Yes. It's good. Very good. I read select passages to

Jed, too, and he agreed. It's good."

"It's good," Jed said, shuffling into the hovel while gnawing on a week-old doughnut.

"You *really* liked it?"

"I did."

"You have any editing experience?"

"A little."

"Would you be willing to edit for me?"

"Nothing better to do."

"You think we should leave the country? Go down to Mexico for a while? You're an accomplice now, you know."

"I'm not going to Mexico."

"Yeah. You're right. We're probably safer here, even with the cops looking for me." I looked down at my manuscript and rubbed my fingers over the dirty, creased binder cover.

"You really liked it?"

CHAPTER 40

The gravity of my situation sank in when Detective Kuklinski showed up in Malpaís asking questions about me. He'd followed the bayou and emerged from the woods, phone propped between his head and shoulder while writing in a notepad about fifty yards from where I sat on a cinder block. His badge hung from a chain around his neck and glinted in the sun. Jed was zipping up after urinating on a tree.

"Shit." I said and ducked around the particle board side of Jed's hut.

"Gotta dig a hole for that."

"What? No. That's a cop over there."

"You wanna see if he wants to stay for lunch? Ain't got nothin' but Ramen noo—"

"I need to hide, Jed. He can't find me here," I whispered.

"There's a tarp back there. Could crawl under it."

"Yeah, okay." I lifted the blue tarp and slithered

under. I didn't move, tried not to even breathe. I was an honest-to-God fugitive now. *Me*. A wanted man.

Hemi appeared like Thalia used to, under the tarp, gruesome face inches away from mine, bathed in blue light. "You're screwed now," he said at full volume.

"Shh."

"Howdy," I heard Jed say. It sounded like he'd gone out to meet the detective.

"Afternoon," Kuklinski responded. "Just wondering if you've seen this guy around?"

A long pause. "Yeah, he's right over there."

Hemi laughed as if this sudden misfortune was too good to be true.

"Shut up," I whispered. Son of a—Jed, you senile old—"

"The Mexican guy by the oil drum?" Kuklinski said.

Oh, thank God.

"Yep."

"Uh. That's not him, man. Take another look?"

Hemi vanished in a disappointed huff.

"Uh. Right there?"

I could hear Kuklinski sigh. "That's a dog."

"You sure?"

"Pretty sure."

It felt like I was suffocating. Sweat stung my eyes.

Jed took it up a notch. "That's a nice gun. Can I have it? As a tax payin' citizen, ain't it part mine anyway?"

"And when was the last time you paid taxes, sir?"

"I paid sales tax on the noodles I bought at the store yesterday."

Silence for a moment. "Jesus Christ. Never mind," Kuklinski said.

I stayed under the tarp for another fifteen minutes until the detective finished poking around. When he was gone, Jed pulled the tarp off me and yelped as if he'd forgotten I was there.

I stood up and brushed myself off. "Thanks, Jed."

"Fer what?"

#

The narrow escape with Kuklinski frightened me. I spent most of the next week in or near Jed's hovel on high alert. Didn't eat much. Jed and Phil kept inviting me to go to the nightly campfire and get to know everyone, but I just wanted to be alone. Unfortunately, being alone meant being with Hemi. I thought about suicide and figured it was imminent, but exhausted and freshly resigned to my fate, I finally accepted their invitation.

They met at night and built the fire on the patch of land farthest from view to the outside world. Logs, cinderblocks, and old ice chests formed a circle around it where everyone sat and they cooked Ramen noodles in a teakettle that hung over the fire. We sweated profusely, savoring what sporadic breeze there was.

"Glad you came, Ches," Phil said. He sat in an old lawn chair. "Have a seat."

He told me everyone's names, but I wasn't going to remember them all. I gave the group, about ten in all, one of those timid, "I don't know what the hell I'm doing here" waves as I sat on a dirty ice chest.

Hemi stood on the other side, just out of the circle of light. I ignored him.

"How you like it here?" a middle-aged woman with tattoos on her face asked me.

"It's okay. It's nice. Better than I would have

imagined. No one hassles you guys about being here?"

Phil said, "Jed holds the deed to this little piece of land. His uncle left it to him when he died about fifteen years ago. Police come in every now and then, but most regular people don't want to dig too deep here. Don't want to get in a position where they somehow feel obligated to help us."

I considered Jed. "You don't mind sharing?"

"Sharing what?"

"Your land?"

"What land?" Everyone chuckled. I wasn't sure if he was crazy, senile, or just screwing with me.

I looked around the group as the tattooed woman handed me a Styrofoam cup of noodles. Everyone was slurping. The fire crackled. "How did you all come together?" I asked.

A young guy, maybe twenty-seven, twenty-eight, seated in a shoddy wheelchair because his legs were missing said, "Only a few of us are here all the time. Most people just come and go." I'd find out later that he lost his legs in Afghanistan. Chris was his name.

"We try to maintain a community here," Phil said. "We share what we have and we'll take in anyone as long as they stay off the drugs and don't cause trouble. Junkies are always a problem. Drunks can go either way."

A man about my age with hair like Sideshow Bob and a guitar propped up next to him asked me to tell them a little about myself.

Jesus, where to start? I had to assume Phil was the only one there who knew about Hemi. "Well ...I uh, I recently lost my job, my house, my car. I have an ex-wife. Full disclosure, I should probably be on meds, but I'm not. Depression. Anxiety. The scar on my face is from a suicide attempt. And, let's see, I'm in trouble with the law for reasons I'd rather not share."

"Those are your circumstances, man," the guitar guy said, "tell us who you *are*."

I shrugged. "Oh, okay. Well ...I'm a writer. A storyteller."

"Whoa. Tell us a story, man."

"Nah. My stories are weird. I only have one on paper anymore and it's too long to read around a campfire. Anything else would have to be from memory."

"Tell us one from memory."

Everyone nodded.

"Okay. Alright. Here's one I wrote a few years ago. It's really, really strange. Come to think of it, this story might be the one that first landed me in therapy."

"That's why you gotta tell it."

I told them the story—more of a confession, really—of the prior week's events which I'd yet to commit to paper. They didn't recognize it as true, as my protagonist, *me*, remained unnamed. It had all the cadence of a work of fiction, an *absurd* one at that. I told it straight, fueled by the misery that'd powered me most of my life, but they received it as a work of black comedy and laughed, especially at the "fuckwit" of a main character—their word, not mine.

That was the first time I'd ever seen one of my stories bring people genuine happiness and all I had to do was kill a man.

CHAPTER 41

Five years passed unceremoniously.

I remained in Malpaís and grew my hair long and my beard swallowed my scar and I lost weight to the point of looking sallow. Phil and I became close. He was gay, but not extravagantly so. Occasionally, his inner perv rose to the surface, which was okay. My inner perv needed the company. He was just a little off, like a slightly crooked picture on the wall, but was good company and, delusionally speaking, made me feel close to the publishing industry.

Other than what we saw passing by on the streets and what we read in the paper, the world just kind of existed out there, somewhere. We weren't really a part of it. We had a guy who made a little cash from a paper route and every day he'd stiff a different house and bring us the news. We mostly just wanted to make sure World War III hadn't started, but I also kept an eye out for news of an arrest for Thalia's murder. As far as I knew, they never caught Leslie.

We ate Ramen noodles, and rice and beans, and potatoes. A Mexican restaurant and a bakery were in the strip mall backed against our land. We had a steady supply of day old corn chips and stale bread. Every now and then, someone would catch a live chicken from God-knows-where and we'd cook it and eat like kings for an evening.

Various church groups visited and did work for us, calling themselves missionaries, and bringing us canned food liberated from the darkest corners of suburban pantries. The churches were particularly interested in a schizophrenic woman named Ruthie Mae who lived among us and talked to Jesus. Jesus hovered six feet in front of her and wore a poncho. One church built us an open-air chapel. When the people of God came, we cried "Hallelujah" and "Praise Jesus" and took turns praying for God to forgive us our sins so that the church left feeling as if they hadn't wasted their time meeting only material needs. Kept everybody happy.

At night, that chapel was mine, I was its pastor, serving the God of slipstream storytelling. Like all pastors, I preached fiction to my flock.

Living in Malpaís wasn't easy, though. Chris, the vet, rolled himself in front of a bus. Hector and Alejandro, brothers from Eagle Pass, fought over a woman and almost killed each other with broken beer bottles. Cold spells in '17 and '18 forced us to take umbrage in overcrowded shelters. Floods in '18 and '20 forced us to rebuild what little we had. There was the flu outbreak of '19 when we had to take Jed to the emergency room. I got dysentery in April of that year.

Hemi continued to torment my waking life *and* my dreams. What I did to him was unforgivable. No matter how many times I reminded myself that he was a child rapist, I couldn't recover the little piece of my soul that died with him.

Years prior, the prospect of divorce had prompted me to shoot myself, yet the current reality of homelessness didn't. I owed it to Hemi to endure the pain. And for the first time in my life, I was part of a true community. Malpaís. Brothers and sisters in agony. I wrote every day using pens and paper I bought at the dollar store with money I cobbled together panhandling. I wrote extra small, and in the margins, and on the front and back of the pages, to conserve as much space as I could. Mostly short stories. Hemi usually stood over me offering shitty advice I almost always ignored. He never stopped being my voice of doubt—always scratching at my psyche— but that was one part of me I refused to let him have. *All* writers have an intense voice of doubt. Mine just happened to belong to someone I'd murdered.

Anyone who could read in Malpaís loved my book, officially called *The Author is Dead*. I'd like to say the title was an intelligent homage to the literary deconstruction movement kicked off by Jacques Derrida in the late '60s, but the truth is I just thought it sounded cool. At night, they'd ask to hear one short story or another, inviting friends, gathering in the chapel to hear my dramatic readings. I felt like a tribe storyteller of old, always constructing some new tale. It gifted them the fanciful mind vacations the rest of the world took for granted. One couldn't ask for a more appreciative audience.

I refined my book as far as I could in light of my

situation and limited resources. I had a notebook full of agent and publisher addresses that I assembled at the library on one of their free-for-all computers. Each week, I'd hustle up money, make copies of the manuscript, and mail it to three or four of them. The owner of the Mexican restaurant let me use the restaurant's address because one time I chased off a burglar who'd kicked the back door in. The burglar was Jed, who'd had a powerful desire to eat guacamole that night, but the owner didn't need to know that.

The world just went on without us and I think most of us liked it that way. I'm sure the world did too.

CHAPTER 42

"Maybe it's the ending," Phil said, flipping through *The Author is Dead.*

"Yep." Hemi. Sitting behind us on the sidewalk with his back against a stucco wall. "All the stuff before it might be a problem, too."

"Ending it with Hemi's death makes it seem unfinished," Phil continued, unaware of my hallucinations. "There should be a better resolution to it all."

We were sitting on a bench across the street from a mom and pop bookstore on Tenth. Phil held a rejection letter, my one hundred and twenty-third. I always made him read query responses first to soften the blow. I'd rewritten *The Author is Dead* six times and not a single bite from anyone in publishing.

"You sure the rejections aren't because I haven't typed it up?" I said.

"No, no. They don't mind, as long as it's good. They

have people to type it for you."

"Bullshit!" Hemi sang with his hands cupped around his mouth.

"Spare some change?" I said to a woman who walked by. She didn't make eye contact but walked a little faster so I know she heard me. The next lady told me to get a job.

"What would you do if you got a book deal?" Phil looked at me. "Would you leave us?"

"I don't know."

"Aren't you content in Malpaís? You write. You have an audience who loves your stories. You have friends."

I leaned back on the bench, pulled out a cigarette, and lit it. Jed still wouldn't let me smoke in Malpaís. I capitalized on every chance I got.

"Where did you get that?" Phil said, frowning. His hair was almost completely gray now, but he had found a razor in a dumpster and had kept himself pretty well shaved ever since.

"Lifted the pack off some guy who was waiting for the bus the other day. Want one?"

"No. Don't let Jed catch you."

I watched the bookstore across the street. An old woman flipped the closed sign to open.

"Did they write anything personal or was it a form rejection?" I asked Phil, taking the letter from him.

"Form. You've never gotten anything but."

I tossed it in the trash receptacle by the curb.

"I'm thinking of starting a second book. Maybe sci-fi this time."

The old woman across the street was stacking books in the window.

"I've been saying you should do that since I met you."

"I'm not giving up on this one, mind you. I just need to focus on something else."

"Good to get your mind off it. Come back to it later with fresh eyes."

The old woman set a book on a stand on top of the stack.

The face on the cover ...

I stood up and dropped the cigarette.

It couldn't be.

CHAPTER 43

A Beamer almost ran over me in the southbound lane as I crossed the street. The guy honked but I didn't look. Phil chased after me. I stepped up on the curb and could see the book clearly.

Thalia. She was on the cover, in black and white, staring back at me. It was that horrible photo of her Calli had given me. The title of the book, in stark red letters, was *Strange Obsessions*. In smaller, but no less stark red letters at the bottom, it said, "by Elvira Moon."

"Erotica?" Phil asked.

I shook my head. *Where do I know that name?* "Elvira Moon?" I said. "Elvira Moon."

"Know her?"

I looked at Phil, and then back at the book. I couldn't even begin to explain.

The old woman inside turned away, trying not to stare at us. I opened the door and snatched a copy of the book. She grabbed my wrist, but I jerked it away. "Let go of me, you old bag."

"I'm calling the police," she yelled, but I was already running down the road with Phil close behind. Two hobo track stars, kicking our knees up, pumping our arms. My beard flitted over my shoulder. We cut around the corner to a back alley and then scampered down to our bayou and back to Malpaís.

#

We sat on a stack of old tires. Phil was reading the back cover of Elvira Moon's true crime book. It was a windy spring day and the trees *swooshed* in waves. Four Mexicans were cooking goat meat over a fire they built in a hole in the ground. Didn't know where they got the goat.

Strange Obsessions was a bombshell of a book that moved Thalia's story to the national stage. The bombshell was that Calli, Thalia's own sister, was involved in her murder. Thalia dumped Leslie. Calli, seeing an opportunity to manipulate a scorned, stupid man, paid him $200 and an iPod to kill her. She even hid the fucker in her own garage apartment right next to her dad's house, relatively safe from police scrutiny. Her dad never knew Leslie was there.

By the time police caught wind of Elvira's findings, Leslie and Calli were gone.

"Jesus Christ, I'm stupid," I said. "And Elvira wouldn't have even known about this whole thing if I hadn't approached her about it. I bet she didn't even mention me in the acknowledgments."

"She didn't," Phil said. He flipped through the book. "She does, however, discuss your involvement in the events that transpired after Thalia was killed. Mentions how you killed Thalia's father and her third-grade boyfriend—"

"I didn't kill them. Those two jackasses killed themselves."

One of the Mexicans was sampling the meat with a pocketknife in his hand. Ash covered his fingers.

"It mentions the dead teacher. It doesn't paint you in a favorable light. I wouldn't imagine she'd thank you after all that." He flipped to the very back and read the biographical information on the inside cover flap. "Miss Moon's only nineteen. That's impressive. She's really got a way with words, from what I've seen so far."

"Let me see that." I grabbed the book from him. "Yellow Brick Books. This is a local publisher. Small one. Never heard of them. Did we submit there?"

"No. This Leslie de la Muerte guy is still at large. Did you know that?"

"Yeah. Maybe we should stop by their offices. They might have an interest, ya know. There's a tie-in here."

"Maybe."

"They're on the north side."

Ruthie Mae was just outside her makeshift tent, swatting at Jesus with yesterday's newspaper. I went over and took the paper from her. We always discouraged her from swatting at the Lord and Savior in case she ever tried it with something potentially lethal to the other residents of Malpaís.

I sat back down next to Phil and pulled out the Arts section, the only part I really cared about. Thalia was staring back at me from page thirteen.

"Look," I said. "Elvira has a book signing event next Thursday at that indie-bookstore over on Parker."

One of the Mexicans brought us an old pizza pan with goat meat and some sort of salsa that smelled hot as hell.

I nodded my head appreciatively. "Gracias."

"De nada." He waved and jogged back over to the fire.

"Plan on going?" Phil asked.

"I just might."

"Pretty big risk."

"Worth it. If I can wriggle my way into this deal, I just might get my book published yet. Maybe her agent will be there." I sampled some goat meat. Greasy. Gamey.

"I've got a date, so I can't go with you."

I lowered the pan and looked at Phil. "With who?"

"T. J." He pointed at a little man who'd only been there for a couple of weeks. T. J. didn't have teeth. I think that's what Phil found enticing about him.

"You dog." I shoved him playfully.

He laughed. "I think he'll be good at—" He mimed a blowjob with his fist, pushing the inside of his cheek in and out with his tongue. Phil was a dignified, well-spoken individual except where his sexual proclivities were concerned.

"Good God, don't put that image in my head, man."

At least he was getting some. I hadn't had sex since Libby left, and that last time didn't count because the phone rang and I heard her mother's voice as she left a message and couldn't finish.

CHAPTER 44

Doorways Books on Parker was decently sized for an indie shop. Modular bookshelves on wheels could be arranged to accommodate events like book signings and kiddie story times. It had been a long time since I'd stepped into a bookstore without immediately being chased out by staff. Maybe it was because I hadn't stolen anything from this particular one. Their employees were watching me, but waiting to see how the situation might evolve. I had *Strange Obsessions* in my hand. They had to know I was there to see Elvira. I'd missed the quiet dignity of bookstores, the crisp new-paper smell, and stacks of bestsellers on little square tables. God, I wanted to see my name on a stack of those books.

A small line was forming at the signing table but Elvira wasn't seated there yet. She was walking around doing the meet and greet thing. She'd grown since I last saw her five years ago, Five-four, five-five, with long, brown hair in slight disarray. She still wore glasses, but they were dignified, black framed glasses that made her look smart and pretty. The glasses she had in middle school made her look like Mr. Magoo.

She spotted me by the door and considered me a moment, realized who I was, and cautiously approached. "Please don't make a scene."

Her voice sounded mature.

"You remember me?"

"Mister Computer Man."

"Smith, actually. Ches Smith."

"Please. Don't make a scene."

"Tell you what, I won't make a scene if you promise not to call the cops. Deal?"

She considered me with suspicion. "Okay." She spotted the store manager. "Can I have a moment?"

The manager nodded, clearly curious, but sensing the situation's need for privacy. The way I looked by that time, no one would know who I was based on a years-old picture in the paper.

Elvira turned back to me, then back to the manager. "Is there somewhere quiet we can go?"

"You can go out the back door to the alley."

Elvira nodded toward the back for me to follow.

As soon as we were in the alley, I lit a cigarette and sat on a couple of stacked milk crates, her book in my lap.

"Got one for me?" she said.

"How old are you?"

"Old enough." She held out her hand, palm up, and gave me one of those gimme wags with her fingers.

I nodded and gave her one. She put it between her lips and I lit it for her. She took a long drag. "What are you doing here?"

"Just came to say 'hi.' Congratulate you."

"You pissed?"

"No. Why?"

"Look, the publisher made me change things a little, ya know. Make it more sensational then it was. Sorry if you didn't come out of it looking too good."

"Is all that shit about Calli true? She was in on it the whole time?"

"That appears to be the case."

"How'd you find out?"

"If you'd read the book, you'd know."

"I didn't even know the book existed. I've been a bit out of the loop."

"Uh-huh. Well, I ended up in juvie briefly, because of the whole testing fiasco. You'd put me up to writing that book and I had nothing better to do. So I just kept working on it. Turned out, Calli had a cousin in juvie the same time I was there and the cousin saw me doing some research in the library one day. This cousin *hated* Calli and was more than eager to tell me that Calli had been involved with de la Muerte. I had a hunch. Where's the one place no one would suspect de la Muerte to be? With his victim's family, right? I spent all my free time for weeks watching her house. Her dad left it to her after he—well, burned to a crisp over at *your* place. Finally, while Calli was out, this pizza guy shows up and leaves the pizza on the porch. As soon as the pizza guy left, out comes de la Muerte to retrieve it. When I saw him ...oh my God ...it was like finding money. Even got a picture of him. It all just kind of snowballed from there."

"And the police?"

"Fuck the police. That Kuklinski guy was a dick."

"Wow. Never figured you for a trash mouth."

"I cuss when it's appropriate."

I felt like a fool. Calli had duped me. I failed Thalia. I should have known. "How'd you recognize me so quickly, anyway?"

"You always had a kind of odd presence about you. I remembered your eyes."

"They're nice?"

"No. Desperate."

I lowered my head, took a drag, and nodded. "How old did you say you were?"

"I didn't. I'm nineteen."

"Nineteen and a bestseller."

"One of the youngest ever. Even sold the movie rights. Johnny Depp's in talks to play de la Muerte."

"Isn't he a little old?"

"He can pull it off."

"Who's playing me?"

"Steve Buscemi, I think."

"Shit. Well, Hemi said you were a good writer."

"Mister Hemingway. Right." She looked briefly ill at the mention of his name.

"This the part where you call the cops?"

"No. He was a pig. Not saying he deserved what you did to him, but he was a pig. After he died, a long line of girls came forward, dating back years, to report what he'd done to them. Bastard ended up in a pauper's grave."

That made me feel a little better about the whole thing. "Whatever happened with all that testing stuff? After juvie, I mean?"

She sat down on a milk crate of her own, knees together, still nursing the cigarette. "Got released from juvie early. Ultimately, ended up speaking before the Texas Education Agency, the governing body of public education in the state. Some things changed for the better the next year so it was worth the trouble. My manifesto was the first thing I ever got published. Small alternative press, but still."

"Did you give credit to the team of lawyers who helped you?"

"No. We'll just say they were ghostwriters."

"Yeah."

She pointed at me with the cigarette between her fingers. "You did your part."

I leaned forward with my right forearm resting on *Strange Obsessions*.

"I've been wondering something." Elvira tilted her head. "Did you love her? Thalia?"

I looked down the alley. "Yeah. Yeah, I guess I did."

She nodded and flicked some ash down onto the concrete.

It felt strange to admit that out loud.

"Why'd you come here?" she said. "Why the risk?"

I stood up and tried to be casual. "Well, I was wondering if—"

"I'm not going to set you up with my agent if that's what you're thinking."

It was. "No, no, of course not."

The store manager poked her head out and whisper-yelled, "We've got a lot of people waiting."

Elvira dropped the cigarette and stomped it out with her foot. "Right." She looked at me. "Gotta go back in."

As I followed her past the office and restrooms, she stopped and turned back. "Take care of yourself, ya know. But, if you don't mind, I'd like you to leave."

"Making you uncomfortable?"

"No. You smell like shit, man."

I did. I really did. "Oh," I held the book out for her to sign. She smiled, pulled out a pen, and wrote something on the title page, shaking her head at the absurdity of the situation. She met my eyes and held the book out.

"Thanks," I said.

"Sure, Mister Smith."

I waved insecurely and walked to the exit. Then a pop. A small, penny-sized hole appeared in the front window. Elvira went down, I ducked, everyone gasped.

I looked outside and couldn't see who fired the shot. Nothing. Just a kid on a bike, a paletero pushing his ice cream cart, and a yellow moving van in the parking lot across the street. No cars speeding off, no one running away. No more shots.

I looked back at Elvira. She was okay. The shooter was an amateur. Between the relatively low caliber rifle, the moderately long distance, and the storefront glass, the bullet didn't have enough velocity left for her flesh. It hit her in the shoulder but didn't even break the skin.

"Jesus," I said. Who in the hell would try to kill her?

Someone was calling the cops. That was my cue to leave.

I ran a safe distance away, wondering if the shot was really intended for Elvira. Maybe someone just didn't like the store's refund policy or their unacceptably small horror section. What if it was intended for me?

I was out of breath. I plunked down on some stairs in

front of a bank and opened *Strange Obsessions*.

On the title page, in chicken scrawl handwriting, she wrote, "Sorry I got you in so much trouble. You have a rebel's heart and that makes you mighty. Without you, there wouldn't be a book. Thank you. Sincerely, Elvira Moon."

That was it. Time to get a book deal of my own.

CHAPTER 45

"How do you think this will play out?" Phil said.

"What?"

"Going to Yellow Brick Books. Pitching your manuscript. Getting a book deal."

"Don't follow."

"You're a wanted man. You scuttle into the light, you might as well scuttle right on to prison."

We were leaning forward on a concrete barrier surrounding a hotel soon to be demolished. We'd watch demos anytime we caught wind of them in the area. Men in orange hard hats walked with trepidation around the perimeter of the building, inspecting blast points and running wire here and there.

"It's worth it," I said, lighting up. "See, if I go to trial, I figure my lawyer will play up the pedophilia angle when it comes to Hemi. Nobody likes a pedophile so I think I've got that going in my favor. Sure, I smashed his head in, but he was already dead at the time, the death itself was accidental, and he was diddling kids for Christ's sake. People love a vigilante. Sell it right, and I come off like Batman, only broke. They'll be lenient. You watch."

Phil took off the beanie he was wearing and scratched his head like a dog with fleas and put the beanie back on and straightened it so the label was centered on his forehead. "You're putting too much faith in the judicial system."

"Nah. You're black. You don't fully understand white privilege. They'd send *your* ass right up the river. Me? Maybe not."

"Do you already have a lawyer?"

"No, I don't have a lawyer. Christ, man, how long have the two of us been out here with jack shit in the way of money? What, do you think I've had one on retainer the last five years? That I'm paying him in glass bottles and blow jobs?"

"You'll get a public offender."

"*De*fender. I think it's public *de*fender."

Phil nodded. "Right. Do you think they'll find out I helped?" Phil said, as if slightly embarrassed to ask.

I looked over at him, made eye contact. "Is that what you're worried about? Look man, I'm not gonna sell you out. You know that."

The construction workers were retreating to a safe distance in an urgent jog that suggested they wanted to get the hell out of the way, but their beer bellies wouldn't let them do it quickly.

Phil watched the shell of a building with mild curiosity. "There's always an insanity defense."

"What's that supposed to mean?"

"That you're insane."

"Maybe. I guess I can see a lawyer making the most of

phrases like 'mental degradation,' 'temporary insanity,' and 'off his meds.' They could bring my dad's suicide into it, ya know, for the sympathy vote. And there's good behavior too. Good behavior can chip a sentence right the fuck down. Hell, I'll give the prison guards sponge baths, wash their balls and everything, if it gets me out a little earlier."

"You've never offered to wash my balls."

"That's because I know where your balls have been."

Phil hit me with the back of his hand and directed my attention to the building.

Three ...Two ...One

The charges popped in quick succession. The building imploded in a magnificent cloud of smoke and dust that rolled out and back in on itself, threatening to envelop us and obscuring the wreckage at the center of it. It made me think of the time I killed a man.

The crowd applauded, but I felt a brief wave of regret. When the smoke cleared, we marveled at what was left. Just a pile of fractured stone with rebar jutting up at severe angles. Months, maybe years, to build. Mere seconds to destroy. All those in attendance quickly resumed their normal lives and I turned to Phil and softly backhanded him on the chest. "Come on. Let's get outta here."

As we set off back to Malpaís, Phil said, "All in all, you're expecting a reduced sentence, not an acquittal."

"I'll be free by the time my book hits shelves. I'll have notoriety. Notoriety sells."

"You're an underdog."

"People *love* an underdog, Phil."

\#

On the last free-standing wall of a collapsed gas station at the edge of Malpaís, I'd spray painted a mural of the denizens of our little community—Phil, Jed, Ruthie Mae, Chris and the rest. The night before I left, I stood before it trying to think of something to add. A way of saying goodbye. Saying remember me.

A rusty can of red spray paint bulged out of my pocket. Hemi was there, standing next to me with his arms crossed. "This moment here is what writers call a 'turning point'," he said.

"I don't follow."

"The day you met Thalia, you were looking for inspiration. You found it in her, wrote your book, but your story isn't complete until the book *lands* somewhere, right? Until you have something to show for all your long suffering. This is the part where you confront a dark truth about yourself and decide to make a change for the better." He pointed in the general direction of Yellow Brick Books. "Your climax waits about fifteen clicks that way."

I pulled out the can of spray paint and rattled it. "What dark truth am I supposed to be facing right now?"

"That you've succumbed to the most superficial American cliché of them all."

"Which is?"

"Fame."

"You're saying I should stay here. Appreciate the audience I already have."

"Staying here is the healthy thing to do. The smart thing to do. But that's not what *you're* going to do, Ches, is it? Because *your* big finish requires you to learn *nothing*."

"Well, a story needs its big finish." I stepped forward and raised my arm to the wall, index finger on the nozzle of the can. A cloud of red enveloped me, sharp and intoxicating, as I added the final touches. When finished, I tossed the can aside and it clacked to a stop next to an old log.

"Fuck you, Hemi," I said and then walked away.

On the wall, in big red letters, it said, THE AUTHOR IS DEAD.

CHAPTER 46

Yellow Brick Books was housed in a brick building painted yellow. It stood between a taquería and a rim shop. The taquería smelled delightful—meat, garlic, roasted tomatoes—while the rim shop smelled like rubber fried in motor oil. We arrived at about 4:45. There was no sign in front of the publishing house, just a small, stenciled name and address on the door above the mail slot.

Some teen in a low rider drove by and the bass from his speakers rattled my ribs. I watched him pull into the rim shop next door.

"Well, go on," Phil said. "You're stalling."

"This would have been a lot easier if Elvira had put in a good word for me."

"In light of your involvement in this whole nasty affair, under what circumstance do you think she could have done so?"

"What if they won't even look at it?"

"We're here. Why *wouldn't* they?"

I tried the door. Locked.

I looked at Phil again. He was pressing his hand against the window to look inside. "Someone's in there," he said.

I knocked and after a moment, the little metal flap over the mail slot flipped out and a woman said, "Yes? What is it?"

"I'd like to talk to you about a manuscript," I said, leaning over with a big, friendly smile.

"What manuscript?"

I held up *The Author is Dead.* "I have a manuscript here. I'd like you to have a look."

"Sorry," the woman said. "We don't accept unsolicited manuscripts. Get an agent and have them submit through the proper channels."

I handed it to Phil. He held the book up and smiled. "*I'm* his agent and I'd like to submit this." He tried to shove it through the mail slot, but there was resistance. The two of them got into a shoving match, Phil pushing it in, the woman pushing it back out. She prevailed and the manuscript fell onto the sidewalk. The rubber band holding it together broke and a few pages blew away.

"Bitch," I muttered and bent over, scrambling to catch the windswept pages. I snagged them all before they drifted into the street and handed them back to Phil as if he might be able to give it another try.

"Go away," the woman yelled.

"Now listen," I said, "You guys published *Strange Obsessions.*"

"Yeah, so?"

"I'm the guy."

"De la Muerte?" She said, clearly frightened.

"No, no. The other guy. See, I was supposed to write that book, Thalia's sister strong-armed me into it, but I enlisted Elvira Moon to write it for m—"

"You're one of the ones the cops were looking for. The one that killed that poor English teacher."

"No." *Why back down now?* "Well, yeah. Yeah I am. And I think you mean poor *pedophile* English teacher. Don't you see? I already have a platform. A tie-in to a book you've already published. How can you go wrong?"

"He's got a point," a male voice said from beyond the mail slot. "It would definitely grab headlines. Headlines mean sales."

"Shut up," the woman hissed. "It'd never get through legal. Get out of here, you two. We're calling the police right now."

"No, wait. Just hear me out."

"Hello, Detective Kuklinski, please."

"Dammit," I said. Phil and I dashed around the corner.

As I was about to run to the back alley, Phil said, "This way," and hustled back toward the street. I don't know why he did that, but he ran directly into the path of a candy red caddy with dice hanging from the mirror. He rolled up onto the hood, shattered the windshield and rolled back onto the street. Legs askew. Mouth bloody.

I could already hear sirens in the distance.

"Phil?" I said, looking down at him.

The driver climbed out of his car and inspected the windshield.

"Phil?"

He nodded slowly.

The sirens were closing in.

The Author is Dead was still in his hand.

I kneeled over Phil. "If you talk to the news people, don't forget to mention my book."

He smiled. Could have been a wince. He coughed some blood out. A crowd was forming.

He grabbed my hand and struggled to raise his head. "I hope you find what you're looking for."

"GodGoddammit." I grabbed the book and sprinted to the alley behind Yellow Brick. A police car skidded to a halt on the other side of the street. I pushed through the thin crowd and cut around to make a right between a grocery store and a twenty-four-hour video establishment—the kind with the peep show in the back.

Another police car approached. I ran across the street, directly in front of it, and cut around to the back of a dilapidated Mexican church called Iglesia Bautista Nueva Vida. New life, my ass.

As I rounded the rectory, a man in a yellow moving van whistled and waved me into the back. Against my better judgment, I jumped in the back and he pulled down the rolling metal door behind me.

"Shh," he said.

I could barely see anything except for a small sliver of light seeping in from under the door. It smelled like gasoline. The cop ran by outside, his radio beeping and broadcasting the outburst of activity. The man in there with me may have had a gun in his hand, but it was hard to tell for sure.

"Be still," he whispered.

Something clicked—maybe a safety.

We waited for quiet and then he leaned over and put

his face to the floor so he could see through the crack beneath the door. He stayed that way awhile and then slowly lifted it and looked out. He *did* have a gun.

He climbed out and snuck around the side of the van closest to the wall on the right. He came back from the left, took a step out to look at the street down the way, and then turned back to me.

After all that time.

Leslie "John de la Muerte" Olenbacher III.

CHAPTER 47

If Leslie knew who I was, I'd probably be dead soon, but he didn't seem to know.

"What'd you do?" he said.

"Nothing. Nothing. Mistaken identity, I think. I'm homeless. They don't care much for people like me, ya know. They'll hassle me no matter what I do. I ran."

He nodded.

Out came the breath I'd been holding. The afternoon sun was penetrating. His face looked washed out in the harsh light.

I threw my legs over the bumper of the van and sat there, trying to calm down.

He didn't seem terribly interested in me.

"Mind if I smoke?" I said.

"In a van full of gasoline?"

I turned to see six full drums of it.

"Oh. Right."

"Climb up in the cab. You can smoke there if you don't mind sharing."

"Not at all."

"I'll take you up the road a bit."

The man who killed Thalia wanted to share a smoke with me. He also had a van full of gasoline. What was he up to?

We climbed into the cab. The interior was that old plastic faux leather that makes fart sounds when you move. Duct tape covered a couple of gashes and the windshield was cracked. It smelled like diesel and sausages.

We rolled down our windows and I handed him a cigarette and lit it for him.

"Name's Mark," he said and then tucked the gun under his left leg.

Fake name. Nice.

I nodded to acknowledge it as I lit my own cigarette.

He looked over at me as if waiting for *my* name.

"We going far?" I said.

He smiled and started the engine. The van grumbled, sounded like it was going to die, but then he revved it up and it was fine.

"No. Not very."

We pulled out of the alley and turned left. I wondered how Phil was. Somehow, I didn't think I'd ever see him again.

I took a long drag, rolled a plume of smoke out. "What's with the gasoline back there?"

"Let's just say I've got a little house cleaning. A reckoning, if you will."

"Uh-huh."

He nodded at *The Author is Dead,* which was in my lap. "What's that?"

"My writing. I'm a writer."

"Oh, yeah?"

"Mmm-hmm."

"*Everyone's* a writer these days."

We drove down the road a way and then he pulled over in front of a small hardware store. He flicked the cigarette out of his window and looked over at the door as if waiting for someone. He checked his watch.

In the window of the store, I saw Calli walking toward the door, two large bags in hand. My heart raced and I slid down in my seat. Maybe she wouldn't spot me.

What's she doing here? Or Leslie for that—

Calli's greasy visage filled my window like creeping death.

"Miss me, sweetie pie?" she said.

CHAPTER 48

"This him?" Leslie said.

"Oh, yeah. It's him. I told you. Didn't I tell you?" She looked at me. "Saw you hanging around Yellow Brick back there. Still trying to get that stupid book of yours published?"

I didn't answer.

"He ran right up to me," Leslie said. "Didn't have to chase him or nothing. Cops were after him and he hopped right in the back. Like a fly to honey."

"What are the chances this would play out like this?" Calli asked, as if God himself ordained it.

"Been staking that fucking place out long enough," Leslie said.

"Waiting for me?" I asked.

"Don't be stupid. You get the stuff, Cal?"

"Yeah." Calli opened the door. "Scooch over."

I didn't, but she shoved me over with her bony hips anyway.

"Should've shopped your shit somewhere else," she said. "Yellow's going down."

"What are you talking about?"

"You'll see."

Leslie pulled away and started down the road.

"You two were in cahoots all along?" I said to Calli.

"Cahoots? Who uses that word?" Leslie smirked.

I took one last drag of my cigarette and flicked it out of the window. I looked at Leslie and then back at Calli. "She was your sister."

"I hated that bitch. I was *never* going to get out of her shadow. And technically, she was my *half*-sister. Different mothers."

"Really? I had no ide—"

"Our mothers were sisters. It's a whole big, weird story. Look, shut up."

I turned back to Leslie. "Here's good. You can drop me off here."

"Are you having trouble understanding the situation you're in?" he said as he slipped the gun into the van's door compartment for quick access.

"No. Just hoping I was wrong."

We turned into the parking lot of an abandoned strip mall. He parked and shut the engine off. "Let's hang here 'til tomorrow," he said.

Calli shook her head. "No, let's just get this done."

"It's going on six. They're gone by now. Besides, maybe Elvira will show up tomorrow. You never know. If not, we'll catch her on the way out of town."

I was beginning to understand. "You're out for revenge?" I turned to Calli. "You two took that shot at Elvira?"

Calli punched me in the upper arm. It was like a hit with a small rubber mallet. "Just shut the fuck up."

"Oww," I said, rubbing my arm.

She pointed at me. "What do we do with him in the meantime?"

"We'll tie him up and put him in the back with us."

\#

They sat me in the back corner of the van next to the drums of gas, hands tied behind my back with twine. A camping lantern glowed by the door, sitting in a nest of wires and other electronic parts. Merciless August heat, virtually no ventilation. They had a small, battery-powered fan on them, but I could tell by their sweat it wasn't much help.

"It's too hot," Calli said, scraping her can of beans clean.

"It's fine. It'll cool off in the night," Leslie said, his can empty and set off to the side. "Tomorrow night, we'll be in Mexico."

"Where it's cool and breezy," I said.

"Shut up."

Leslie stared at me awhile. I guess he made out the scar amidst my beard. "What happened to you face?"

"Sex injury."

"Fine. Don't tell me."

"Shot himself," Calli interjected.

"Why? I never understood how someone could do that to themselves."

Of course, he couldn't. "Some people get to a point in their lives where the emotional pain of living becomes unbearable. You know how when you have a toothache and you start to think that ripping the tooth out with a pair of pliers is preferable to enduring the agony a single minute longer?"

"Can't say I have."

"Yeah, well, you've given me a reason to live, Leslie."

"Don't call me Leslie." He pointed the gun at me. "You're the guy Thal was talking to that day, aren't you?"

"You recognize me?"

"I don't recognize you from Adam, but Calli kept me filled in. Wish I'd walked up to that fuckin' table at the mall and shot you *both* in the head. Would've saved me a lot of trouble. You're the reason the shit hit the fan."

"*Me?*" I pointed at Calli. "What about her?"

"Whatever," he said. "You ain't right in the head."

I surveyed the shoddy wiring attaching the gas drums together. "You just have drums of gasoline and some sort of detonator? Can't be that easy. I don't think it'll work. If it were that easy, terrorists would be a lot more successful."

"What if he's right?" Calli said.

"He's *not* right. I followed the directions I got on the internet."

"Oh, the internet," I said.

"Shut up."

I watched Leslie awhile. I thought about Thalia. About what might have been. I missed her. I barely knew her and I missed her. All that time, I imagined her having been mad at me, disgusted, outraged over what I did to Hemi. Why did she care, anyway? She wasn't real. Now even more.

Humph. Even imaginary friends grew to hate me.

"Did you really kill her for $200 and an iPod?" I said.

"The iPod didn't even work."

Son of a bitch piece of shit motherfucker.

Calli tossed in her two cents. "Shooting her in broad daylight in the middle of a crowded parking lot wasn't the smartest thing you've ever done."

Leslie reared up at her. "Would you stop bringing that up, Cal, Goddamn it? It was almost six years ago."

"I guess the upshot," I said, "was it looked like a crime of passion rather than a hit."

Leslie nodded. "Yeah, yeah, that's right. See. I did you a favor, Cal. No one ever even suspected you."

"It *was* pretty stupid, though, Leslie," I added. "Your picture was on the news that very night."

"Don't call me Leslie." He scuttled over to me, held up a roll of duct tape, snapped about six inches off the end, and smoothed it over my mouth. I pooched my lips in and out and wiggled my cheeks until the right side fell aside. He snarled and proceeded to wrap a long strip of it all the way around my head a couple of times, ensuring I couldn't get free. It tugged at my hair and the sharp pain made my eyes water.

I could feel a tube of something under my hands, maybe lubricant, but I wasn't sure since I couldn't turn around to look at it.

Calli picked up *The Author is Dead* and flipped through it. "Still carrying this around, I see. Any good?" Leslie asked.

She rolled her eyes. "God, no."

He took it from her and thumbed through the pages. "No pictures?"

"Most books don't have pictures, John," Calli said. "You ever finish this dumb thing, dude?"

Thought I had.

Leslie shook his head. "Who the fuck you think's gonna read it?" He flipped back to the beginning and started skimming then tossed the manuscript down and brooded. Calli turned away. All that talk of Thalia seemed to bother them. Did they secretly regret what they'd done? Leslie pulled Calli's face around and kissed her. She pulled away, but he persisted until she gave in.

It was awkward and I nervously fumbled at the tube that I'd wrangled into my fingers. It had one of those flip tops.

Oh, God. Leslie was caressing her right breast. I'm surprised it didn't come loose in his hand like the leprous mound of gelatinous flesh it was. I looked away, but in the corner of my eye, I saw her caressing him back.

CHAPTER 49

"Wait," she said, pulling away. "Not with him watching."

Leslie came back over to me and put another strip of duct tape over my eyes. He didn't wrap it all the way around my head this time. I thought maybe he didn't mind if I watched. He had to have known I could probably blink the tape off. Not that I *wanted* to watch or anything.

I flipped the tube open with my thumb. *Was* it lube?

I heard clothes rustling and sucking sounds, maybe a little licking. The side of the van thumped and one of them went, "Shh."

I squeezed the tube and a warm, thick liquid ran out between my fingers. It was slippery.

"Where's the lube?" Leslie said.

"I don't know. It doesn't matter."

I squirted some of it onto my wrists and rubbed them together. It smelled like strawberry and grew warm on my skin. The twine began to slip.

Slapping. I heard slapping and I wanted to vomit.

The twine was giving way, sliding over one finger and then the next. Soon, my hands were free. I kept them behind me and started blinking the tape off, scared of what I would see.

Calli was completely naked, straddling him, moving on him. His jeans were around his ankles, gun off to the side and within reach.

He looked over at me, surprised. I grabbed the gun and Calli jumped off him, pulled her discarded shirt over her chest. She stared at me in a stupor. Leslie held his head off the floor of the van, scared to move.

I shot Calli through the hand that held her shirt in place over her black bean of a heart. The bang in such an enclosed space left my head ringing. Blood soaked through her shirt as she took several deep gasps and then tumbled to her side. Her eyes didn't close. Leslie held a hand out in front of him and sat up cautiously.

"No man. No man," he said, shaking his head.

"You stole her from me," I said.

"*What?*" He couldn't understand me with the tape over my mouth. I pulled it off. It ripped some of my hair out. I went teary-eyed with searing pain. "You *stole* her from me," I repeated.

"Calli?"

"No, you prick. Thalia."

"Calli," he said, and looked down at her. He looked back up at me. "All this is because of that bitc—"

I shot him in the face. A black, nickel-sized hole above his left eye. His head fell sideways and bled out like a toppled jug of red paint.

I was scared to move, kept expecting to hear sirens. Everything remained quiet.

I'd now killed three people. That's serial killer territory. My old neighbor would have been proud. I wasn't thinking clearly and no matter how I looked at the situation, I seemed to be screwed.

I put the gun to my temple. Wait. A bullet through the temple might just leave me blind. I put the gun to my chest. Wait. I can never remember, is the heart to the left, right, or dead center? Don't want to spend the next few hours bleeding to death. I put the gun in my mouth. Well, no. I've been down this road before, haven't I? Aim up. I need to aim up not to the side like last time. A bullet through the roof of the mouth? Ick. Finally, I placed the muzzle just behind my right ear, settled on pulling the trigger, until *The Author is Dead* caught my eye. Calli's left calf was resting on top of it.

I lowered the gun, tucked it into my waistband, grabbed my manuscript, and quietly opened the back of the van. A refreshing breeze blew over me. It carried the thick smell of garbage with it. No one was around. I climbed out, pulled the door closed behind me, and walked around to the back of the abandoned store the van was parked in front of.

Stupid to stay in the area, but I didn't care. The cops didn't show. I fell asleep in a dumpster.

\#

The burning monk appeared to me that night.

"It's time," he said.

I felt cold. The fire that engulfed his body looked inviting, like a blanket.

I longed to be enveloped in it.

\#

The next morning, I crept around the corner and peeked out at the parking lot expecting to see yellow tape and a flurry of red and blue. The van stood alone, the back door still closed. I approached it, admiring the dawn sky on my way. It was pink and baby blue with beams of sunlight shooting over the eastern clouds.

Peace. I felt peace and I scarcely thought about my actions from that point on. I wasn't worried about anything. Today, the world would hear.

I pulled my shirt collar over my nose, looked around, and opened the door. I couldn't be sure the bodies would stink yet, but I didn't want to find out. The blood had dried in maroon, almost black pools. I climbed in, fished the keys out of Leslie's pocket, and then grabbed a couple of small gas cans before shutting the door for good. I climbed into the driver's seat and put the gas cans and *The Author is Dead* on the passenger seat.

I started the van, pulled out onto the street, and drove to Yellow Brick Publishing and parked on the side of the building. Cars were in the parking lot. I hopped out of the van and walked to the passenger's side door. I pulled out a can of gas, unscrewed the metal lid off the top, and poured the can over my head. The fuel was cool on my body. The smell was pungent.

I walked around to the front door, *The Author is Dead* in one hand, lighter in the other, and banged on it. Someone peeked through the blinds. I sat down, cross-legged, and set my aspiring book out in front of me, far enough that it wouldn't burn. I held the lighter in my right hand.

Someone came out of the door, a man in a light gray

suit with a black tie. He had impeccable hair.

"Oh God, not another one," he said. "Margie, bring the fire extinguisher."

I looked at him in inquiry. "Stay back. You don't want to get burned."

CHAPTER 50

"**D**o you realize how many authors have sat right there, doused in gasoline, demanding we read their manuscript lest they immolate themselves? I mean, Jesus, it's *so cliché*."

"Cliché? Trying to use an author's dirty word to embarrass me out of this?"

Margie brought the extinguisher and set it on the concrete. It made a deep resonating clang.

The man squatted, keeping his distance, and rubbed his index finger on the ground. "Look at the sidewalk, man, it's all black from writers burning themselves here. Hell, the hospital down the road set up a special burn unit just for people like you. And we're a small publishing house. Imagine how many of these Random House or Harper gets. It's got to be a Goddamn weenie roast on those Manhattan sidewalks every day."

"I'd have heard about that on the news."

"Do you hear about *every* mugging? *Every* burglary?

No. It's too mundane to be spotlighted. I, for one, am tired of it and I'll tell you this much: you set yourself on fire, I'm going to throw that fucking manuscript of yours right on top of your roasting carcass and let it burn along with you."

"You wouldn't." He was trying to bluff me out of this, I was sure.

"The hell I wouldn't. You can't bully people into liking your manuscript. If it sucks, it sucks. That's life. Life sucks. The problem with people like you is you want so much to be heard, but you don't really have anything to say that's worth listening to. If you did, you wouldn't resort to this sort of nonsense." He paused, recognition on his face. "You're that guy who was here yesterday, aren't you?"

I nodded. The lighter was still in my hand, my thumb on the wheel.

"The guy that killed that teacher."

I nodded.

"The police are on their way." He flipped through *The Author is Dead*. "What is this? Some kind of memoir? We don't even publish memoirs."

Sirens approached.

"Just read—"

The man shook his head to stop me.

A police car pulled up, the officer leaped out, gun drawn. "Oh shit, not another one," he said.

The man in the gray suit stood and looked back as a second officer pulled up.

"Who are you?" I said to the man.

"Senior editor, Yellow Brick Publishing," he said, still looking at the cops. He turned back to me. "Might as well be God to you, though."

A third officer ran over to the moving van. I couldn't see him from where I was. I heard him open the door and say, "Oh God." He backed up and into my line of sight. "Get the bomb squad down here. *And* homicide."

The senior editor raised his eyebrows as if the developing details were too good to be true.

A nearby bar with an open patio played a Beatles song. "I Am the Walrus."

"Did you know John Lennon wrote that song just to fuck with people?" I said.

"No, no. He wrote it to cryptically recount the death of the *real* Paul McCartney. This current one is an imposter."

"Damn," I said. "McCartney's reaping all the benefits of a dead artist while he's still alive. That's a creative supernova right there."

"Yeah, whatever, man." He turned away and walked around the corner to see the commotion around the van. As he did, I pulled out a cigarette, put it in my mouth, and lit it.

"Sonofa—" the editor ran towards me.

The fire was quick and searing. The world turned wavy and orange, clothes melting off my body.

Time slowed. Hemi, malformed yet judicious, watched me burn. Someone behind him. A plastic bag over his head, encasing it, pulled tight. He struggled side to side, went limp and fell down.

Thalia. The merciful Goddess had come back to me.

"Shh," she said. She had tears in her eyes and her voice cracked. "The credits are rolling. Quick. What song do you hear?"

"Pink Floyd. 'Wish You Were Here'," I whispered.

She dropped to her knees, straddled me—warmer than the fire, wet enough to put it out. Kissing me with sweet divinity, she ripped her button-down shirt open and cradled my head between her bare breasts as we moved together.

"Tell me you love me," I said.

"I love you."

She loves me.

Everything's foggy.

Can't breathe.

This is it.

CHAPTER 51

Well, shit.

Self-immolation isn't as instantly fatal as you might think. Fucking Margie with her fucking fire extinguisher. Now I share a hospital room with a guy who shits himself and talks to unicorns. I'm slathered in burn cream and wrapped in gauze all the time. Something like fifteen to twenty skin grafts are in my immediate future. My left wrist isn't burned, but handcuffs are on it, locking me to the bed rail. Gifts are on the flimsy end table on the other side of the room. Daisies from Libby. Stargazer lilies from Elvira Moon. A dirty, one-eyed teddy bear from Phil.

Thalia sits in the chair in the corner, one leg over the other, reading a magazine. She looks up and sees me watching her. There's a new kind of bond between us, that of the freshly consummated.

"And I thought the scar from the gunshot looked bad," she says and giggles.

I laugh.

Ah well. At least I got a book deal out of it.

Biography

Ches Smith was born in 1974, spent six confused years in elementary school, three awkward years in middle school, four invisible years in high school, found Jesus, went to college, graduated, got ordained, got married, went to seminary, had a kid, dropped out of seminary, went back to seminary, had two more kids, became increasingly insane, dropped out of seminary again and then lost Jesus. He soon discovered there isn't much an agnostic atheist can do with a degree in Biblical studies and half a Masters of Divinity and there isn't much *anyone* can do with a minor in philosophy. So, to kill time until his inevitable demise, he works to support his family and writes to support his mental well-being. He lives in Houston, Texas with his wife, Silvia, and their three children, Sarah, Cristian, and Max.

CPSIA information can be obtained
at www.ICGtesting.com
Printed in the USA
FSHW02n1107080518
47804FS